A JOURNEY TOWARD TOMORROW

The Beginning

A Science Fiction Novel

J J Eckhardt

A JOURNEY TOWARD TOMORROW

Cover art: Aspire Book Covers, Sharon Brownlie
shazziebrownlie@gmail.com
Website: https://aspirebookcovers.com/

Editing: Tanya Oemig & Meg Richardson

ISBN: 979-8-9863632-0-2

This book is dedicated to my family and to all the generations to follow.
Always remember, it is never too late in life to start something new and explore something you never thought possible.

J J Eckhardt   May, 2022

"The best dreams to achieve,

are those you never knew existed."

J J Eckhardt

A JOURNEY TOWARD TOMORROW

THE NATURE OF HUMANITY I

What are Humans, beyond the collection of memories which makes each unique? All beings have form and function, dictated, and controlled by the laws that make up the universe we know and the environment the universe chose to provide. If you strip away a Human's memories, are they the same person?

Can new memories replace a distinct individual, creating in the process a new being? Does the person still exist, buried deep and hidden, continually struggling to reemerge and take their rightful place of consciousness?

Can emotional pain be buried so deep below consciousness it can never again be experienced or managed? Does the pain haunt the dreams even if it is not free to build, strengthen and remind the being they are of Humanity?

DREAM A LITTLE DREAM OF WE

He followed her out to the patio to discover her unconscious body lying on the multicolored flagstones. His body drenched with sweat, his head pounding, he could do nothing to help her as another round of sharp pain overtook his mind and body. He clutched his head as the pain moved through his neck and back. He screamed from a final burst of agony as he fell onto the patio and into darkness. The house was quiet as blood flowed over the colorful stones.

His unconscious mind drifted from one suppressed memory to another.

They stood looking at the Eiffel Tower, multicolored lights, traffic noise, and shadows swirled around them, with the spray from the fountains blowing behind as he took her hand. They came for a vacation, but he had planned so much more. He turned to the woman beside him as distant music played. He got down on one knee . . .

Walking through the woods in darkness, lit only by their flashlights. The crunching of leaves and twigs as they walked became the only sound. The light they followed disappeared beyond the next rise. They crested the hill, saw below them a body in the clearing; Bart, their friend . . .

The memories swirled and blended, glimpses of an unremembered past.

Her blond hair flowed over her shoulders. She was beautiful; soon, they would become husband and wife. He walked along Jewelers' Row to pick up the rings. A man he had met before, but didn't recognize, stopped him. He asked the man to find his fiancée. The man explained she was not there; the woman he met was not . . .

He stood next to Bart, looking down onto the planet. A man bumped him while he stood in a new place. Bright and tall, trees and odd creatures all around. The man walked away, glancing back. He recognized the man as . . .

Images of past and present appeared and departed. Confusion permeated his mind. Seen and unseen by his mind's eye, as more non-distinct images followed, of new places, unfamiliar, familiar, disjointed, unclear.

The creature exhaled on them; all he could feel was the anger. Anger, they took its land, anger it could not reach its prey. He experienced no fear as the creature lunged with mouth wide open and teeth ready to . . .

Calmness arrives, his heart rate slows, he hears the song and sees one last image or memory of her as things become clear.

He sat at the piano, playing the song for her. He remembered who she was and why he had such an attraction. He swept her off her feet, carried her into his bedroom, and began to make love to . . .

The music played on in his mind as his unconscious, having completed its mission, returned him to reality.

Warren awoke and reflected upon the strangest dream of his life as it slowly faded away, but this time not forgotten. His mind cleared, the memories returned, and reality hit him hard; his home was now an empty, lifeless piece of rock.

A single tear fell from his eye.

He was not surprised to find himself lying on a bed in a hospital.

THE BEGINNING

Dad, the car, look out . . .
Graduated with honors . . .
Introducing at the piano . . .
Heading for war, Russia attacked Israel. The United States vows . . .
China is promising to attack any country who uses nuclear weapons . . .
Bright light, not in my bed, pain, light, movement, prodding . . .
We will help you, the species will survive, a new beginning, another place . . .
you will be together . . .
Samantha, Samantha . . .
My life, my friends, my love . . .
Is it time, I'm ready . . .
It is time.

Day One

The man awoke to nauseating pain in his head and along his back, lying in what he thought to be a field. He stared up at a clear blue sky but had to immediately shut his eyes to block the sun's brightness, which caused a blinding irritation. The sun beat down, from almost directly above, while he waited for the throbbing in his head to go away. As he listened to a familiar babbling sound coming from his left, the pain began to ease and he enjoyed the gentle breeze blowing across his face, which fought to cool him as the sun worked to keep him warm.

If not for the pain still in my back, I could lie here enjoying the breeze and the sound forever. After all, what good would come from getting up—there remains no point?

The thought made no sense to him as his head cleared, and he took a deep breath, further enjoying the fragrance of the flowers that surrounded the clearing in which he lay, their pleasant scent carried by the wind.

A minute or two passed. He turned his head away from the sun, opened his eyes, and slowly sat up, feeling lightheaded for a brief moment. When he looked down, he discovered small rocks mixed among the grasses on which he had been lying had caused the pain in his back. He looked toward his left to see a small creek splash over the polished rocks on its way to a larger stream below, leading off in the direction he had to go.

How do I know where I need to go? Why am I starting to feel it urgent to get there when I don't even know where I am?

He turned toward a rustling noise to his right and saw a family of deer. They seemed not to care about his presence as they walked below a dense forest of evergreen trees, eating berries from a group of bushes while the trees above swayed in the gentle breeze.

Ten minutes had passed while he had looked around. He wasn't sure where he awoke, but he knew sitting there on his backside wasn't the best way to find out.

Time to try and stand, if I can manage to make my body move.

His hands tingled, and his legs had occasional muscle spasms. He didn't think his legs could take the exertion yet, so he sat and looked for anyone, any buildings—any signs of life. There was no camp, no sign of a campfire, and no smoke—only the clear blue sky, snowcapped mountains, the deer, and numerous trees as far as he could see. The view was beautiful, but nothing felt right.

The boots he wore didn't look familiar, and he could find no tags or logos to identify a brand. His clothes, like the hiking boots he didn't remember buying, also appeared new and clean. Considering he awoke lying on the ground in what certainly looked like the middle of nowhere, he expected at least some dirt on the boots.

Nothing around him indicated how he got there. He could see no car, no motorcycle, no ATV. His head cleared, and the pain no longer bothered him as he thought about the last thing he could remember—going to bed in his Philadelphia apartment after watching the latest news about the spreading strife in the Middle East and Europe. The news report said Syria, backed by Russia, was advancing troops toward Israel, and Israel was threatening to use nuclear weapons. In Europe, Muslim extremists backed by Russia were rumored to be planning attacks with chemical and biological weapons against Germany, France, and England.

No, that's not correct!

The terrible news wasn't the last thing he could recall. He could remember walking along a street doing something important, something he had to pick up—something special for . . . her.

I can't clearly remember what happened before I woke, yet I can remember details from the news. That makes no sense.

His immediate concern remained, where the hell was he? The area could be the Pocono Mountains, but the mountains seemed larger to him than the Poconos, and the highest peaks here had some snow. He didn't see anything he could have fallen from, such as a hiking path or a ledge. The area around him for at least thirty feet in any direction was flat with a slight incline toward the little creek. The dry grasses and blooming wildflowers danced slowly in the breeze as he looked for any sign of civilization, finding none.

How the hell did I get here, he wondered? *Who would abduct me from his home, put me into apparently new clothes, do God knows what else, and dump me, alone on the ground?*

He didn't think anyone had dragged him there, in fact, the cleanliness of his clothes indicated he had walked of his own accord, yet he saw no footprints or even tire tracks.

Fifteen minutes had passed since he sat, and it was time to stand. He moved slowly at first, and nearly fell forward but found standing wasn't as hard as he had expected. His legs no longer had spasms, and his hands no longer tingled. He remained disoriented and saw spots in his eyes that cleared while he found his balance. He gazed around, hoping standing would allow him to view something familiar; it didn't.

The boots were comfortable, fit him perfectly, and looked more than adequate to handle his surroundings. He wasn't sure how he knew this, but he did. The family of deer had gone, which left him alone and frightened, his heart pounding in his chest and his hands moist with sweat. He checked his body for bruises and scrapes where he could, without removing some clothes, but found none.

The pockets of his pants were empty, but strapped to his belt was a small leather bag. He opened it to find packages he thought were snack bars, wrapped in blank, nondescript silver wrappers. Curious and hungry, he took one out and unwrapped it to see what appeared to be a nut and fruit bar. He popped it in his mouth before thinking how stupid it was to eat something he happened to find strapped to his body without knowing the circumstances that brought him there.

He dug around in the bag, and under more supposed fruit bars, he found an old, flip-style cell phone. The excitement of calling someone and getting help gave way to confusion when he turned it on to find no signal and no contacts, like a blank slate. He could find no way to open it to look for a SIM card, and if not for the pure, bright blue screen, he wouldn't even have thought the phone was operating.

In addition to the boots, which he was sure were not originally his, he wore well-fitting blue jeans with no label, a heavy flannel shirt, and a red V-neck undershirt. He never wore flannel, even when he went out hiking with . . . with someone. He closed his eyes, desperately clutched at the memory, and could almost see a face, but no name came to mind. He figured there would be time later to check out the socks and underpants, but was sure they would also not be his style or brand. He liked to wear boxers, but he could tell without looking he was now wearing briefs. He pushed the thought from his mind of someone changing his underwear while he lay there out cold. It was a little too disturbing as if the whole situation he found himself in wasn't unsettling enough.

He hoped he hadn't done something to cause his memory loss and then stolen the clothes from someone. But if true, the clothes wouldn't fit him so well, and the question of how he got into the middle of nowhere remained.

"Hello!" he yelled, and practically jumped out of his skin. His voice was . . . different. He didn't recognize it as being his. At first, it sounded as if someone yelled at him. He started to think he had fallen into some strange dream, like when as a child, he would have vivid nightmares. The more he thought about it and looked around, the more he came to understand this experience wasn't a dream.

If this is reality, I may be screwed

He yelled again—no response and no sounds other than birds, insects, and the light breeze through the trees. Another ten minutes had passed since he stood. He hadn't moved more than a foot or two, but he knew he needed to do something other than stand there if he wanted to find his way to where he had to be.

A thought came into his mind. In an instant, it disappeared. No, not a thought—an image of a place—a house he didn't recognize even though it seemed familiar. Panic again set in; he needed to find help, something to drink, and a way to get back home.

Sweat appeared on his brow. The weather had warmed a bit, but it wasn't hot. There was still the light breeze that smelled of flowers and the scent from the evergreen trees. The sky was bright blue with some puffy gray clouds in the distance and a few birds he could see flying from tree to tree. The breeze was cool, but the long sleeve flannel shirt made him hot.

I appear to be dressed for colder weather, maybe because it had been cold when they had dumped me on the ground. They, but whom could they be?

He unconsciously clenched his hands at his side and was taken aback by the bitterness and anger he now experienced.

Although not uncalled for, the hostility seemed odd to him. He wasn't typically quick to anger; he somehow knew it as a fact. Even if he had no certainty of where he now was or how he had gotten there, he knew himself, even if he couldn't recall his name. He suddenly had a chill run down his entire body—something didn't feel right. He thought of the phrase, 'someone is walking on your grave.'

Was it possible he died? Could this be Hell? It looked more like Heaven, but it could become Hell if he stayed forever lost. He couldn't remember the kind of life he lived, who he was as a person, his beliefs, his cares, or his desires. Did he live his life as a good person; was he a criminal, a murderer, or God forbid a rapist? His disdain at the thought convinced him he was not that type of person.

The chill left him, and warmth returned to his body. He removed the heavy flannel shirt before he overheated and grew even further in need of water. He tied it around his waist and looked down at his arms and chest. His body was different. His arms and chest were larger, bulging with muscle, but that wasn't possible. What he could see of his body looked and felt unfamiliar, and he realized he was better built than he thought he ever had been before. It wasn't possible unless he was having a complete meltdown or an unwilling participant in a nightmare he couldn't escape.

His hand caught his attention—his left one. He recalled a bandage on his left hand and a bleeding cut. Yes, he remembered it now. He cut his hand with a knife making breakfast. He was chopping scallions for an omelet when he fumbled with the knife. He couldn't remember any other details, such as when or where, but he assumed it was his home.

Anger built inside him from the frustration. Why can I remember some strange details while other memories are so out of reach? The point was, he now had no bandage, no cut, and no scar, but he knew he had recently cut himself. He recalled bleeding on the floor and needing to clean it up before heading out to work . . . where? He felt sure he had a job, another thing, another memory gone as if wiped from his mind.

"What did they do to me, and why?" he said to himself in a low voice, as if afraid someone would hear. His head was once more starting to hurt as the things he tried to remember slipped out of his grasp. How long ago did the last events he could recall, actually happen? Why was he having trouble with his memory, and why didn't he feel like himself? He knew his name was Warren Est . . . Eston, maybe. He lived at . . . in the city of Philadel . . . his age at his last birthday was—dear God, he didn't even know his age or his birth date. He wanted to scream.

"What is happening to me?"

He couldn't stand there any longer talking to himself; of that one fact, he was positive. He wasn't sure how, but he knew to find help, he needed to follow the stream down. Eventually, it would meet a larger body of water and civilization. Worst case, he walked all the way to an ocean. In his mind, he knew it to be the natural thing to do. He felt compelled to move, but he didn't know where he had to go.

The day remained bright, with the sun shining off the water tumbling over the rocks. The sound calmed him, but he couldn't spend the day squinting. He wished he had some sunglasses to shade his eyes. The desire for sunglasses made him stop in his tracks as he realized he should have eyeglasses.

"I'm sure I wear glasses, but my vision appears to be fine without them; I have no problem seeing far or near. Reading glasses must be what I'm thinking of, but there is nothing around for me to read to verify if I need glasses."

He had been talking out loud and laughed to himself about how he would look if there were someone around watching. He glanced around, hoping maybe he had missed something. There was nothing, yet he felt he wasn't alone. Everything looked and sounded natural, but it didn't feel normal. Something was wrong or out of place—even the air felt different.

Warren heard the whine of insects and had seen bees and other flying bugs, but nothing came at him, bit or stung his body.

He always was a mosquito magnet, which he somehow knew for sure, but apparently not today. The observation was another odd thing in a day filled with the bizarre. The world had turned upside-down even though it looked normal.

His attention was drawn to the sky by the sounds of humming overhead, but all he could see were eagles soaring above on the winds and updrafts, while off in the distance, other birds circled, dancing across the sky. A tingling ran up and down his arms, and he experienced a chill before his muscles tensed. He quickly looked around and turned, expecting danger, but nothing was there, at least nothing he could perceive.

A few squirrels jumped in the trees while one sat on a rock about ten feet in front of him. Warren walked closer, but the squirrel didn't move or run away as he approached. The fluffy little animal stared at him as if he were something new, never encountered before. He knew squirrels ran as soon as they saw people, but this one acted as if it had never seen a person. Only one foot apart, the squirrel still didn't run, he contently sat there looking back at Warren, while Warren stared back as if in a trance.

Walking Down To . . .

When did he start walking? He couldn't recall. One moment, Warren had been watching the squirrel, but now he walked down a rocky path, and the scenery had changed. The worn path he followed had narrowed, more bushes and branches encroached along the sides. Up ahead, the path meandered along the bottom of a small hill of exposed rocks. Large fallen boulders littered the trail in some spots, and he had to climb over them or go around into the woods. A few yards into the trees, more deer foraged and ignored him as he found his way back to the path.

"Who's there?" He turned quickly, expecting someone behind him. He was sure he had heard a noise or sensed a presence, though he recognized the thought made no sense. As he stood there, the hairs on the back of his neck stood straight, and he experienced another odd chill across his body, different from the last.

What made him think someone was coming behind him? He had thought he heard a voice, but the only sound he continued to hear was the breeze and the buzz of insects. Everything still seemed off. Familiar and unfamiliar at the same time. He had an intense feeling like something was hiding over the horizon, something, or someone. It made him think about the time-eating lango . . . langol . . . something, coming closer but always unseen.

"How the hell can I remember a story I must have read in the past by Stephen . . . Stephen someone, but not remember my full name and where the hell I live?"

He practically screamed the rant, happy to hear the voice, he still couldn't reconcile as his. Still, the sound made him feel alive and helped assure him this nightmare wasn't a dream. Whatever event was playing out, the one thing Warren understood—he had no control, and he wasn't alone.

"Who's there? What do you want and why are you following me?" he yelled once more, a touch of panic in his tone. "Show yourself!" Warren didn't expect an answer, but screaming made him feel better, real, and alive, and not dead he hoped.

What am I feeling?

He had to stop. *Look out, move!* The thought surged into his mind.

He watched as large stones tumbled onto the path ahead of him, exactly where he would have been if he'd kept walking. He waited for the rocks to settle, looking up to see if someone could have caused the small but potentially life-threatening rockslide, but saw no movement.

Good thing I stopped. How had I avoided stepping in the way of the rockfall? Did the rocks at that moment fall on their own, or is someone up there?

Again, he called out, almost screaming, and still, only the sounds of the forest greeted him. He thought he had been walking for about two hours, but he never was good at judging time without a clock. He had the oddest feeling, it was getting late, and he had to move faster.

He walked well beyond the rockslide with nothing new in his surroundings, only more of the same—while someone or something watched his every move. He knew it without a doubt. Much stronger than before, he could sense something out there, something or someone observing him, maybe following him but too far back to be visible.

He had an idea. Warren sat on a group of rocks, hidden beneath the trees, and waited to see if anyone or anything followed. While waiting, he ate another of the odd bars that were in the pouch. They tasted pretty good, certainly better than anything else he could remember. He thought it strange he couldn't remember the last time he had eaten before waking in the forest. More importantly, he was thirsty and needed to have a drink, but he had no water.

What would happen if he didn't get water? He could drink from the creek and hope it didn't make him sick. And what happens if he didn't find shelter before dark? He would need to find something to make a spark and some dry brush to start a fire. Should only take a few minutes to . . . he had never built a fire in his life, had he? He could end up freezing to death out in the middle of, only God knew where. His heartbeat increased; he stood and staggered as sweat formed on his brow.

The sound of something ringing came from the pouch he had around his waist.

The day warmed, as the sun moved toward the horizon. Warren knew it meant the time was now late afternoon. While he sat there, near a collection of moss-covered rocks, a loud screech from a hawk flying above startled him. He thought he might have dozed off for a minute or two. He was no longer thirsty, which he found odd. He had waited a while but saw no one coming along the path.

It must have been my imagination.

He didn't sense anyone following him now, but he remained sure someone or something watched him and was certain he had forgotten something important. He rubbed his head, feeling pain starting to return to his head as he stood.

"I need to keep moving." He whispered.

It looked much closer to sunset than he thought it should be when he emerged from the trees, and he wondered how long he had been sitting on the rocks. The sun was going down behind him, so he thought he must have been heading east. Amazing, he knew something important which might help him, not that it mattered because it wasn't going to assist him in figuring out his situation.

After walking for another half hour, he again started to panic. He knew things were not right; someone was playing with him, a game he didn't want to play. He knew he was different, both mentally and physically.

How long ago did they take me?

He remained certain he forgot something, a fact or task he needed to know or do. What was he unable to remember, and why was he so unnerved? Why were his hands sweating and the pain in his head and neck becoming stronger?

The sun began to touch the horizon, darkness was closer, they were closer, watching, and he didn't know what to do, except he had to keep moving; he needed to keep moving. The sky darkened with no moon; he needed to find a place to rest and shelter for the night. He sensed there was shelter ahead a few hundred more yards around the bend.

What is waiting around the bend, how would I know? Have to keep moving, have to get there, get to the shelter!

He hurried along a few minutes, and stopped, startled by the sight now in front of him; an improvised shelter consisting of sticks and grasses, occupied space under the trees and against a large rock.

What in the world . . . how did I . . . how did I know?

The pain grew stronger, his vision began to blur. His face dripped with sweat?

"I should sleep here; I need rest. It's dark now and—"

A ringing sound interrupted his thoughts. The sound startled him and brought him out of his panic.

A phone. Where? In his pocket. He had a phone? Pick it up. Quick! "Hello?"

There was no answer. Fatigue overwhelmed his body, and Warren couldn't stay awake as he slowly collapsed to the ground.

Day Two

He awoke to a cold chill his body acknowledged with goosebumps. He rolled to his side, his face, and hands itchy from the twigs and grass on which he had slept. The long shadows on the ground cast by the thick stands of trees indicated the sun had recently come up, and some wisps of fog remained in the air. He didn't know where he awoke and wondered who built the shelter. He knew he couldn't have made it, as crude as it was; it was not something he knew how to construct.

He saw a creek about thirty yards off to his left. Beyond the creek and also to his right stood a dense forest of evergreen trees. He looked around to discover if anyone was in sight or if there were any buildings. All he could see was the clearing sky, snow-capped mountains, the creek, and trees. There was nothing to indicate how he got to the clearing, no means of transportation, and not even a dirt road.

The last thing he could recollect was walking around somewhere in the woods. So maybe he camped here yesterday, but he didn't know where here was. He began to wonder if he had fallen and hit his head before going to sleep in the shelter, but he seemed fine, with no bumps or bruises on his head, or anywhere else on his body he could see. He knew his name was Warren . . ., he stopped, not sure how to proceed. Maybe he did hit his head if he couldn't remember his full name.

He must be here with someone who knew what they are doing in the wilderness, someone who knew how to build a shelter that offered suitable protection from the elements out of debris lying along the ground.

He yelled a couple of times, but there was no response except for a few birds he startled out of the trees. When he looked at the shelter again, he grasped it wasn't large enough for more than one person. If he were here with someone else, where were they, and where did they spend the night?

"Hello," he yelled. "Is anyone nearby? Hello, can anybody hear me?"

More startled birds flew out of nearby trees as he waited a while and listened, but heard only the rustling of leaves and the insects in the grass. He realized he had a small bag strapped to his belt. He opened the bag and found packages of snack bars. He unwrapped one and found it was a nut and fruit bar. After eating three of them, he wanted a drink of water. A canteen sat against one of the shelter's posts, and without thinking about it, he took a couple of long drinks and was ready to go.

Go? Where am I going? Down, yes, down along the creek, because that's what I have to do.

Warren grabbed the canteen and followed the path, which meandered beside the creek. He walked for a couple of hours, at times wading in the creek as a tree or two blocked the way. The path was a good sign, he thought; it meant he couldn't be too far from civilization. It wasn't perfect or well maintained, but a person made the shelter, not an animal. If the path were from the animals, it would have been more uneven and narrower; how he knew such an odd fact, he wasn't sure. He didn't remember ever doing anything like this before, but he appeared prepared and dressed for a long hike.

He remained concerned about his memory since he had no idea where he was, or if anyone was with him. He knew his name was Warren, and his age was twenty . . . something. He had been born . . . he didn't know where, or for that matter, where he lived. He stood there a moment, trying to remember but could picture no house or apartment. His head hurt, and he wished he had some aspirin in the pouch.

He remembered nothing of detail from before he woke up in the morning. He must have had a severe head injury, but he didn't feel any blood or bumps on his head when he checked. His senses seemed to be working. He could smell the scents from around him. His vision was clear, and he could hear the water in the creek and animals in the woods.

He started to panic as the pain in his head became worse. His hands were wet; his head throbbed between his eyes and at the base of his neck. He started screaming. "Help! Is anyone out there?"

He wondered why he experienced so much anxiety. Something in the sky, watching, coming, they were coming for him, they were going to hurt him, they were getting closer; he knew he had to hide.

Warren saw a pile of rocks he could hide behind. He wanted to get away until they passed, needed to get away before the ringing started; before they took control. He ran to the rocks and sat behind them in a fetal position, his head buried in his arms when he heard the ringing.

He believed he had dozed off, which was odd since he awoke only a few hours ago. He didn't remember sitting behind the rocks, but it was cool and the day was getting warm. He stayed a little longer, ate another mysterious fruit and nut bar, and drank some water.

"I need to keep moving." He said to the empty forest.

Still hungry, he munched on another bar. He knew he needed to keep his strength up so he could make it to . . . the place. What place? Where was he going? What if he didn't want to go? They couldn't make him! Not again.

He stood, determined to hold his ground, and wait. He knew someone was nearby; he could feel it; he wasn't moving until they showed themselves. His hands were clenched tight against his legs as he yelled into the forest, "I'm here, what are you waiting for?"

Ring, ring . . .

Warren thought he dozed off for a while. Odd, he thought since he had woken up only a few hours ago. He rose and moved farther along the path, feeling invigorated and ready. The sun was much farther across the sky than when he had sat in the shade behind the rocks.

I must have taken a long nap back there in the shade.

He didn't remember going to sleep in the shelter. Maybe he hadn't slept there long, and that's why he fell asleep sitting behind the rocks. He knew it would be getting dark in four hours. He had no idea how he knew or why the hours remaining before darkness were important. Warren hoped he wasn't losing his mind.

Yet so much seemed so close, nevertheless out of reach to him. Flashes of what he believed to be memories popped into his mind and disappeared again before comprehending what he saw. The images were, at times, so powerful, he had to stop and sit on a boulder or downed tree to wait for his normal vision to clear.

When he felt better, Warren understood he needed to pick up his pace to arrive by nightfall. He still didn't know where, but he knew something waited for him, and he needed to get there soon. A storm was coming; Warren could sense it, and soon he heard the storm's approach.

It started as a low rumbling behind him, like thunder, but he could only see a few clouds around the mountains. The wind began to pick up, and he squinted to keep the dust out of his eyes. Even though the sky remained clear overhead, he could feel the storm coming. It would be violent and dangerous. The birds had disappeared from the sky, and he saw no more deer or other animals as he increased his pace.

<<<>>>

Warren walked for over three hours and knew he had only a little farther to go . . . for shelter. The storm was getting closer; he hoped the thought was correct. He wasn't sure what he had done for the last few hours other than walk, but he moved forward, between rocks and trees blocking his path, as if in a trance. They no longer followed him; they were watching and waiting. Of that, he had no doubt.

The weather had gone downhill quickly as the storm moved in. The thunder was much closer and louder; the wind was picking up, and the sun now hid behind a gray sky filled with a mixture of light and dark clouds, rolling in like waves in an ocean. An odd tingling started on the back of his neck, and he leaped to the side as a large tree limb crashed across his path.

Wow, the branch almost hit me. Good thing I had moved out of the way.

Warren didn't see the limb as it fell, but he knew he had to get out of the way of the danger and knew he needed to move faster. The storm was coming; he would be in trouble if he didn't get there in time. Lost in his thoughts, he kept moving.

The wind ripped through his hair, and it started to rain as Warren managed his way down the slippery uneven path. Leaves and twigs blew into him as he walked, his pace increasing minute by minute. A flash of bright lightning was brighter than any he could remember, followed by a deafening clap of thunder directly overhead.

A little farther, just *a little more now. Walk. Walk! Faster!*

He cut through the last of the trees, moving aside in time to miss being hit by a large branch blown from above. As the rain increased, he emerged into a clearing, and the wind blew more forest debris into his hair and face. He looked up while trying to protect his eyes, and there stood a house. His house? Maybe! He didn't know, and he didn't care; he just needed to get inside. Move! Move! Almost at the door.

How do I get in?

"How do I get in?" He yelled, hoping someone heard him over the noise of the storm. He was afraid, wet, and shivering. He wanted this to end.

From inside his pant pocket, a phone began to vibrate and ring.

"I had a phone?"

He pulled it from his pocket, nearly dropping it out of his wet hands, and after a brief pause, said, "Hello?"

"Hello, Warren, the door is open for you. Come in; I have been waiting."

A NEW WORLD

Heading for war, Russia attacked Israel. The United States vows . . .

China is promising to attack any country who uses nuclear weapons . . .

Bright light, not in my bed, pain, light, movement, prodding . . .

We will help you, the species will survive, a new beginning, another place . . .

My life, my friends, my love . . .

No, I don't believe, take me back, let me go, what did you do to me . . .

Day Three

Warren awoke, lying on his back in an exceptionally comfortable bed, with fluffy pillows and soft covers he had wrapped around his body. At first, he wasn't sure where he was until he looked around and recognized his bedroom. A strange dream about places and events he didn't understand slowly faded from his memory. His head hurt for a short moment, but the pain quickly disappeared as he sat on the side of the bed.

He stretched, his hands and arms high above his head, before standing and looking around the bedroom. Though it appeared familiar, Warren didn't remember having ever purchased or used any of the furnishings. A medium tone brown wood paneling covered the walls. Against one of the walls, a mahogany desk with a computer accompanied a matching chest of drawers. Two doors led off to the left and another off to the right. The room was warm, welcoming, and safe.

He walked to his right and opened the door to the bathroom, wondering how he knew where to go. The standard bathroom included a single sink and a brightly tiled shower. There was fresh soap by the sink and a new, full bottle of shower gel. It wasn't until he looked in the mirror that he found it odd that he had slept naked, which he thought was unusual. He turned on the water, adjusted the temperature, and stepped into the shower, the odd thought fading from his mind.

As he showered, his mind replayed images of walking in the forest and an approaching storm. He had the feeling of being out of place as if he were only a guest. Wherever he happened to be, it didn't belong to him; he had to be a guest. The place he lived in was . . . was where? He couldn't remember where he lived, what it looked like, or even if it was a house or an apartment.

He found towels under the sink, dried his body, and returned to the bedroom. He paused a moment looking for clothes and remembered they were in the chest of drawers. He found only long, basic, white boxer briefs when he opened the drawers—not what he expected. They were unfamiliar to him, but he pulled them on anyway, seeing no other choices. There were no socks, but black slippers sat next to the bed. He needed his shirt and pants.

I can't go anywhere in only my underwear, but where am I going?

Warren expected the rest of his clothes to be in the closet; however, he didn't find the shirts and pants he anticipated when he opened the closet door. Several one-piece overalls hung neatly on hangers, all the same, off-white color and made of a fabric that didn't look or feel familiar. He thought it odd but pulled one out of the closet anyway, put it on, and found it fit him perfectly.

As he finished with the zipper, he became startled by the sound of thunder. He hadn't noticed the rain and wind hitting against the window until he heard the noise. He felt his mind sluggish as if still in a morning fog. Now paying attention, the rain sounded intense, and there was something about the sound of the thunder that gave him a brief chill.

Warren didn't recall a storm when he went to bed the previous night. He couldn't recall going to bed as he thought about it either. He found he didn't remember yesterday or anything beyond getting up earlier. Even the night's dreams had faded from his memory. He peered out the one window in the room as long rolls of thunder followed the huge flashes of light he saw in the distance. The rain was heavy, the sky extremely dark with fast-moving clouds, and the wind violently strong, pushing the trees back and forth. He found no clock in the room and had no idea what time it was, but he believed it to be still mid-morning.

He turned away from the window and again surveyed the room. Adequate size and well decorated, but something wasn't right. It made him comfortable, but it didn't feel like his even though he thought otherwise when he woke. He walked over to the computer wanting to turn it on; however, he couldn't find a power switch and found no visible cords.

Time to explore, something isn't right, and the answers I need are not to be found in this room.

Hello Again Warren

Warren opened the door to the left figuring it must lead to the rest of the house. A short wood-paneled hallway opened to an area he could only describe as a great room. The words popped into his mind, but he wasn't sure if he could explain the term if asked.

Similar to the bedroom, but in a lighter shade, the floor was wood, with a few area rugs scattered around in colors that matched the soft-hued walls. A small office area occupied a corner of the large space, and instead of books, unlabeled binders filled the two middle shelves, while the others remained empty as if waiting to be filled with personal items. To the right of the office was a kitchen, which would be the perfect size for one or two people. A small table was positioned to one side against walls covered with unadorned, off-white tile.

An exquisite black baby grand piano and a matching bench sat in front of a large picture window. To the left of the window was a sliding glass door leading out to a flagstone-covered patio. The view out the window, dark from the storm, but breathtaking all the same, looked down into a fog-covered valley. The building seemed to be on a mountainside, with a rolling field of grass and flowers descending into the fog.

To his far right, a sofa and two chairs, separated by a throw rug, formed a cozy sitting area in front of an unlit stone-clad fireplace. Between the fireplace and the hall back to the bedroom was another door, currently closed.

A beautiful place, but to whom did it belong? He wondered.

He walked into the kitchen to check out what food might be stocked in the refrigerator when a voice came from behind.

"Hello again, Warren, I am glad to see you are doing well. You almost did not make it here. You had us worried."

Warren turned and was only slightly startled to see the man who stood in front of the door on the far side of the room. "Hello, Lan," he responded, as he frowned trying to remember how he knew the person standing across from him. Lan was slightly shorter than Warren and of average build with sandy-colored hair. Lan approached him and stuck out his hand, which Warren tentatively shook.

"Come sit with me by the fireplace, Warren. How are you feeling?"

"I feel fine, but a little confused. I don't know where I am, how I got here, or why I'm here."

"Good, that is precisely as it should be and how everything was planned."

Warren's mouth fell open as he wasn't expecting Lan's statement.

"I have many things I must tell you, and as I tell you, it will become familiar, and you will begin to understand this is all part of the process. You must now relax, listen, answer any questions I ask, and do not interrupt. I will answer all of your questions later.

"Let us begin." Lan paused a moment in thought before speaking. "What does the word earth mean to you?"

"It's the ground, the soil," Warren answered, and then hesitated. "It's also something familiar . . . I can't remember. Where am I?" He rubbed his temple and took an aggravated breath, feeling momentarily light-headed.

"Warren, be calm; you must relax, while I explain everything. Your mind is still processing all that has happened. You should only know the earth as the ground under your feet, but there is more I need to tell you Warren, relax, and listen."

Warren paused, confused by the words he was hearing. After a moment, he understood he didn't have another choice, so he sighed and took a seat across from Lan. The pain and anger momentarily left him when told to relax.

"The Earth is a planet on the other side of this galaxy, which some have called the Milky Way galaxy. It is many thousands of light-years away from where you are now. The planet does still exist, as does the entire solar system to which it is part, but it is no longer able to sustain life.

"Our scientists and others studied the Earth for hundreds of Earth years, and we were distressed to learn its sun was quickly becoming unstable. The sun began to shoot out vast amounts of solar flares, more massive than had ever been seen in the solar system before. The Human population perished almost immediately. Over a span of one Earth month, the sun tore through all of the magnetic fields protecting the planet. Afterward, it became, and always will be, a dead planet."

Warren sat across from Lan feeling like he had lost something great but didn't understand what exactly he lost. "A dead planet," Warren whispered, burying his head in his hands.

"We were prepared many years before the destruction began. We became aware of the sun's instability about seventy-five Earth years before. We knew we had to do something to help the intelligent life on the planet avoid extinction. We developed a plan to seed a new Earthlike world with species from the Earth and to populate it with individuals from the planet."

"Everything gone. Everybody dead."

"Yes Warren, please relax. Our scientists knew we would have to alter your bodies and suspected also your minds. They feared we could not simply retrieve people and move them here; the shock to their minds would be too much. You have experienced some of this, as I will explain later.

"This planet is like Earth, but in many ways, it is also different. This planet is twenty percent larger than the Earth, which means the gravity is twenty percent heavier. To you, it feels normal because we adjusted your body for the gravity of this world, and your mind knows no different.

"This planet has a vibrant ecosystem filled with a large variety of plant and animal species. In addition, we wanted to bring as many of the Earth's species here as possible. The intention was not just to preserve the Earth's variety of life, but also to build an ecosystem in some regions of this planet to make your new home feel familiar, to help in your transition."

"Why are you telling me all this useless information. So many dead."

"You need to understand why you are here. The information will help you further adjust."

Lan began to worry. Warren should not be so distressed, but he had no choice but to continue the program. He feared they might have to start over.

"We began by bringing plant life from all over the Earth, planting and cultivating in the appropriate areas of this planet. After fifty Earth years, we began to obtain and modify, as needed, animals and insects. The insects adapted quickly, but with the larger species of animals, we found we had to genetically adapt them to exist in this planet's gravity, atmosphere, and weather patterns. The process took over one hundred Earth years to complete.

"We brought fruit trees, vegetable plants, and other food seeds to allow your bodies to have access to natural types of nutrition. We could have altered your DNA further, but we already had enough manipulation to manage for you to survive on this planet. After we finished bringing what we thought was needed, we allowed the two ecosystems in some places to grow and merge for the next fifty Earth years. In other areas, we preserved the natural ecosystem. We built the necessary infrastructure, and the time came to bring the Humans we rescued."

When Lan said, 'bring the Humans,' Warren stood—prepared to run away, but Lan grabbed his hands and sternly told him to sit, relax and listen as instructed. Warren sat; he had no choice; his body wasn't his own to control at the moment.

"As I have mentioned, we were visiting the Earth for hundreds of years, but we never interfered or made our presence known. We were there to learn and study, but everything changed when we discovered the planet's ultimate fate. The decision to act came after much debate among the broader community. To help you, we needed to study you much closer, so we began to take people from across the Earth. We studied and experimented on them, some we returned, and some I regret, we could not."

Warren began to sweat as his heart rate increased even more. He wanted to run, to get away, but he couldn't make himself stand. At his side, his hands clenched, and his arms shook.

They had no right.

"This was not something we did lightly, and the process was disturbing to many of us, but to save your species, these were the things we had to do. The experience was difficult for many involved."

Lan stopped a moment as if lost in thought or silently in another communication.

Warren didn't notice, as his mind had started to block out everything his subconscious didn't want to hear.

"Many of the returned managed to remember some of the experience, while other Humans spotted a few of our ships about the Earth. We tried to avoid it, but on more than one occasion, we had mishaps which led to the capture of some of our people and ships by several governments of the Earth."

Lan's words jogged something in Warren's memory, clearing his mind and calming him.

"What happened to them, Lan? Were they returned?" He asked, sitting at the edge of his seat.

Warren was unsure why he now experienced concern instead of anxiety, but he could sense a feeling of loss from Lan. Although it made him sad, it did lessen the anger and fear he could detect in himself.

"They were not returned. When discovered, our people were already dead, and the Earth's governments kept the incidents a secret. I lost a good friend in one of the first crashes."

Lan paused again before continuing.

"After many years, our experiments were a success, and time was running out. We started taking people off the Earth for transplantation five years before the sun was about to cause the end of the planet. We took people with little emotional attachment to others, in most cases twenty-two to thirty-five years old. We brought people from all over the Earth, from every continent and every race. Those we took were healthy with no sign of disease, people with higher intelligence, and no propensity toward mental illness or criminal behavior."

Warren's lips quivered, and his body began to tremble. The house monitors informed Lan the subject was in distress.

"I have much more to tell you, but I see you are under much stress. Your brain must rest again to adjust."

Lan took a small instrument out of his pocket, which Warren had never seen before, yet it looked familiar. He told Warren to take it and open the top. With his hands shaking, he took the device, opened the lid, and saw a blue screen.

Day Four

The next morning Warren felt refreshed at first and ready for anything. He was prepared for the new day until he experienced a burst of panic, followed by anxiety, then by calm excitement. The mixed emotions quickly flowed over him as he lay there with the previous day's memories playing in his mind. He thought about everything Lan had told him yesterday and was frustrated he could remember nothing from before the morning. He recalled wanting to jump up and run away, but Lan put him in some form of trance. Now thinking back on it, He didn't understand why he was upset or afraid.

How do I even know Lan is telling the truth?

Nevertheless, something inside him knew everything Lan told him was true.

What was my life before yesterday, and what would it be after today? Where was everyone else?

All these thoughts rolling through his mind brought on the pain in the back of his head for another visit. He knew it was time to get up, and he hoped a long hot shower would ease the pain.

An hour later, with the pain in his head gone, he walked out to the great room to find Lan sitting in the chair by the fireplace. Between the chairs stood a small table with a tray of fruit, some variety of cake, and cups of tea.

Warren walked over to Lan and said, "One thing I do remember, Lan, is the idea of privacy. Will you always be here waiting for me every day, and how exactly did I get into bed?"

"Good morning, Warren. As I said yesterday, we still have much to discuss. As to how you got into bed and why you do not remember, let me explain. Please sit."

Lan reached into his pocket and pulled out the same device Warren remembered from the day before, and for a moment, it made him anxious. It resembled a cell phone, though he could not recall if he ever owned a cell phone or if this particular one was his.

"What is that?" he asked Lan.

"This is a simple communication device, an old one from Earth you will be able to use for some limited communication. It is also a trigger. We altered the device to display a message you cannot see and sounds you cannot hear, but they trigger your body to go into a protection mode, like a catatonic state. We followed and watched you, waiting for your brain and body to adjust to their new situation. We used this device to put you into the protection state when you became agitated or in need of your next rest period. After you entered the rest state, we came and took care of you. You remember none of this, and you remember nothing specific of your former world, as it is all part of the transition process.

"As to the matter of privacy, this should be the last day I need to be waiting here to talk to you and guide you, but there is a long process ahead, which I will explain. Though we may not be watching you directly, we will be monitoring you and your progress."

"May I ask a question of you, Lan?"

"Yes, today, I expect you to have many questions, most of which I should be able to answer, but first have some nourishment."

They ate the food that had been laid out and drank the tea. Warren admired the fireplace and looked over to the office shelves, curious about the binders in varying colors and sizes. He assumed Lan would explain them, but he made a mental note to ask Lan about them if no explanation came.

"With everything I have apparently forgotten, I do remember apples, berries, and tea, although I would prefer some coffee." After a few berries and another sip of tea, Warren resumed the conversation.

"I'm still trying to understand and, I guess, process all of this. I remember you mentioned yesterday; you had to adjust the animals. Did you also adjust me and others like me you had taken and brought to this place?"

"Yes, we did. We had to alter your body on a molecular level to allow you to survive on this planet. In addition to the higher gravity, air pressure is also higher, and this planet has a different ratio of nitrogen to oxygen than what was on Earth. This planet is considerably like my own, but it is not the same in many aspects."

"Is that why you look like us?"

"No, Warren, we do not look like you. What you see before you is a clone of another individual from Earth who did not make the transition. My mind can inhabit this body while my body is resting in stasis. I also feel I should point out this world had no intelligent life before transforming it for you. My home planet is many light-years from here, and I have not seen it for many cycles of our time. Someday when we finish here, I hope to return."

Warren took more fruit while Lan was talking; he was hungry, and the fruit was better than anything he could remember. The fragrance and taste were exquisite.

"The terms you're using are not only familiar to me, I also understand what they mean. How is it possible to know or remember those terms and concepts yet not remember my former life?" Warren sighed. "It's frustrating. I feel there are many things, many memories close but out of reach."

Warren stood, walked over to the fireplace, placed his hands on the mantle, lowered his head, and took a deep breath. Standing made him feel better; it made him feel more in control.

"It is all part of the transition process we have developed to ease you into your new life. The Human brain is primitive and delicate. Your minds could not take the quick transition to a new life while remembering all you had lost. As I mentioned, we also needed to adjust your bodies to survive in this new world. We changed you to be stronger, healthier, smarter, and capable of using parts of your brain the Human species had not been utilizing.

"Warren, please sit down."

Warren hesitated, fought an urge to run, and sighed knowing it to be a silly idea. He did as requested, but unlike yesterday, he didn't feel compelled to obey.

"During the transition period, you started to use those new abilities instinctively, and you knew we were watching. It caused you fear and mental distress. We learned from earlier experiences it would take a couple of days of adjustment for your mind to work through the transition. Some things must happen naturally, not in a lab setting."

Warren sat unmoving without saying another word while he tried to absorb everything. As he sat there, his body wanting him to move, he clenched his fists but didn't understand the reason for the returning anger.

"As I stated, we watched you. On the first day, you awoke to find yourself in the mountains, remembering nothing beyond going to bed and a few other minor details from your previous life on Earth. At first, you believed you might have been hiking and fell, you then slowly came to understand someone had taken you and put you there, but you did not know why.

"You grasped you were different, and the clothes you were wearing were not yours. You knew you had to move, and you knew in which direction, but as you progressed, the fear of the unknown was too much for your brain, and you fell into a fugue state. When it happened, we guided you further down the mountain. You awoke from your fugue state and continued on but not without problems.

"Later, your mind started to rebel once more and you became agitated and afraid. That was the first time we used the device. We provided you with water, additional nourishment, and gave you some time for your mind to rest. Later, after traveling a few hours, you became fearful of the coming night and could feel our presence nearby. You progressed to the small shelter we set up in time before any damage occurred, even though your mind was burning. We used the device again to put you into the protection state, and while you were unconscious, we took care of your physical needs and protected you for the evening. We moved back away from you an hour before dawn."

Warren listened as Lan went on, and his anger grew. His hands were sweating, and he started fumbling with his fingers. It was familiar to him and comforting.

"On the second day, you awoke remembering nothing from the day before. It became more natural to you to be in the woods until you realized you were alone. As before, your mind questioned everything. You were desperately trying to remember, and you had a great fear of us behind you.

"You went into the trees as your mind headed into another fugue state, so we used the device. This time we woke you to a controlled state where I introduced myself and pretended to be your hiking partner. I calmed you, put you into a short catatonic state, and left you to wake up on your own.

"You progressed a short way further until your questioning of where you were going and why it was important started to upset you greatly, so we had to use the device to put you back into the protective state. At this time, I was beginning to worry we were going to lose you. You had a way to go yet to reach the house, and a storm was coming. After an hour we sent you once more on your way."

Warren refilled his plate with berries and refreshed his tea as Lan spoke. He was no longer hungry, but eating made him stop playing with his hands. The more Lan talked about how they manipulated him, the more his anger increased. Instead of eating, he played with his food, crushing some of the berries with his fork.

How dare they? The thought ran over and over in his mind.

"You awoke and hurried on until you reached the house. By that time, the storm was upon you and severe. The storm, the fear, and the new knowledge starting to fill your mind caused your brain to overheat. I used the device to put you back into a partially catatonic state. I talked to you and showed you a bit of the house and the bedroom so they would feel familiar to you the next morning. I put you into bed where you remained until you awoke on your own yesterday, day three.

"When you awoke, your entire old-world memories were gone and pushed far below the surface of your mind. The house and the surroundings appeared normal to you. You began a typical morning routine, and I waited for you to come out.

"As I am sure you remember, we talked, and I started to explain everything to you. Even though your old memories remained suppressed, for the most part, your mind started to rebel. I used the device again. I put you back to bed where you remained until this morning, day four.

"I don't expect to need the control instrument any longer. Your mind should have completed this part of the journey. So, how are you feeling now?"

Warren considered it for a moment and realized he had no more anxiety or frustration, only a wave of growing anger. His hands were now still. The lack of memories didn't bother him, which he told Lan before asking his next question as he tried to control his anger.

"Why was all this of the last three days necessary? Why could you not alter my mind as necessary? Fill it with what it needed to know and completely wipe out the old?"

"The Human mind is complex. Although Humans had come nowhere near using it to its potential, it is one of the most complex brains in the galaxy. Many other intelligent species have much less complicated brains and nervous systems. Humanity is unique in the universe. It is one of the reasons we rescued you.

Lan paused to collect his thoughts, and Warren was taken aback by the realization he now experienced.

He's hiding something from me.

"We tried the more direct approach, but it failed. We brought people together for a group orientation, but that also failed; even with changing your memories, the abrupt transition was too much of a shock. After much trial and error, we found putting you into slightly familiar surroundings and guiding you over a few days was the best approach. However, we still occasionally have failures."

"How many are there? How many people have you taken and manipulated to your liking?"

Lan didn't react to the comment. He remained aware of but did not address Warren's apparent anger.

"There are five hundred and sixty-two who have come before you with success, twenty-three others currently in transition, and over four hundred more waiting. Our goal is to have one thousand individuals start a new life for Humanity.

"If all remains working well, everyone will have forgotten the details of their past life, but will remember the concepts that helped shape their former life, such as the concepts of quality of life, liberty, fairness, freedom, and a hunger to learn."

Warren was about to ask another question when Lan suggested they take a break.

The House

"Come, Warren, let me show you around your home," Lan said as he stood and headed to the kitchen. As Warren passed the piano, he dragged his finger across the rich, black mahogany. He stopped and stared at it with a familiar longing; his anger abated; he became filled with excitement about the prospect of creating music with the glistening keys. A tune instantly popped into his mind, but no matter how hard he tried, he couldn't recall ever playing.

Lan turned to watch Warren's reaction to the instrument. When Warren pulled out the bench, Lan directed him to follow.

"The kitchen has all the conveniences you would have been used to operating and everything else you should need to cook meals. It is essential, Warren, for your body to be well-nourished. We have discovered a tendency for Humans to skip meals when they become busy. It is not recommended.

Warren looked around the kitchen and poked his nose into some of the cabinets. The cooktop was familiar, and Warren agreed he knew how to operate most of the appliances, but he didn't think he appreciated much about cooking. The term 'pizza' briefly flashed into his mind.

Lan was standing there watching him, and as the image of pizza slipped away, Lan asked, "So, Warren, how do you feel about the kitchen?"

"Lan, I don't think it mattered much to me one way or the other. I don't expect I will be making any meals in the oven for myself. When will I get to meet the others?"

"That, Warren, will be part of the discussion later. Let us continue. You are familiar with the bedroom. I want to point out you will find a normal wardrobe waiting for you when you return. We learned the plain attire we originally provided helps with the adjustment on the first day or two. You will see we removed the one-piece garments to the lower level. We recommend you use them when working outside."

Before Warren could ask Lan to clarify—work outside, Lan had moved back into the living room area of the great room.

"I expect you will want to use the fireplace in a few weeks. The temperatures in this area average from zero to ten degrees cwantare for about two months. Although not needed for heating, I understand many Humans find the fire relaxing."

Warren had become lost in thought as mountains covered with snow appeared in his mind. He didn't immediately hear Lan's question.

"Tell me, Warren, does the term cwantare mean anything to you?"

"What? Oh yes, it's the measurement of temperature."

Lan was about to resume his questioning when Warren interrupted.

"Lan, you say weeks and months, does that mean we will use the time and day formats I remember?"

"Let me ask you, Warren, did the term cwantare feel as familiar to you as the terms weeks and months?

"Yes, sort of. I know weeks and months are from the planet you called Earth, and I know cwantare is, as I said, a measurement of temperature, but they feel different to me. I understand cwantare is new, but I don't know any other word or term to use instead."

"I find your thoughts interesting, Warren. To answer your question, yes, for the most part. Although you know and will use the Galactic Standard for temperature, measurement, and distance, we found it is best to use the temporal terms you are familiar with from the past, but with some changes. We decided to base everything on tens like Earth's metric system. This planet has a different amount of time for rotation and movement around its sun. We broke the year into ten months, each month having five weeks each broken down to ten days. Each day has twenty hours, and each hour one hundred minutes, and each minute, one hundred seconds. We did rename the days and the months based on a variety of Earth's languages because the number of days and months are different."

"So, there are five hundred days each year."

"Yes. It may take some unconscious adjustment on your part, but we did modify your body rhythms to the twenty-hour daily cycle. If you search your mind, you should find you do not remember the old names of the months or days, nor do you remember holidays of any sort. None of those concepts are part of your new life. You will learn the names of the days, and months later, when you start your self-taught education, we call Learnings."

"Lan, we didn't all speak the same language, did we?"

"How do you know, Warren?"

"I'm not sure, but I'm correct, I believe."

"Yes, you are correct. Not that you will comprehend the difference, but your mind can now understand all the old languages spoken by all whom we brought to this planet. For example, each of you knows weeks and months in your previous language, but others will hear you say it in their old original language.

"Your question was interesting, now let us continue.

"I'm sure you noticed the desk and computer in the corner. The operating system works with a keyboard, the hand tool you would have called a mouse, as well as gestures and voice. The operating system is easy to understand, and details are part of your memory."

Warren's head started to hurt, but this time he was sure the headache was from all the information Lan expected him to take in at one time. It was like being back in college at the University of . . . the name wasn't coming to him.

"You will be spending much time here at first since this is where you will learn about the process we have been discussing, this planet and the universe. You will also learn about the other races that inhabit the galaxy, and you will learn general scientific theory to help you develop a new civilization."

"Lan, you keep talking about this planet. Does it have a name?"

"At this time, we refer to it as the Human Project Planet. The Council decided the residents of the planet should pick its name. When a government is set up here in the future, it will be one of its first tasks.

"Let us continue."

"You say that every time I ask a question! You said you would answer my questions, but I feel like you're brushing me off."

"I assure you, Warren, I am not trying to brush you off or hide anything from you. You will have plenty of time to learn the details of anything and any topic you like, but for now, I still have much to tell you before I leave."

"Where are you going?"

"I am here to get you started on your new life, and I will always be in contact, but there will be others to guide you into this life.

"Let us—come, Warren."

"Great, now I feel like a dog."

Lan stopped for a moment and smiled, though Warren sensed surprise.

"I am glad your sense of humor is emerging. It is one of your traits we tried to carry forward. Although I do not fully understand Human humor, it is better than your anger."

Warren ignored Lan's reference to his anger as he headed over to the piano, feeling drawn to it. again. Lan grabbed Warren's arm and directed him toward what he thought was a closet between the bedroom hall and the fireplace. He was wrong. The door opened to stairs leading to a lower level. On one side of the lower level's hallway was a room with workout equipment, including what he recognized as a rowing machine.

"This, Warren, is for you to keep your body strong. You cannot become fat and lazy like many humans before, and you can only walk outside, not jog or run. In addition, there is a hot tub and a small lap swimming pool in the other room down the hall, plus shower facilities and your laundry area."

Warren walked around the room and examined the equipment as Lan watched in silence.

"The rowing machine is more familiar than the others, and the treadmill."

Lan led him across the hall to another door.

"This room here is your storage."

The room contained shelves filled with food and two freezers. Along another wall were generic supplies like light bulbs, paper towels, and various tools.

Lan took some time to point out a few specific items, such as the environmental and emergency systems if the automatic systems failed, and led Warren to a door for access to the outside from the lower level. He showed Warren where he would find the coveralls and a variety of garden tools.

"In addition to the supplies of food here, we planted a garden outside filled with mature vegetable plants that we expect you to maintain and harvest. All you need to learn is available to access on the computer.

"Speaking of food, it is time for lunch. I know it feels like you recently ate, but your body will need much energy for your full development. Let us go back upstairs to the patio where you can enjoy the view."

They went upstairs, but Warren sat on the piano bench before Lan could stop him. He sat there a moment, and without thinking about it, began to play a tune. Since he first was drawn to the piano, the melody had been in his head. He knew how to make the music come out of the piano with little thought or effort.

"Lan, I have no idea what I'm playing or how I know the tune. I feel I should know its name, but I don't."

"I am glad you have retained your ability to play. For some Humans, if you had a talent or passion for something in your past life, it carries through to your new life. I can confirm you were a musician and you loved the piano. It is good to see you retained your talent. We were not sure if you would retain enough knowledge and skill, nor did we expect you to remember any particular melody."

"Sitting here playing, makes me feel relaxed and happy. Is there . . . sheet music?"

"You will be able to find and print sheet music from the computer; however, for the time being, it will be only the music, not the words, as I will explain over lunch."

Warren played for another minute to finish the song, something he had to do. When finished, they proceeded through the glass doors to the patio, where the table had been set up with sandwiches and drinks.

Apparently, they were not alone.

Lunch is Served

The first thing Warren noticed as they walked onto the patio was the spectacular unobstructed view. Glancing out the window from the house didn't do it justice. The valley below almost vibrated with a variety of colored flowers. The trees filled the remainder of the landscape up to the rolling hills and steep mountainsides topped with sparkling white snow.

The second thing he noticed was the lunch. A sandwich on some type of roll sat on a bright yellow plate. A colorful bowl of salad sat in the middle of the table, filled with vegetables he recognized, such as tomatoes, multicolored peppers, and a mixed variety of lettuce. In another bowl sat what appeared to be fruit, but Warren wasn't positive.

"I recognize the vegetables, but these, I believe to be, fruits, are strange to me."

"We brought many species of plants, vegetables, and animals to this world. We wanted to save as much as possible, not only intelligent life. You are correct about the fruit. They are from trees native to this planet that are safe for Human consumption.

"As you become a full participant of the society here, you will find cuisine from Earth different from where you lived, so you may not recognize the variety. You can find out more about the entire process from your computer."

They ate and talked more about how Warren was feeling. Lan was pleased Warren was well but concerned when he complained he had nothing by which to compare.

"You stripped away my memories, so maybe I'm well, and maybe I'm not! How would I know?"

Lan ignored the comment but noted it as a possible issue. After lunch, he talked about the land around Warren's house, although Warren was still having trouble with the concept of this being his property.

Try as he might, Warren couldn't keep his focus on Lan's words. He was distracted by the breathtaking vista below. Mixed within the evergreens were a vibrant combination of trees starting to show their colors. Lan had indicated cooler weather was coming, so Warren assumed it to be the fall season. The house sat on a hill, looking over the broad tree-filled valley. Below the patio's right side, he saw another sitting area with chairs, including what looked like a place to cook. While he admired the view, Warren enjoyed the gentle breeze and the sunshine, interrupted only by an occasional passing cloud.

"Each house is surrounded by one thousand cusalns of land that has been terraformed, planted, and populated with Earth's species. In addition to preserving some of the lower species from Earth, it also helps with adjusting to your new life by surrounding you with things your subconscious mind will find reassuring. The area around the houses we partially controlled, but we try to let things progress on their own as much as possible.

"We scattered across this world, preserve areas terraformed solely to create a habitat for animals that do not always get along well with Humans. For instance, larger bears and many predators which inhabited the region of Earth called Africa."

"I don't recognize the name," Warren said.

"You would not. We have removed most of the names of areas, countries, and large cities from your memory to help with the transition. You will remember the names of some animals, but not remember where they lived."

"What of the animal species who inhabited this planet, before you took it over to do with as you pleased?"

Warren grasped as he was speaking, his voice was forceful, accusing, and somewhat angry. The feeling left him quickly, and though he did catch a slight reaction on Lan's face, he said nothing.

"The land outside of the housing area has been left largely untouched. The two ecologies are slowly merging and will eventually become one new ecology."

Warren finished his sandwich while the breeze blew across the patio carrying a fragrance of fresh flowers which danced in rhythm to the wind, as another question came to mind.

"Are any of the natural species of this planet dangerous?"

"Yes, Warren, there are many larger and more aggressive animals on this planet. We moved all of those species to another continent where they can live as they would have originally. We did have to adjust them to the changes we made to the planet, but the ecology is mostly intact."

They were silent for a moment when Warren realized he had many questions about the larger purpose behind all they had done. For some reason, he again grew angry and now suspicious. He wanted to know what was in it for them.

"So, who exactly are you," he said more forcefully than he intended, "that you feel you can manipulate other beings to your liking?" Warren quickly apologized, feeling embarrassed but still angry, and his head started to throb. "I'm sorry, Lan. I don't understand this anger I'm having."

"I'm glad to hear, Warren; you acknowledge your anger toward me and the circumstances. I was getting concerned you denied your resentment. Humanity believes in freedom and self-determination. These traits serve you well but do cause some issues with the transition. We cannot, nor do we want to suppress it entirely. Unless they fail to go away, your occasional bouts of anger are nothing to be concerned about unless they fail to go away.

"To answer your question, we are Jonton, one of many species in the galaxy. Our civilization had existed before the time Humanity discovered fire. We have been a spacefaring civilization for over one thousand of this planet's years.

"Twenty-two spacefaring species exist in the known galaxy, and over one hundred more worlds have intelligent life. There is peace among the spacefaring now, but that has not always been the case.

"The decision to help you was extremely long in coming. The debate persisted among our people for over ten Earth years. We had never done this before, and we were not certain it would be successful. We knew there would be some degree of manipulation needed to make the transition a success. That is why some argued against the mission, but eventually, we did decide it would be better to alter Humanity rather than let it be extinguished."

Warren thought for a moment while dishing more salad onto his plate. "I believe from what I remember we were not spacefaring."

"No. You were in the very early stages of exploration. You had landed a few times on your moon and planned a crewed trip to one of the outer planets."

Warren shifted in his chair, uncomfortable for a reason he couldn't explain. He stood, walked to the patio's edge, and gazed into the valley below. *She would love this view.* He watched the breeze moving through the trees, pushing out of his mind her image, and spoke to Lan without turning around.

"Even though I don't remember Earth, I feel a great loss. What of all our civilization had accomplished—music, art, literature?"

"Before I answer, I must ask how bad is this feeling of loss? We have tried to prevent you from feeling any loss; it is one of the reasons we wiped part of your memory. Most of the other Humans awakened have not expressed this feeling. It is crucial if the feeling persists, you let me know so we can give you help and guidance."

Warren sat back in the chair, and uneasily assured Lan it wasn't that bad, and he promised to keep Lan informed. He hadn't exactly told the truth; however, Lan was satisfied, so he proceeded to answer Warren's question.

"We have preserved significant amounts of original pieces of art as well as many documented copies. We have digital files of over seventy percent of your literature and ninety percent of your music. We also have as much of your history as we could save, but you will not be allowed access to all of it for many years."

"Why?"

"You will have access to some of the music and art, but we feel it will be best if you do not have access to anything which details the less desirable aspects of your culture's prior existence until you are a fully settled culture on your new world. That is why the sheet music will not have lyrics. After some time has passed, your history will be fully available to you for study.

"I believe a significant member of your past society once said, 'Those that fail to learn from history are destined to repeat it.' We do feel it vital you know of your past, but not until you have adjusted to the present. Of course, repeating the mistakes your civilization made along the way would be harder considering the circumstances; however, we believe all species have something to teach."

"When do I get to meet the others?"

"You must first get accustomed to your new life and learn about the universe of which you are a member. You have much to learn, and you can consider this a learning vacation. Eventually, you will meet others of your species. When we finish settling everyone, it will then be time for you to form a government, an economy, and a full society.

"You will have to determine a direction for your life, establish a career, maybe find a mate, and then when you are ready, join the Galactic civilization. We cannot guide and direct your new world forever. You will need to become a fully self-sustained world, part of the larger galaxy of intelligent species.

"You will probably not live to see all of this happen."

Warren thought for a moment then replied, "How long do you expect this all to take before we become fully independent? I feel like I'm going to miss the best of this new life."

"It will perhaps take close to one hundred of this world's years before Humanity is ready for complete independence."

"How old am I, Lan?"

"You were twenty-seven Earth years old when we retrieved you. We estimate if you live well, the male of your species should live from ninety to one hundred of this world's years."

"So, I will be close to seeing a complete new rebirth of our civilization, but the new world will belong more to my children."

"That is correct, Warren."

After a brief pause to let everything he said register with Warren, Lan stood and indicated it was time to leave. Warren noticed Lan's movements to be stoic and stiff. He wondered if it had to do with his use of the body or maybe only a trait of the Jonton.

"I have given you much to think about and digest. I suggest you go rest again to give your body and mind more time to adjust. Tomorrow is the true beginning of your new life."

"How do I contact you?"

"You will see a link to my communication device on your computer and your device. If you need me or want to talk, please do not hesitate. You can also instruct your CA to connect us."

Warren didn't know what his CA was but figured he would learn later. He stood and shook Lan's hand. "I'll contact you if the need arises, I promise."

Lan walked down the steps from the patio and disappeared into the forest off to the right behind the house. Warren wondered where exactly Lan was going and how. Oh well, a mystery for another time.

Warren recognized his body and mind were tired. His head ached, so he went to the bedroom and went to sleep without even taking off the silly all-in-one overall.

Warren slept but not peacefully as his mind drifted back to memories he no longer was to possess. He stirred briefly as a strong storm blew through in the early evening, but he fell back to sleep and dreamt until morning.

WARREN'S NEW LIFE

Heading for war, the United States vows . . .
China is promising to attack . . .
Bright light, movement, prodding . . .
We will help you, new beginning, another place . . .
Congratulations Warren & Sam . . .
No, I don't believe, take me back . . .

Morning Routine

Bright sunlight pushed through the window. Warren was excited to start his new life even though he remembered nothing of his old one. He vaguely recalled an odd dream about people he didn't recognize and a party, but the dream quickly slipped away as he stretched.

He didn't need a shower; however, he had to complete his routine to start the day; it's what he always did in the morning. He removed the jumper he slept in and stood there, wondering where it should go. Lan told him there would be other clothes now, so would he need the garment another time?

After some searching around the bedroom, Warren found what he believed to be a hamper in one of the bathroom closets. After dumping the overall, he decided instead to start the day off right in the workout room.

He found workout clothes in one of the drawers and a full selection of socks and underwear. There were also drawers of shirts and pants and a closet he decided to check out after the workout. Lan said there was a shower down there, but he didn't know if there were any towels, so he grabbed one from the bathroom linen closet and headed downstairs.

He glanced out the large window in the great room and saw the sun shining on his patio while the leaves on the trees gently swayed from the light wind also blowing through the wildflowers. He watched for a while, feeling at peace.

Warren looked around the workout room to figure out where to begin. He didn't have any actual memory of working out, so he decided to start on the treadmill. He soon became bored; something was missing. As he jogged at a fast pace, he thought about everything Lan had told him the day before. He remained amazed he could remember things like the workout equipment and names of animals but not remember specifics about his life or past experiences on the planet Lan called Earth.

The skills needed to do such a thing to a person's mind were hard to grasp, and he began to feel angry again about what they had done, but it quickly passed. What would happen to him if the anger didn't stop? Lan had indicated it could be a problem, but what did that mean? He was afraid to ask and decided he would not be mentioning this latest episode.

After the treadmill, he used some of the lifting machines. The machines tracked how much he lifted and how many reps he performed and displayed the information on a small screen. A similar record was projected onto the wall after he did a set with the free weights. He had no clue how it got there, how it updated, or how he would get rid of it if desired. He needed to get on the computer and hoped there were some general and specific instructions for the house.

After the weights, he spent time on the bike and soon became tired and hungry. He decided to check out the pool and hot tub on another day and headed into the shower area. The shower room included multiple showerheads, which he thought would be great if he experienced muscle pain. The room included a sink and a full supply of personal items—and yes, some towels. "They have thought of everything," he said to the empty room.

He found another hamper and tossed in his clothes. Score! He thought, not having any idea what the term meant. The multiple showerheads were fully adjustable and were great even if he didn't need them yet to work out any muscle kinks. He could get used to this life.

Warren finished, dried off, tossed the towel into the hamper, and it hit him—there were no clothes down there, and he had brought none with him. He panicked a second until he realized being alone in his own house meant he could walk around all day naked if he wanted. He headed back upstairs to find something to wear.

When he glanced out the large window, he became self-conscious, as if someone were watching him. He felt vulnerable and nervous, but he didn't understand the reason. He recollected Lan mentioning they had improved upon his senses, but who would be watching if his senses were correct?

Warren hurried into the bedroom, and immediately his anxiety disappeared. He looked through the selection of clothes in the drawers and moved on to the closet. He noticed there were no dress clothes or shoes, but it did contain a variety of casual pants and shirts, many of which were a shade of blue. To one side of the closet, he found hiking boots plus rain and snow boots. The snow boots made him wonder about hats and gloves for winter. Lan had told him everything he would need to know would be on the computer, so he decided that would be his next step after some breakfast.

He sat for a moment on the bed and experienced a brief moment of sadness. He couldn't understand where it came from—maybe an old, suppressed memory. When the melancholy passed, he thought about his new life, the only life he knew and would ever know. He thought about the house and was excited it belonged to him. He wondered if it was a permanent situation or if they would move him elsewhere in the future.

Warren knew he would accomplish nothing sitting there. He headed to the kitchen to see if he knew how to make breakfast. After some searching, he found coffee grounds and made a pot of coffee. In the refrigerator, he found a dozen eggs and sliced cheese. He expected something else for breakfast but had no idea what might be missing.

He knew how to make fried eggs and believed he knew how to make over-easy eggs without breaking them. After successfully cooking two eggs with some cheese, he toasted a bagel, feeling he preferred it to toasted bread. He sat at the counter, ate his breakfast, and drank his first cup of coffee, still having the impression something was missing. It was as if he'd lost something or should have been doing something else. More mysteries he figured he should get used to as a daily occurrence. Lan told him there would be a continuous adjustment period, and he wondered how long the period would last.

When he finished, he moved to check out the computer. His excitement was mounting, like a kid on . . . something, some event that wasn't coming to him; another odd thing, another memory hiding in his mind.

Computer

In front of the partially filled shelves sat a wooden desk. Warren recognized the classical style and beautiful tones of oak wood. He spent almost a full minute admiring the desk's construction before bothering to look at the materials on the desk. In addition to the computer, he found a lamp, notepad, pen, and a printer. He opened the drawers and discovered they were primarily empty except for some additional notepads, pens, and pencils.

Warren put down his cup and went over to the shelves to look at one of the binders, but it seemed to be stuck when he tried to pull one out. They didn't really appear to be binders, but the term popped into his head when he had first noticed them. Feeling frustrated and, for some reason, a little embarrassed, he sat at the desk. After looking at the keyboard and monitor for a few seconds, he couldn't find a power button, so he moved the mouse.

The computer screen came to life with a blue background and the words:

TURN ON COMPUTER PROTOCOLS

He reached for the mouse again, and a cursor appeared. He hovered above the words and clicked.

The blue faded away to be replaced by a picture he recognized as the view from the patio. When he noticed the leaves of the trees moving in the image, he comprehended it was a live feed.

In the top right corner of the screen in white type on a black background were words and numbers.

Tembre 35, 006 – 08:74.

He believed it to be the month, day, year, and time.

To the right side of the screen was a column of icons, which he believed to be a list of programs. He moved the mouse, clicked on the top icon, and became startled by a voice that seemed to come from all around him.

"Hello, Warren, good morning. Please stand in the circle on the floor for your morning physical."

He looked around, thinking Lan or someone else was in the house, but no one was there. The voice didn't sound like Lan; in fact, it sounded almost like a woman. The voice repeated.

"Hello, Warren, good morning. Please stand in the circle on the floor for your morning physical."

The voice did sound Human, but something was off, and he realized the sound wasn't coming from behind or around him, but in his head.

"Hello," he said, but he didn't get a response. "Hello."

After a few seconds, he heard in his head, *"Hello Warren, good morning. If you are speaking to me, please say the word 'computer' first."*

He stared at the screen expecting something, but the same image remained.

"Computer, are you speaking to me?"

"Yes," was the reply.

Okay, he could play this game. "Computer, what did you ask me to do?"

"Please stand in the circle on the floor for your morning physical."

Warren looked a few cux over and on the floor was a red circle that wasn't there before. After a few seconds, the computer repeated, *"Please stand in the circle on the floor for your morning physical."*

He walked over to the spot on the floor, and immediately a bright blue-white light enveloped his body. He found he could not move at all, no matter how hard he tried. He stood frozen for what seemed like a full minute, feeling no pain or other sensation while the scan was in progress. When the light went away, and he could move, he asked what had happened and received no answer.

"Oops, I forgot. Computer, what happened? What did you do?"

"Warren, i gave you your morning physical. I am required to do this every morning to make sure you are staying healthy. I am pleased to report all your systems are in order."

"You make me feel like a machine," he said, before repeating it proceeded by "computer."

"Warren, i am sorry."

"Computer . . . oh, this is . . ." He paused, annoyed, and before he could collect his thoughts, the computer again spoke in his mind.

"Warren, i did not understand."

"Computer, can I change what I call you?"

"Warren, if you are referring to my initiation word, yes."

"Computer, from now on, your initiation word will be . . . nag. That is more fitting."

"Warren, confirming, initiation word is now nag."

"Good, and please stop using my name all the time. Oh hell. Comp . . . nag, stop using my name every time you address me!"

"I understand."

"Nag, do you have to be in my head? I feel like I'm being violated."

"Is this better?"

The voice was now coming from somewhere above him instead of in his head. "Much better."

The only voices I want inside my head are my own thoughts.

"Nag, yes, that's much better. Nag, are we able to communicate in every room of the house?"

"If you are addressing me with multiple responses or questions, you do not need to repeat the initiation word. To answer your question, yes, we may communicate in any room of the house and outside the house using the audible house system for about thirty cuselts away. However, when you are outside, i must respond via the communication implant."

"Well, I guess I have a lot to learn," he said out loud, but of course, the computer didn't respond.

He spent the next hour communicating with nag, or the CA, which he now understood to mean computer assistant—and learning the daily routines he had to follow. His regular activities included the morning physical and exercising, among other things. The CA instructed him on using the interface via the mouse and keyboard and showed him the various programs installed in the system.

The CA informed Warren he could do everything by voice command if he wished, but he preferred to use the mouse and keyboard while sitting at the desk. Using the computer, he could study maps of the house and his property. The property appeared on the map as the Warren Estridge Estate.

My last name must be Estridge. His full name was something he never thought to ask Lan before he left. It sounded right and familiar.

Outside his territory, little was visible, and the areas displayed on the map as wild, resources, or Estate followed by numbers. When he asked the CA if he could walk to one of the other estates, it said no, but didn't elaborate.

"Nag, why can't I see more information about the other residents or the other continent Lan mentioned?"

"You will not be able to see information about the other inhabitants of this planet until you have met them, and they allow you the privilege."

"When will that happen? When do I get to meet the others?"

"As Lan mentioned, you must first adjust to your new life and routine, and learn about the world you now inhabit."

Warren was about to argue, then decided to move on when the CA displayed the other continent on the map he had been viewing.

"Here is the other major landmass of this world."

The screen now showed both continents on the map. The other continent was smaller than the inhabited one he lived on and had markings in three areas. One was 'natural'; one was 'resource,' and the last, 'spaceport facilities.'

In the middle of the last was a small area identified as Port Nateria.

"Nag, what does Nateria mean?"

"It does not mean anything. It is the name of the spaceport."

"Who named it?"

"The name was given by the Trandel."

"Lan's species are the Jonton, so this must be another alien," he said out loud, thinking he had better not make a habit of it, but then again, to whom else could he talk? It was only him and the CA, for now.

"Nag, who are the Trandel?"

"They are the species most advanced with space travel, planet transformation, and construction. They built most of the facilities on this planet."

"I thought the Jonton built this."

"No, the Jonton do the scientific, genetic, and medical work, as well as administer the reclamation process."

"Nag, you answered without me addressing you."

"As I indicated before, if we are in conversation, it is not always necessary to address me first."

"So much to learn."

"I have confidence; Warren, you will get there."

Oh great, a pep talk from a computer, or maybe the computer's attempt at humor. He needed to remember to ask Lan if they programmed the computer with a sense of humor.

"Nag, you said 'reclamation project.' Is that what they call this transition process?"

"The term reclamation applies more to the planet, but the transition process is the part the Jonton also control."

"Display the map as a spinning globe with actual satellite images, if they exist."

The planet appeared on his screen showing the two major continents, a few other small islands, and the poles' ice sheets. Most of the world was oceans, and the two continents had many lakes, which had not been shown on the maps.

"Nag, display all names of places on the globe and slow the rotation by half."

Not much changed.

"That's it?" He asked.

"Yes, only major areas have been named on this planet. The task is to be assigned to the inhabitants when the reclamation process is complete."

"Show me where Lan lives."

"That information is not available."

He sat there for a moment, thinking about what the CA had said. He guessed Lan didn't want visitors, or maybe he would tell him when the time was right.

He had been quiet for a time, thinking and watching the planet spin by, so he figured he better use the initiation word.

"Nag, can you zoom in to show me more detail of the spaceport or the natural area of the planet?"

The map zoomed to show the port marked only in outline with all detailed grayed out.

"Nag, show me the natural area in detail and freeze the rotation."

The globe stopped spinning and zoomed into the natural area. The image now showed a combination of forested land with areas that slowly rose to high snow-covered mountains and down to some desert-like regions.

"Show me some of the animals."

The CA didn't respond.

Must have been too much time since his last question. The process was going to be frustrating. "Nag, show me some of the animals."

"I am not permitted to do that at this time." Before he could respond, it continued. "Warren, you now have the privilege to access Learnings One from the knowledge wall. It contains information about house maintenance and daily routines you must observe."

He thought about the implications of the word 'must,' and the silliness of the term 'knowledge wall,' as the top left binder or Learnings popped out a bit from the shelf.

"You will be able to read the material in the volume in book format or scan the chip to access the information on the computer monitor."

Warren was about to walk over to the shelf and grab the Learnings when he heard, "It is time for you to have lunch and then go outside to tend to the garden."

Tending to the garden must be another of those things I 'must' do.

He questioned how many tasks were there he must do, and what happened if he didn't?

He wondered what time it was, so he looked at the computer monitor, which flashed 10:86.

The information made sense; he guessed when his day was twenty hours long. He had no memories of any time tracking, aside from days, months, or years, but he did know breakfast was in the morning, lunch was around mid-day, and dinner was in the evening. The knowledge he had along with the gaps were going to be an odd thing to deal with going forward, but he guessed it would get easier. He knew what amnesia was and began to realize how bad it must be for others, as he was now struggling with a partial, forced type of amnesia.

"Nag, I am a bit hungry, any recommendations for lunch? Do you have any idea what is available?"

"I have a complete inventory of all available foodstuffs and supplies. All items are tagged and tracked; you do not need to worry about running out of supplies."

"That's good to know, even though it didn't answer my first question."

"I do not know what you like Warren; however, i would recommend you eat at least twenty grams of protein."

"Sounds yummy! Only one way to find out."

Thinking ahead about dinner, while listening to his now rumbling stomach, he went into the kitchen, looked in the freezer, and saw an assortment of clear containers filled with a few varieties of food. Different colored lids differentiated between fish, meat, and vegetable meals, and each had a label with a brief description. He pulled out one he recognized as chopped steak, baked potato, and carrots and placed it in the refrigerator.

He looked in the cabinets and found a variety of familiar food items; soup, vegetables, and pasta. All were in glass jars so he could see them, with basic informative labels. He picked a pasta jar, opened it, grabbed a bowl, and put it in the microwave to cook. He waited as the food cooked and momentarily felt dizzy as an image of another kitchen flashed in his mind. The vision disappeared as rapidly as it came, and in a couple of minutes, he sat and ate a delicious pasta meal with a tomato and cheese sauce. He also grabbed what he thought was a juice bottle, and to his surprise was an iced tea.

Not bad. Cooking for himself wouldn't be too hard, but it was only the first day on his own. After his meal, he asked the CA where he could find the garden. It told him to go out the back door, and the garden would be off to the left. Warren thought for a moment but couldn't remember where to find the backdoor, so he had to ask nag, which made him feel a little foolish. He felt sure Jon showed him, but he couldn't remember. Thankfully nag did not bring up the fact he should know.

"The back door is down the stairs and through the storage pantry area off to the right side. You will find clothes and shoes by the back door you can change into if you like. It would be best not to bring dirt into the house."

"Nag, thank you."

Almost like being married.

The thought came out of nowhere. Based on what Lan had said, Warren was sure he never married or even became engaged, or they wouldn't have taken him. Must be based on an old memory of what married life was like for others I knew; people who are now gone.

The thought made him feel sad even though he had no memories of anyone in particular.

Outside

Warren found the clothes and boots, nag suggested he wear for working in the garden. There was also a pair of gloves, an assortment of garden tools, and a basket. He took the basket as he stepped outside into the bright sunlight and appreciated this was the first time he had ventured beyond the patio. He breathed deep, enjoying the fragrance of the fall air.

He stood below the patio off the main living area, looking down into the valley he had seen through the window. It was magnificent, with the sun illuminating the different greens of the valley and the trees' multicolored leaves. He looked around at the landscape with a feeling of contentment. Unlike the last time he walked outside, based on what Lan told him, he felt completely safe and comfortable.

She dreamed of a house like this looking over a lush valley.

Warren rubbed his head, wondering from where the strange thought emerged. Lan told him he didn't have a girlfriend. If true, who was she?

A gentle slope led away from the back of the house, and to the right, a few trees provided shade over a picnic table and a gas grill surrounded by stone. Stepping stones provided a path from the back door to the picnic area and to the front. After admiring the view for a few minutes as the pain subsided, he walked over to look at the garden. He found an assortment of familiar vegetables and also a variety of herbs, some of which were recognizable; however, recognition didn't matter since his hosts marked everything with a small placard.

The warm breeze caused him to wonder about the seasons of this world. If this garden were seasonal, he would probably need to harvest and store some of those vegetables. As Warren stood there, he comprehended he knew how to can some veggies to have during the winter months, yet he could not remember ever having done so.

"Nag, how long is the growing season?"

"The growing season in this area lasts five to six months."

He had spoken his question aloud, but the CA answered him using the implant, so he tried only thinking his next question.

"So, what do I do for fresh vegetables when it isn't the growing season? Will I only have what I prepare and can for myself available to me, or will there be fresh vegetables from other sources?"

"You will preserve some vegetables and others you will grow in the greenhouse during the colder months. You will also be supplied with vegetables as needed as part of the regular stocking program."

Warren found it odd and disturbing, but it wasn't difficult to communicate with the CA using the implant. He wondered if the CA could read his mind. Could it hear his thoughts and questions even if he didn't use the initiation word? Warren felt like he had fallen into a sci-fi movie, and he didn't appreciate the feeling.

He picked a few ripe vegetables and filled half the basket before going back inside. The CA told him he could wash the vegetables in the sink and take them upstairs in another basket, so he didn't dirty anything in the living area.

"Nag, have you always been such a clean freak?"

"I do not understand the question."

"I guess they didn't program you for humor. Too bad."

The CA didn't have a response as Warren cleaned the vegetables and left them to dry. He decided to go back outside and explore the rest of his house and the surrounding area.

Beyond the garden and around the house, he found the greenhouse. It appeared small, maybe ten cux by twenty cux with two rows of tables. On shelves were containers of various shapes and sizes, all containing soil ready for planting.

"Nag, when would I need to start planting in the greenhouse? How long until it gets cold?"

"We are a month away from the time to plant the seeds."

"Where are the seeds? I don't see any here."

"The seeds are stored in the house in the garden section of the storage area. I will let you know when it is time to start planting."

Warren left the greenhouse and walked to check out the other side of the house while enjoying the pleasantly warm temperature. On the way, he decided to first check out the grill in the picnic area. It wasn't large, which made sense since food for one, would be the norm until introduced to the others. Even when he did meet the others, how many would be over at one time? From what he saw on the map, the houses weren't close together.

He looked back toward the house and saw the steps leading up around the bedroom to the front with another set of steps leading to the patio. Attached to the house, below the bedroom, was what looked like a large shed made of the same material as the outside of his home. It had a sloped roof, which matched the rest of the house, and was only as high as the lower level. He went over to what looked like the door. There was no doorknob or handle to pull on to open it, even though it was obviously a door.

"Nag, what's in the shed below the bedroom?"

"I am not at liberty to tell you at this time."

What could be in the shed that would be so important? After trying to find a way to open it to no avail, he decided to let it go for now and made a mental note to ask Lan about it the next time he saw or spoke to him.

He walked to the front of the house, taking in the scenery. In the distance, he could see a tall and strikingly beautiful mountain range with snowcapped peaks. To one side was a large field of yellow and orange wildflowers with a few deer running about through the field. There were some small bushes around the house and flowers lining a pebble path leading up to the front door, which had a little deck area with a roof over the door.

He noticed a more significant path that looked like it could be a roughed-in road leading away from the house to the left and right. Seeing the pathway made him think about a car. There was no garage near the house and not even an ATV anywhere on the immediate grounds. Apparently, he couldn't do more than walk around his land. How was he going to interact with the others if he couldn't get to them?

"Nag, do I have any kind of personal transportation available?"

"No, you do not. It is not needed."

"I thought some form of transport was in the shed, but it didn't look large enough."

Warren was hoping the CA would take the bait and respond, but of course, the thing was a computer, not a person. He intended to press the CA for more information, but on second thought, figured it could wait. He started toward the house to do some research.

At the door, he recognized two things: one, there was no doorbell; and two, he didn't have a key. He tried the handle and found the door to be unlocked. For a brief moment, he had the impression he walked into someone else's house; he still didn't at some level accept it as belonging to him. As he entered, the sense of this being someone else's house turned to a sense of loneliness. He pushed the feelings out of his mind and thought about all he had received from his benefactors.

"It's going to take some time getting used to the fact this is all mine," he said, before mentally scolding himself to not be like a crazy person talking to no one—all the time.

"Nag, is the door always unlocked, and do I have a key?"

"No, the door is locked unless i unlock it. I control all the security of the house; you do not have or need a key."

Hearing the CA say it was in charge of all the security sent a brief chill down his back. He didn't know why, but he started to feel like a captive, and he knew he didn't like the feeling.

Dinner

Warren prepared his meal, as the sun was setting with a beautiful show of color in the sky. The snowcapped mountains displayed brilliant shades of yellow and orange, matching some of the leaves on the trees below. He thought something so beautiful should be shared, and he had a brief image of someone in his mind. As quickly as the vision came, it went, and he forgot about it as he again began to feel lonely.

"Nag, it's too quiet in this house. Play some music for me."

"What would you like to hear?"

"How the hell do I know, nag? My memory of such things was wiped from my mind, yanked out, and tossed into the garbage pile of other old memories."

Warren recognized the hostility was building and it made him nervous. His head was wet with sweat and his heart racing away. He went to the sink and threw some water on his face; sure nag was documenting all this for Lan. The loneliness he understood, but he didn't know why he kept experiencing bouts of anger, and fear. He knew he had to get it under control.

"Nag, play something soft and soothing. Surprise me!"

He communicated his request silently; worried his voice would betray his anxiety.

A pleasant piano and violin melody began to play, and Warren found himself calming. Nevertheless, he couldn't get the fear or anger out of his mind as the episodes of almost rage were beginning to frighten him.

What happens if I became unstable? Would they terminate me like some failed pet project, or would they put me away somewhere never to be seen again?

"Nag, what happens to the people who fail the transition process—the failures, as Lan called them?"

"Warren, i am not at liberty to discuss what happened to the failures in the beginning. Those who physically adjust but have mental stability problems are taken back for further adjustment, and the process is restarted."

"And if the process fails another time, what then?"

"I am not at liberty to say."

"Of course not," he said, thinking again, it wasn't a good idea to talk to himself. "Nag, the music selection is enjoyable, but it's still too quiet. How about you give me some education while I'm sitting here eating?"

After a brief interval, it answered. "On what topic?"

Warren noticed the hesitation from the CA as if it were waiting for directions. He answered using the implant as he did remember it was rude to talk while eating with your mouth full; not that the damn computer should care.

"Well, nag, I don't remember anything about the solar system in which Earth was part, but I do remember the concept of a solar system. Please tell me about this one."

"I am permitted to give you this information. However, i would like to remind you Learnings One is still waiting."

"Six major planets are contained in this solar system. This one is the second.

"Planet one is the smallest. It is close to the sun and is non-habitable and also not suited for any industrialization."

"What do you mean by industrialization?"

"Many planets in the inhabited solar systems are used for mining minerals, fuels and, gases for a variety of purposes. The first planet is too hot to allow any mining or other development."

After another brief pause, he asked the CA to resume the presentation.

"This planet, planet two, the third in size and mass, is in what the scientists of Earth called the Goldilocks Zone. It is a zone, not too hot or too cold to allow for life. The area allows for a planet, containing water as a liquid, which promotes the creation and existence of life.

"Planet three is slightly smaller than this planet and is in the Goldilocks Zone's outer edge. It has some animal and vegetable species and vast oceans filled with life. Humans could easily survive in the equatorial zones.

"Planet four, the largest, is what the scientists of Earth called a gas giant. There is no life on this planet, but the atmosphere's gasses, are minable for many uses.

Nag instructed Warren that the last two planets were cold, rocky worlds of valuable minerals, devoid of life.

"Nag, do the Jonton or any of the other species in the galaxy currently use the planets in this system for mining or other uses?"

"No, this solar system is reserved for Humanity."

"So, there are no bases or facilities in this solar system owned by other spacefaring aliens?"

"Port Nateria is currently operated by the Jonton but belongs to this world. Control of the facility will someday be turned over to your world's governing body when one exists.

"A base exists on the second moon, which the Jonton use to supply this world. Ownership of this facility will be negotiated with the future government."

"Nag, stop. Second moon? How many moons does this planet have?"

"This planet has two moons, unlike Earth, which has one moon."

"Why did you call it the second moon?"

"It is considered the second moon because it is smaller than the first and rises second."

"Okay, nag, that makes sense. You may resume."

"A refueling platform is orbiting the gas giant. The platform is owned and managed by the Satorie. Ownership of this facility will also be negotiated with the future government."

Warren sought to ask more about the Satorie but decided he could wait until later. He finished his dinner and took his coffee out on the patio. The weather was cooling, but he wasn't cold. He enjoyed the crisp cool air; it made him exhilarated and ready for anything. The sun had set, but the last bit of sunlight reflected off the clouds on the far horizon painting a fantastic landscape of color.

It was nice to sit, relax, and listen to nothing but the whispering sounds of nature. He wondered what, if anything, kept the wildlife away from the house. He didn't ask nag, as he wanted to enjoy the lack of its voice as long as possible.

Warren sat a while, and when the night became completely dark, he asked the CA to turn out all the exterior lights so he could look at the stars in all their glory. He didn't know what to expect since he didn't remember the night sky from his past life, but he was taken aback by the abundance of stars filling the sky in all directions. As his eyes adjusted, more and more pinpoints of light became visible. He recognized the many clusters of stars as other galaxies far away and possibly still unattainable even for Jonton technology.

Above the mountains, one of the two moons, the first based on nag's information, rose into the sky. The moon was full and bright, and through its dense atmosphere, Warren could see what looked like oceans. Fifteen minutes later, a smaller disk followed behind the first. The second moon wasn't full, and he couldn't perceive any signs of life or the spaceport.

The second moon looked much smaller than the first, but he knew that might have been an illusion of distance. The second moon was only three-quarters full, making him realize it probably was at a different distance than the first.

Something about the moons bothered him, and he started to doubt if any of it was real. If this were all fake, if it were all a lie, what better way to fool him than to fake a couple of moons? Was he crazy? How could anyone fake a moon unless everything was all in his head? Maybe, none of this was real. Perhaps this was all an illusion like a story he almost could remember but remained out of reach. After a few more minutes of looking at the moons and stars, he became more relaxed; no more fear or doubt—for now. He went back inside and cleaned his dishes from dinner, ready to spend some time with Learnings One. The idea of having to listen to, read, or watch all the information contained in the Learnings wall made him a bit anxious.

All work and no play makes . . . something, Warren thought, but the idea wasn't coming to him. It must be something he knew from his past life. As he headed to the computer, he noticed a glint of moonlight coming through the skylight and reflecting off the piano. The piano beckoned to Warren. He walked over, pulled out the bench, and sat. Something remained wrong; he re-positioned the seat and let the tune in his head flow out through his hands. Without thinking about it further, he began to play.

Warren didn't know what his hands were playing, but he thought it was a beautiful, haunting melody. His hands moved effortlessly across the keys as if he had been doing this all his life. As he played, his mind filled with images of candles and flowers and the face of a beautiful woman. After he finished, he sat there a moment, stunned but also relaxed and content.

"Nag, do you know the name of the song I played?"

"What you were playing was the first movement from Piano Sonata no. 14, by Ludwig Von Beethoven, also known as 'Moonlight Sonata.'"

"How appropriate, I should choose to play that selection. Not that I consciously selected it in the first place. Standing outside, looking at the moons, and then seeing the moonlight reflected off the piano must have triggered the memory."

He wondered if that was supposed to happen.

Lost in thought, he walked over to the terminal on the desk and asked the CA how he should proceed with the Learnings process. It reminded him he could read the material in the binder or scan the chip to view on the terminal screen.

Warren was too tired to read and didn't feel like sitting at the desk, looking at the computer.

"Nag, is there any other way or any other place to review this material?"

"You can view the material on the bedroom monitor or the monitor downstairs in the workout room."

"Can you read it to me?"

"I can, but this binder includes video as well. I could initiate a three-dimensional visual rendering with the health monitoring algorithms system."

"I have no clue what you said, but it sounds interesting. Please show me."

"Look behind."

He turned to look, and in the area where he stood for his physical, there was now an image of a blue background with the words "Chapter One – The House."

"Really, nag? Don't I already know enough about the house?"

"There are maintenance, security, and emergency procedures you must learn."

"But you take care of security, at least that's what you told me."

As Warren expected, the CA didn't respond. He thought about pursuing the discussion further but decided it wasn't worth the effort of arguing with a computer.

"Okay, please begin the presentation of Learnings One."

Learnings One started with rudimentary information about the house, most of which he already knew. The CA read the text and showed the video where included or needed. After the housing overview, nag gave information about the land around the house, followed by a video tour of the continent. One interesting thing he discovered was his house was close to an ocean. He wasn't sure why he hadn't noticed when looking at the maps earlier. He decided the ocean was somewhere he wanted to visit.

The video moved on with chapters describing and showing some other areas of the planet, followed by general information about the project. The footage provided some wide-ranging statistics about the residents of this world, but still no names or contact information.

"Learnings One is now complete, Warren."

"Nag, is there anything else you can tell me about the other citizens of this world? It's very frustrating not to know more about this world or how long I'm going to be stuck at this house."

"No, Warren, there is no information about the other citizens that i am at liberty to tell you at this time."

"Great, I guess I should go to bed."

"Warren, Lan is requesting communication."

"Guess I was asking too many questions," he said. Or just coincidence, maybe. The CA, of course, didn't respond. "Nag, what do I do? Do I need to sit at the computer?"

"The communication is voice only. If you accept, i can use the audible house system, and you can proceed with retiring. Or you can use your direct internal link."

"I don't want to be having a mental conversation. I accept. Use the house system."

"Hello, Lan."

"Hello, Warren. I wanted to communicate with you to make sure the first day on your own went well."

"You expect me to believe, you have not been following my every move today through nag?"

After a pause, "What is, nag?"

"Oh, sorry. I didn't want to say 'computer' all the time, so I changed the initiation word. Since it's my only company and it tells me what to do, I consider it to be a nag."

"That is interesting. To answer your question, no, I did not monitor you. I know Humans value their privacy. I read a few standard status updates your house provided, but I knew, nag, as you call it, would alert me to any significant issues. The house systems automatically notified me when you finished Learnings One, so I thought it would be a good time to check in as Humans like to say."

"Well, Lan, I guess I'm adjusting okay. How would I know? Learnings One was a bit basic and mostly left me with more questions than answers. I guess it's a good system though. Since I don't know what it is, I don't know, it's hard to ask the right questions, and nag won't answer most of them anyway."

"That is normal, Warren. You will have many questions as you proceed. Future Learnings will answer some questions, and others will have to wait until you are ready to join the larger community. I will come to see you in a few days, and I may be able to answer some questions for you at that time."

Warren went into the bedroom and proceeded to change into pajamas as the conversation continued.

"And when will I be able to join the others?"

"To be honest, Warren, it will take you two months to get through the required Learnings even if you did one a day. You will find they do get more involved, and for some, you will have to pass tests to proceed. While you are learning, you must also exercise your body, relax, and take an occasional hike to explore your property and take care of the house and garden.

"Some of your fellow Humans have been able to join the community in three months, while others have taken six months to be ready. We have studied the individuals and looked at their history, but there does not appear to be any pattern."

"I guess I'll have to take things one day at a time. If there's nothing else, I'm ready to hit the bed and get some much-needed sleep."

"I will bid you a good night, Warren, and communicate with you in a few days."

"Communication ended."

"Nag, turn out the lights and bring the temperature down five degrees."

The CA took care of the lights as Warren got into bed, thinking about everything he learned. He tried to clear his mind and relax but he couldn't. He began instead to think about everything he had forgotten; his family, friends, education, country, and even more, his entire world, wiped from his memory, maybe forever.

I must remember to ask Lan if I will ever be able to get back my old memories or learn about my past.

ROUTINE OF LIFE

War, the United States, China, weapons . . .
Bright light, we will help you, another place . . .
Bart, Sam . . .
Why . . .

School is in Session

Warren stood on the patio, watching the morning fog drift through the valley. His sleep seemed extremely brief, and he didn't feel well-rested. He recalled a dream about walking outside holding someone's hand and other images he couldn't place. He wondered if the dream was due to his feeling of loneliness or was what he had dreamt of an actual memory? He wished he knew; not knowing was frustrating, and Warren decided he would keep the emotion to himself. He didn't know precisely what reactions Lan expected as part of the process, and he worried he would fail.

While going inside for his daily physical, he decided to check out the pool after a light morning workout. After nag completed the physical, Warren asked the CA about a bathing suit. Although he could swim in the nude, the idea made him uncomfortable. In the back of his mind, he still had an occasional sensation of being watched.

"What you call a bathing suit is in the closet by the lap pool. If you intend to use the whirlpool, i can turn it on for you and adjust it to an adequate temperature for a Human."

"Yes, nag, I like your idea. I knew I kept you around for some reason." There was, of course, no response to his humor. "I'll use the whirlpool after swimming, but I want to exercise first. I found the experience boring yesterday; can you prepare some music and have it ready? Anything you think I would like."

"Yes, Warren, i will pick some music I believe you will enjoy."

"I bet you know what I listened to in my past life back on Earth. In fact, I am positive you know everything about me there is to know."

Warren waited for an answer from the CA while his muscles tensed, thinking how everybody probably knew all about him except himself. A response to his statement never came, and the silence only fueled his anger. He pushed the resentment away, went back to the bedroom, changed into some workout clothes, and went downstairs. He did a few rounds of weights for his arms and followed with sit-ups and rowing. Feeling energetic, he decided to spend time on the bike.

"Nag, I'm getting bored. Time for that music I requested."

Immediately a song flooded the room. There were no words since they weren't allowed, but the selection had a catchy melody, up-tempo, and suitable for a workout.

As he rode the bike, he thought how nice it would be to ride outside with the wind in his hair and the warm sun on his back, but he suspected there were no bike paths. He wondered if they could give him an ATV. Although he knew what an ATV was, he didn't know if he had ever owned or used one. Another topic he would bring up with Lan when he had the opportunity. He was getting a long list of things to ask about, as Lan had indicated.

He finished with the bike and moved on to the treadmill while the music played. He enjoyed the music; the song was familiar as well as comforting. For a computer, the CA did an excellent job of selecting music he liked. Warren was sure it wasn't a coincidence, and if he could order nag to cooperate, he would learn a lot about himself.

Having soon tired of the treadmill, Warren found a bathing suit, changed, and stepped into the oversized lap pool. The taste of the water started a memory that wouldn't complete in his mind. He recalled swimming in larger pools with multiple lanes, but he didn't remember using a lap pool. He felt sure this one looked larger than usual. It appeared wide enough for two to swim abreast.

Warren set the controls to the halfway position and started doing the breaststroke. The movement felt natural to him—obviously something he had done in his past. After a minute, his feet touched the foot of the pool, and Warren realized he had set the water speed too high. He lowered the pace and moved to the foot of the pool, kicked off from the wall, and started doing a backstroke. As he swam, he gazed at the lights in the ceiling and used them to verify he wasn't swimming too fast or too slow. He spent the next half-hour alternating between the breaststroke, backstroke, and what he recalled was the butterfly. The different strokes and their names were all-natural to him. He thought he must have swum many times during his past life on Earth. Though tired when he jumped into the pool, the water and the swimming invigorated him, and he could have done another full workout. He enjoyed the entire experience and felt relaxed and carefree, all the earlier fears and anger gone.

The music soothed his mind while Warren enjoyed the refreshing water. When he finished, the song playing gave him a familiar urge to play the melody at the piano. As the song ended and moved on to the next, Warren turned off the water jets and floated in the pool. He closed his eyes as he floated while the music relaxed him further.

Minutes later, his mind drifted away to be touched by something unknown and unexpected, vast, and all-encompassing. He immediately jumped up and looked around. Someone called his name, or he thought someone did, but nag confirmed no one else to be in the house. He thought about the experience and wondered if it had been just another odd daydream.

No, I sensed something.

He stood in the water and recalled an image—a massive complex of what appeared to be metal floating amongst stars. Warren could feel the accelerated heart rate the experience had brought on, and he was ready to enjoy the hot tub the CA had prepared. The temperature wasn't bad. It seemed at first slightly burning but easy to slip into, and after a few minutes, he again relaxed and let his mind wander.

You're on stage in a few minutes, Warren. Your fellow students are looking forward to hearing you perform the new arrangement . . .

"Warren, it appears you are falling asleep."

"What! Oh yes, thank you, nag, you're correct. I was having an odd dream about being on a stage, but I'm sure I would have awakened if my face went underwater."

The hot tub had been further relaxing, but the rumbling in his stomach indicated he needed to eat, plus he believed he had a lot of learning to do today. He decided he would shower upstairs since his clothes were up there. He didn't want to drip water through the entire house, so he removed the suit, and hung it on the back of a chair by the pool. Warren reached for the towel and could instantly sense someone watching him while he stood there naked and vulnerable. He wrapped the towel around his waist and quickly headed upstairs. He reached the bedroom, closed the door, and the anxiety vanished as fast as it started.

When he took off the towel, the feeling of being watched didn't return. There were no windows in the pool or workout area; he wondered how anyone could see him unless Lan was using hidden cameras. As he stood there wondering about the feeling, he grasped both times it happened he had been naked.

He stood in front of the mirror in the bedroom looking at his body, feeling it to be wrong. He recognized the little birthmark on his neck, but his body proportions seemed off. He remembered Lan saying they altered everyone for the higher gravity, maybe that's why his body appeared off. After a minute of staring at his image, he woke from the trance, he seemed to have fallen into and headed to the bathroom, talking to himself.

"Why do I feel safe now, but I didn't before?"

"Nag, remind me after breakfast to gather up all the clothes I have left lying around and do the laundry."

He didn't wait for an answer, but the thought of the clothes lying down by the pool and in the hampers bothered him.

The term he had used to describe nag, 'clean freak,' leaped into his mind as he turned on the water for the shower.

Warren enjoyed a breakfast of poached eggs with sausage, toast, and coffee on the patio. He took in the perfect day, warm and bright, the fog gone with wild turkeys and ducks wandering below the barbecue pit.

These surroundings are not a terrible setting for school; I could get used to this style of life. Better than . . . better than what?

He pushed the incomplete thought from his mind. As he prepared to go inside, he had the feeling of being watched again, but this time it was different. He quickly turned his head to look beyond the barbecue area and thought he saw a flicker of movement. It could have been the turkeys or ducks, but he didn't think so. He put the dishes on the table and quickly ran down the stairs, heading toward where he thought he saw movement.

"Warren, where are you going?" he heard in his head as he ran past the picnic table and entered the woods. Only a small way into the woods, he stopped and looked around. He no longer had the sense of being watched, and he didn't see anyone beyond the trees. All the wildlife had scattered as he ran past them, and the only other life he could see were a couple of squirrels.

"Warren, respond!"

"Sorry, nag, I saw someone or something in the woods."

"No one could be in the woods, Warren, without me knowing about it. The house sensors go one hundred cuselts away from the house in all directions."

"Good to know, nag, but I also know what I saw."

Warren didn't mention to the CA as he walked back to the patio, he had sensed someone looking at him, and he somehow knew where to look. He grabbed the dirty dishes, cleaned up breakfast, and headed over to the computer area to start the day's Learnings.

Unknown to Warren, the CA had made its report to Lan. If the CA were Human, it would have been confused by Lan's standing orders not to let Warren know if someone were watching the house.

It was about noon when Warren finally sat at the computer to begin Learnings Two. He spent the first hour reading the procedures for ordering supplies when they ran low. The CA kept an inventory but didn't order the supplies itself. The CA was to alert him, and then he would decide when and how much to order. He figured the Jonton thought it would be better for the Human to take responsibility. If there were a food item he didn't like, he could have it removed permanently. There were numerous food items he could order that weren't in the house initially, including alcohol, which surprised him. He didn't feel compelled to order any, so he wasn't an alcoholic, not that they would have chosen him if he were.

The supplies he ordered would be delivered to the house, but the lesson didn't elaborate how. Since he didn't need anything at the moment, he decided it was something to worry about later.

The next part of the day's lesson, provided via video, detailed information about the surrounding area. It talked about the various types of terrain, animals, and plant life that he quickly found boring. There was a brief mention that safety outside would be covered in Learnings Three, not yet available, and a warning to not go in the ocean. He became intrigued and hoped there would be more information about the oceans soon.

"Warren, would you like to take a break?"

"No, nag, please keep going."

The video resumed with a discussion of the seasons. Summer average highs were up to sixty degrees cwantare, and winter lows down to minus fifteen cwantare. The video moved on to the dangers of extreme temperatures when he asked the CA to stop.

"Nag, I know what a cwantare is from my conversations with Lan, but I don't understand where the term originated. Is it a unit of measurement for this planet only?"

"Cwantare is the Galactic Standard measurement of temperature. You will learn about Galactic Standard measurements in the next Learnings module."

"Maybe the lesson on Galactic Standards should have been first?"

"Terminology charts are hanging on the refrigerator, and you can access charts on the computer terminal at any time. Since you won't be going off-planet any time soon, the information on galactic standards is not important at this time."

Typical computer non-answer.

Warren wanted to ask about going off-planet. The thought had never occurred to him, and he found he needed this adjustment process to be done with soon. There was so much available to him now that Humans on Earth never had, and he understood in an instant of sadness, never would. He sat a moment, waiting for his emotions to come under control.

"Nag, continue with the presentation."

The video moved to warnings about traveling outside during extreme temperatures and storms, followed by a discussion of the months of the year and how they corresponded to the seasons. As Warren watched, a listing of the months, days, and a calendar started printing for his reference. The first month of the year was Activite, when winter officially started. Each season was two-and-a-half months long on average, but summer lasted longer than winter.

The information started to get tedious when the topic changed to the planet and the solar system. Warren was fascinated when the lesson confirmed one of the Project Planet's moons—not the one with the spaceport—had an atmosphere. It wasn't breathable for Humans because of harmful particles in the air, but there was a low level of life on the planet plus an abundance of water.

"Learnings Two is now complete. Lan instructed me to remind you to study the documents printed for your reference."

"Great. Homework. The last part was fascinating, but that was a long session, and I need to stretch my legs and clear my head."

Warren got up from the chair, thinking he needed to stretch more before and after his workouts. He also needed to remember he didn't have to sit all the time while the Learnings sessions progressed. So much to learn or relearn—it felt daunting. He stretched his arms over his head before the piano caught his eye once more. He walked to the instrument, thought about it for a moment, and realized he had a desire to sit and play. He sat on the bench with his hands on the keys, not knowing what he wanted to play. He closed his eyes to focus and relax while he sat lost in thought until his hands started to move effortlessly across the keys. He heard the melody in his head a split second before his hands played the tune. He knew exactly what to do and where to place his hands. He could hear other instruments accompanying him as if an entire orchestra played in his head as he played.

The music was hauntingly beautiful; goosebumps appeared on his arms and neck. As he played, he found the song joyful, and the term "rapture" came to his mind. His body ached in a way that wasn't painful—maybe longing. He almost needed to cry, but not tears of sorrow. It was as if his soul had left his body and ascended over a strange and wondrous landscape.

After a few minutes, the song came to an end. His body and mind were more relaxed than they had ever been since being—reborn. It wasn't a term Lan had used, but the expression was now so appropriate to Warren.

He remained at the piano for a minute or more, lost in his feelings, until he closed his eyes and began the song again. All the same emotions and feelings returned like the first time; however, this time in his mind, he heard a different version of the song. The melody flowed without a full orchestra, simply a few low-key instruments following along and adding an accompanying tune.

He hadn't completed the song when he felt pulled back to reality as he suddenly had a vision of outside in the woods, above the ground, looking at his house. The odd thing about the image was he looked at himself sitting at the piano. He opened his eyes, looked over to the woods, and this time, he thought he saw movement in one of the trees. He pushed the bench back to get up and race outside when the CA started to speak, and he sat back in front of the piano, curious as to what happened.

"Warren, are you all right? Your breathing and heart rate slowed to alarming levels as you were finishing the song and then quickly accelerated."

He sat for a moment before answering, still wanting to dash outside.

"Nag, I'm fine. Do you have the song I played in your database of music?"

"Yes, Warren, i do. The song is 'One Man's Dream,'" they said the last word in unison as Warren somehow knew the selection had been his favorite, while nag continued, "The composer was Yanni."

"Yanni, what?"

"I don't understand the question."

"What was the composer's last name?"

"Yanni was his stage name. I do not have access to his full name."

Warren sat there for a moment thinking.

"How did you know my breathing and heart rate changed?"

"I can monitor your basic body functions while you are in the house."

He wanted to ask another question when the CA again interrupted his thoughts.

"Warren, Lan is requesting communication."

"Accept and broadcast."

"Hello, Lan, interesting timing as usual."

"Hello, Warren, what do you mean by that statement, did something happen?"

He hesitated, not sure how much he wanted to tell Lan about his sensation of being watched or his experience at the piano.

"Everything is good. I guess you received notification I finished Learnings Two?"

"Yes, I did. So, when I say I am coming for lunch on Vanday at 10:00, you know when to expect my arrival."

"Not without my cheat sheet. I don't believe I even know what day today is. Why should I, what does it really matter at this point?"

He sensed hesitation from Lan.

"Yes, Warren, that would be true. Today is Gealday, which means I will see you the day after tomorrow."

"Okay, Lan, I will see you then at noon. Goodbye."

"Good evening, Warren."

"Communication ended."

Evening already? Wow, he didn't realize it was so late in the day.

Outside, the sun was setting, casting a beautiful array of colors across the patio as Warren sat there watching. The emptiness in his stomach and slight rumbling reminded him, time to make dinner.

Two hours later, Warren had finished cleaning his dinner mess, and afterward, he spent an hour outside staring at the sky. It had been a long, eventful day—time for bed.

A Visit from Lan

Warren lay in bed with a slight headache and a feeling he had again forgotten something significant. This time he did remember part of the night's dreams. In the shadows stood a person saying something about another place. Warren had responded; he was ready; they were prepared. He never saw who they were. The last thing he could remember before he had awakened was stars.

He looked at the bedside clock and confirmed he had been lying in the soft and warm bed for half an hour. He laid there and wondered if the dreams were some pieces of memory he shouldn't be experiencing, and he speculated for how long they would dominate his sleep. He became anxious, thinking they may never end.

"Warren, are you feeling okay? Your heart rate appears elevated this morning."

"Already, nag. Can't you wait 'til I come out for my usual morning scan? I'm not sure I like the fact you're always monitoring me; it's creepy."

"It is required until you are ready."

"Ready for what?" No answer, as he expected. "And so, the day begins."

He dressed, got his full scan, did his usual morning workout routine, showered, and prepared for Lan's arrival.

As Warren prepared lunch, he reviewed the printed cheat sheet about yesterday's Learnings Four regarding measurements. Not only length and distance, but it also included liquids, volume, and Galactic distance. The only constant was the speed of light. The lesson also included basic shapes in Galactic as well as a touch of geometry, which he did remember he hated. The CA informed him he must study the sheets as much as possible because knowing the information was necessary. He would be required to pass a test before moving on to some other Learnings. So much dull mathematical information had given him a headache, and in the middle of the lesson, he had to get outside.

"Nag, I need a break. I'm going out for a walk."

"You must take the communication device with you."

"Must take? What device are you talking about?"

"The communication device Lan left for you. It is sitting on the table by the fireplace. It will allow us to communicate when you are more than one hundred cuselts away from the house."

"Okay, I remember. Now, let's get back to must. Why must I take it with me? What if I refuse?"

"Why would you refuse? Why would you not want to take it with you? I do not understand.

It sounds like a flustered parent. This is getting to be fun.

"We need to be able to communicate should you fall or have some other type of emergency. It is a rule you must follow."

"And I bet you can also track me with this device."

"Yes, so i can send help to you if needed."

"Okay, you win—mom."

"I do not understand."

"You never do."

Warren had grabbed the device and headed out the front door, smiling.

It had been a beautiful, mostly sunny day with clouds moving in the distance. He knew from the Learnings, fall had arrived, and many of the trees were full of multicolored leaves. The wild-growing grasses were getting a golden hue, and some of the flowers had gone to seed.

He headed east across the dirt road and into the forest, where it wasn't thick with growth. He knew the direction would take him toward the ocean, but he didn't think to check and see how far he would have to go. He knew he could ask, but what fun would that be?

Warren followed a little path where the grass had been laid flat by the passage of animals. As he walked, he hesitated when moving in specific directions. It wasn't a tingling anywhere on his body. It was more a feeling he couldn't put to words—a slight ache, or push in his head. He sensed danger ahead and to the right, so he headed off to the left. As soon as he changed directions, the sense of danger lessened. He had concentrated so much on the feeling; he had wandered off the path.

Warren's anxiety rose with every tentative step, and his heart rate increased. He had trouble breathing and looked frantically over his shoulder at every sound, expecting a bear or some other wild animal to come charging toward his position. He closed his eyes and forced himself to be calm and relax. He took a few deep breaths and started walking back the way he had come. He wasn't on the path, but he was confident he moved in the correct direction. After a few minutes, he found himself back on the trail and headed toward the house. The sky grew darker while the wind increased from an approaching storm moving in from the ocean he had wanted to see. After a few more minutes, he entered a clearing and came within sight of the house.

Warren entered the house feeling refreshed and ready to finish the lesson as the storm moved in with strong winds and heavy rain. He suspected his anxiety in the forest had resulted from the enhancements the Jonton made to his mind and was a response to the approaching storm and possibly an animal or two in his direct path.

Yesterday's storm had moved passed during the evening, and today was a beautiful day, perfect for sitting on the patio with his soon to arrive guest. Lan was due for lunch in about a half-hour, so he had to finish getting everything ready. He made them some tomato and cheese sandwiches with a few bits of bacon remaining from breakfast and a side salad of fresh vegetables from the garden. Lan came up the outside patio stairs as he set the plates outside.

"Hello, Warren; it is good to see you again. It is a beautiful day for a nice lunch on the patio."

"Hello, Lan; welcome back. Can I ask how you got here? I never hear any noise or see any form of transportation."

"You can ask, but my answer will be, it is not something you need to know at this time."

"Am I detecting a note of humor with that response?"

"Yes, I feel it is important in my many relationships with Humans to interject some humor into our conversations. There is an old Earth saying. Laughter is the best medicine."

"I wouldn't know since I recall so little of Earth. Must be something that happened to me, I guess!"

"That was a bit of snide humor, I believe."

"Yes, you're correct, sorry. Please sit, and let's enjoy our lunch."

Lan sat, and they enjoyed the lunch Warren had prepared while a light breeze blew across the patio. Lan inquired about his health even though Warren was certain he got daily reports. He also asked how Warren was adjusting to his new life. Warren gave a few polite answers, saving the more important discussions for after the meal.

"I have a question," Warren said. "It's about the names used for the week's months and days. Of course, I don't remember the months on Earth—just a statement, not a complaint—but I wondered how they came to be since they do sound familiar."

"The days and months are derived from different Earth languages. As you learn and are allowed to explore Humanity's past, you will be able to look up the names and see the meaning from the original language."

"What Earth language are we speaking now, or is this language not from Earth?"

"There is one language used on this world, and it is the Galactic Standard. To you, it feels normal as if you were born into this language. You will discover that you can read, converse, and understand anything in your native language as well as any other language you knew before being retrieved."

Warren poured more to drink. "I took a walk yesterday into the forest. It was good to get outside and stretch my legs. I wish there were better paths to walk along. I know I'm close to the ocean and would love to see it, but I'm not sure how hard it would be to reach."

"The ocean is a little more than nine hundred cuselts from your home. The land is over thirty cuselts above the ocean, and there is no beach to walk down to see or explore.

"Warren, are you okay?"

When Lan had mentioned the word 'beach,' Warren had a flash of memory. There was a smell of popcorn and images of what he knew to be amusement rides. A moment before Lan called his name, the word 'wild' popped into his mind, and he felt . . . happy.

"Oh, yeah, sorry, I was daydreaming." He didn't want to mention to Lan what he had experienced.

He quickly changed the subject, "Running on the treadmill is boring. I feel like I should be doing something else. I would like to run outside, but I don't want to twist an ankle on the rough terrain."

"I find that interesting. On Earth, you used to run through the nearby parks almost every day. I might be able to clear a small area for you to run outside. Winter is coming so you will not be running outside much, but there might be something I could do."

"What about other forms of transport? Can I get a mountain bike or an ATV to get around and go exploring?"

"No, it is best, for now, to stay close to home. You have much to learn here."

Warren sat there a moment, not sure he should mention the incident at the piano or ask about being watched.

"I can tell you have something you want to say," Lan said.

Warren put down his cup and wiped his now sweaty hands on his napkin.

"Yes . . . I . . . umm, well the other day after finishing the Learnings session, I had an urge to sit and play the piano. I started playing a hauntingly beautiful song, which flowed out of me. My hands moved across the keys while in my head, I could hear other instruments as if they were right there beside me." He paused a moment before calling over his shoulder. "Nag, what was the name of the song I played?"

"One Man's Dream."

Lan folded his hands in front of him. "I can tell you; it was one of your most favorite songs. You liked to play it when you were stressed."

"Is what happened to me normal?"

"I am not sure normal is a word we can use in this situation. You are the only person here so far with a strong musical background. We expected you would retain the ability to play; the fact you can remember a song you use to play is not unexpected, but the rest is . . . fascinating.

Lan noticed Warren had stopped listening and was looking toward the forest.

"Warren. Warren. Did you hear me?"

"What! Who is there?"

Without thinking, Warren jumped up and ran to the edge of the patio. He realized he shouldn't have reacted so in front of Lan.

"What is it, Warren, what is wrong?"

"I . . . a . . . nothing. I thought—oh hell; I guess I can't keep it from you now. I thought you were watching me, but since you are here in front of me, it can't be you."

"But you could not have seen anyone from sitting here on the patio."

"I didn't see—I felt! I should explain."

He proceeded to tell Lan about his experiences in the house when he sensed he was being watched, including downstairs and on the patio.

"I can assure you, Warren, I have no cameras in your house. Except for the first day, neither I nor anyone working for me has been watching you."

"So, you were watching me the first day after you left the house."

"Yes, I wanted to be close in case there were any adjustment issues. You certainly could not have seen me from the lower level.

"I can tell you we learned from watching you on Earth that you were a modest person, and you were not comfortable with being naked around other people. If this was happening while you were naked, it could be your modesty coming through and maybe enhanced, unfortunately."

"What about when I was sitting on the patio having breakfast? And when I was inside, I knew I was alone, or was supposed to be alone, and I didn't feel it had anything to do with being naked. No one could have seen me in the gym or by the pool unless there were cameras, so I just don't get it."

His voice had become loud and, on his lap, he played with his fingers. Before Lan could speak, Warren continued while he still had the nerve to tell him everything.

"There is more I should tell you. When I completed playing the song on the piano, I also had a vision. I saw myself sitting at the piano as if I were watching from outside."

Lan remained motionless a moment, staring with a blank look on his face as if lost in thought or in silent communication. Warren detected something else in Lan's demeanor, but let it go as Lan responded.

"This is all very interesting, Warren, and thank you for telling me, but whether it is something to be concerned about, I honestly do not know. No one before has mentioned experiences like yours. That does not mean they did or do not happen. We gave you all abilities the Human mind had not yet discovered, to help you survive, and I cannot say what we do is always perfect. We may have enhanced your faculties in ways we cannot understand.

"There are two possibilities. One is your mind has adjustment issues, and you imagine these things. I am sure that is not the case. The second being, that your mind is enhanced more than we have seen before. If the latter is true, I do not understand who could have been watching you, how they got here, or why they watched.

"What I don't understand, is why you did not want to tell me."

"I don't want to go back to . . . I don't know. I was afraid of . . . of being one of the failures." Warren's brow dripped with sweat and his heart pounded. "I didn't want to be taken and reconditioned like a piece of machinery you can do with as you please. Tell me, Lan, what do you do with your failures?"

Warren continued to play with his hands, and he had a knot in his stomach as he waited for an answer.

"Warren, relax. You have no reason to be afraid. The failures I spoke of before were people who, for whatever reason, could not adjust at all. They were people who became mentally unstable. These people never made it past day two. I can assure you, the visions and feelings you are having would never cause us to take you back and start over."

"I still want to know. What did you do with those who failed?"

"Our first group had an inadequate success rate. We learned from our mistakes, and there have only been three failures since the first successful group. All three were taken back and reconditioned. I know the word may be affecting you. It is part of your Humanity, your independence, so desired by most Humans.

"All three are now well-adjusted members of this society."

Warren noticed Lan only talked about those since the first group. What about those who came before? He was positive Lan was still hiding something from him, but what?

"Warren, all I can tell you is I will be available to help you in any way. From what I have seen and from the reports your computer assistant has sent me, I am delighted with your progress and excited to hear more about your enhanced abilities in the future.

"What I want for you now is to proceed with your Learnings so you can soon join the other members of society."

Lan excused himself and ended the conversation, which didn't satisfy Warren completely, but at least he had some answers. They said their goodbyes, and he watched Lan walk down the patio stairs. He wanted to follow Lan to see where he went but believed after everything that happened; he should let it go and be patient.

After he cleaned, Warren didn't feel like doing any Learnings. He told the CA he would spend the rest of the day relaxing. He took a short walk in the woods and came back to spend an hour listening to music while soaking in the hot tub before he relaxed by floating in the pool.

He made hamburgers outside on the grill before dark and had a late dinner followed by a beer on the patio. After looking at the moons and stars for a while, he headed to bed.

Tomorrow would be another day, another day in the journey of the rest of his life.

I'm ready, a new beginning, safety . . .

Days—Weeks—Months

The next few days passed with a continuation of the usual routines. Morning exercises were followed by afternoons of Learnings, testing, and work around the house. On a couple of evenings, he did an extra Learnings session or spent time playing the piano. He asked the CA to print sheet music of varying difficulties, and he found he could read and play all but the most complex arrangements. There had been no additional episodes of being watched; however, he remained concerned and didn't believe it was his imagination

A week after the lunch with Lan, the CA said, "Warren, I have a message for you from Lan."

"Play the message."

"Warren, I took care of the request for somewhere better to run other than the treadmill. Your CA has the details. I hope you enjoy."

"Warren, I suggest you put on some warmer clothes to go running outside today."

"Thank you, nag; I'll do as you suggest."

A few minutes later, Warren wore one of the heavier sweat suits and stood at the top of the patio stairs, astonished by what he found. A fine-crushed gravel path ran around the house and into the forest. He knew the pathway hadn't been there yesterday, and he wondered how they did all the work overnight and without him hearing anything.

"Amazing," he said, not caring if he sounded like a nut talking to himself.

Excited to give it a try he ran down the stairs. The path weaved into the forest and up some small hills before heading back out into the clearing. He ran along the hills and around the greenhouse side of his home then crossed the broader path, which ran in front of the house. He enjoyed the run; it gave him a sense of freedom, and the cooler temperatures didn't bother him as the crisp air flowed over his exposed skin.

The path headed briefly into the forest across from the front of the house and down a bit before returning him to where he had started. Still full of energy, he went around a second time and a third. After he completed the third lap, he ran around the other way for two more laps.

Nearing the end of what was going to be his last lap, Warren caught a glimpse of sunlight reflecting off something in the forest. He stopped and walked into the tree line and was surprised at what he found. In front of him stood a giant golden statue of a woman sitting on what he recognized as a horse. The trees behind the statue blurred to be replaced by a large building with columns, and to the right, a group of smaller white buildings also with familiar ornamental columns. Beyond the white buildings, he saw a flowing tree-lined river. He started walking toward the river when he was startled by a voice, which caused the image to disappear, and he found himself standing in the trees.

"Warren, have you experienced a problem?"

"No, nag; why?"

"You had been stopped in the forest a few minutes, and then you started walking into the forest, off the path."

"I'm fine. I was looking at a deer that was feeding in the woods. I will be on my way in soon."

He stood there a short while longer, wondering what had happened. Was the vision a memory of his life before?

Why did I not tell nag the truth?

For now, he'd had enough running, so he walked back to the house the rest of the way, wondering if it was a good or bad thing nag followed his every move so closely.

He stripped out of his clothes and jumped into the pool. After a few laps, he spent some time in the hot tub relaxing. He waited for the feeling of being watched to hit him, but it didn't, even when he walked through the house wearing nothing but a towel. As he passed the patio doors, he decided to try an experiment. He went out the door and stood on the patio's edge facing the valley below. He dropped the towel and stood exposed to the world, his arms outstretched, reaching for the sky. The cold air wrapped around his body; he was wonderfully refreshed and liberated. He considered himself free and more in charge than he had ever been since his first day in the house.

Lan's theory just literally went out the door of me being modest or bashful about being naked. I have no discomfort, feelings of insecurity, or of being watched. Is my mind adjusting, or am I not being observed today? And if someone watched me before, who was it and why?

The days and weeks passed. Warren fell into his standard routine, followed by intense Learnings sessions all afternoon and into the evening. He had an insatiable hunger to comprehend everything he could. He learned about the other races inhabiting the galaxy, including those who had not yet developed far enough for space travel.

He learned Lan's native language, or at least as much of it as he could pronounce. Some of the words were not possible for Human vocal cords his CA informed him. He also asked his CA to provide him with some of the Learnings in his native language, which the CA told him was English. As Lan had indicated, Warren could read and understand the material without any problems.

Nag also informed him he had been a student of the Latin language. The CA explained Latin was an older Earth language and was the basis for English and many other languages from Earth. He learned there were far more languages on the Earth at the time of its destruction than he could have imagined. He often thought about how much Humanity lost even though he couldn't remember any of it, at least not consciously. His odd visions of people and places he didn't know persisted, but he kept those visions undisclosed.

After five weeks, the CA informed Warren he needed to order supplies, and the next day there appeared a large container, sitting behind the house. The following morning it had disappeared as mysteriously as it had appeared.

Warren played the piano whenever he could. His hands flowing over the keys relaxed him as his mind drifted. One evening he sat and again played a new melody that flashed into his mind.

"Nag, do you know what I played?"

"The song is called 'Josette's Music Box,' from an Earth entertainment show."

"Can you elaborate? What do you mean, entertainment show?"

"It was from a television show which would have originally broadcast before you were born."

Warren learned about television and how it worked a few days earlier. Maybe, he thought, it stimulated something in his brain. The song was beautiful, yet also haunting at the same time.

A couple of weeks later, the first snow arrived. Only three culs had fallen, and the temperatures had risen enough to melt it all away a day later. He found when he researched the weather that the area wasn't expecting a lot of snow come winter, even though the records he had access to showed an average of over eighteen culs.

When Warren looked out at the snow, he had another urge to play the piano. He sat and played a few slow and solemn songs, which came to him as many others had in the past couple of months. Different this time was he could hear words in his mind and the singing of a choir.

"Nag, those songs I was playing, they feel related somehow. Do you have any information about them?"

"Yes, Warren."

He waited, but the CA didn't continue, and Warren was positive; it was stalling. He believed the CA was waiting for instructions from Lan or someone else who monitored his every move and action.

"Nag, do I have to ask a second time? Please answer the question in full."

"The songs you were playing were Christmas songs. They were also known as Christmas carols. Christmas was an Earth holiday you celebrated."

Warren sat with a smile on his face, and he became excited and joyful. He had no idea why he was smiling or why he felt so happy. He also had a sentiment of anticipation as if waiting for something.

"Tell me more about Christmas!"

"I have no additional information available."

Warren felt let down as if something expected had been taken away. He was sure the CA was lying but knew better than to persist.

Over the next few weeks, he devoured the Learnings at an even faster rate and began to understand the concepts of space travel, general engineering, and advanced mathematics. His mind and knowledge were growing more than he had ever thought possible. He knew his mind and body were ready for anything this new world had planned for him, and most of all, Warren Estridge, a former resident of planet Earth, was happy and, for the most part, content.

On the last day of Nyd, his CA informed him Lan would be stopping by the next evening to talk and have a drink after dinner. Warren thought the timing was strange but told nag to let Lan know he would be looking forward to seeing him again. Warren was sure a new chapter of his life was about to begin. He wasn't sure where this new confidence in himself was coming from, but he liked it and hoped it would remain.

Another Visit from Lan

Warren spent the day like most others, but for some reason, he knew today would be different. He sensed good news was coming even though he thought it odd Lan was coming by after dinner instead of at lunch. He knew Lan had many responsibilities, and probably had a full day scheduled.

He finished the latest Learnings after lunch, and his CA informed him there was not another session available. Warren figured there was something else he needed to accomplish first before the next Learnings course became available. About an hour after dinner, the CA informed Warren, that Lan waited at the front door.

"Thank you, I will greet him at the door."

Warren knew it to be the proper thing to do rather than have the CA open the door. He went to the entrance, excited to let Lan in as if he was his first guest. He realized Lan actually was his one and only guest even though this wasn't his first visit.

It had snowed in the afternoon, and when he opened the door and welcomed Lan, he noticed Lan's footprints went along the walkway and to the left down the path in front of the house. There was no visible sign of any means of transportation.

"Hello, Lan, and welcome back. Glad to see you use the front door. How did you get here?"

"No need to discuss right now. You will understand soon enough. For now, please get a couple of glasses so we can have a drink from the gift I have brought for you."

Lan handed him a bottle, which he recognized as being a type of alcohol. The white and silver label said, "Glenfiddich Rare Collection Scotch."

"This scotch was from Earth," Lan said. "We saved some of Earth's more special beverages for you to enjoy. It was bottled in Earth year 1937 and would have been over seventy-five Earth years old before being taken and preserved."

Warren grabbed a couple of glasses, and they sat by the crackling fireplace. The scene stoked another memory that came to life like the stocking of the fire, but Lan wasn't the person who should be sitting across from him. Lan opened the bottle while noticing Warren's far-away look. He poured a small amount of amber liquid into each glass and warned Warren to sip slowly.

Lan held up his glass and offered a toast. "To Warren Estridge as he completes his Learnings and prepares to join his new civilization. Cheers!"

Warren sat there for a couple of seconds before a huge smile spread across his face as he realized what Lan had said. "Cheers!" he replied and took a sip. The scotch burned going down his throat, but the taste was familiar, and he knew he had partaken of this in his past life. Lan started to speak before Warren could ask for further explanation and confirmation.

"You are unusual, Warren. I have never had someone with your ability to learn so quickly, sense his surroundings, and remember so much of his past life. Congratulations!"

Warren was about to ask a question when Lan continued.

"Soon, you will finish your Learnings, and you will be ready. In a few days, on Activite ten, you will meet your Human mentor, who will begin your integration into society. After some time with your mentor, you will begin to have access to some of Earth's past. Eventually, some of your former personal life as well."

Warren sat there, stunned, and excited. He wanted to jump and shout, but he controlled himself. He hadn't expected to have access to his past, and his body quivered with anticipation. He took another sip of his drink while enjoying the warmth coming from the fireplace. The prior memory returned, clearer than at first; a vision of sitting around an open fire and drinking with a man his age with red hair, wearing a jacket with a familiar logo. Before Lan interrupted his thoughts, the name Bart came to mind.

"I urge you not to be in too much hurry to learn of Earth or even your individual past. Not everyone is successful in handling the knowledge. There have been a few who have needed special counseling and a couple who have needed more time. We saved much from Earth, but still so much has been lost, and not everyone is as prepared as I believe you are today to deal with what they learn."

"Man's youth is a wonderful thing, it is so full of anguish and magic, and they never come to know it as it is until it is gone from them forever."

Warren sat a moment, unsure where the quote originated, but the words made him happy and somewhat sad.

"I'm sorry, the phrase or quote, I guess it would be, popped into my mind. I don't know what the quote means or where it's from, but I think it was special to me."

"Warren, for many reasons, you are fascinating!"

SABASTIAN AND CHLOE

His Name is Warren

"Chloe, have you seen my light blue shirt?"

Sabastian thought the shirt hung in the closet, but he didn't see it. His wife probably couldn't hear him with the shower running. "Hon," he said louder, "do you know to where my light blue shirt has disappeared?"

"I put it in the dressing room for you."

Sabastian knew if she already had the shirt laid out for him, she had been reading the file of his newest mentee. Chloe knew she shouldn't be reading the subject's file, and Lan wouldn't be pleased if he found out. Sabastian didn't see the harm, but he would tease her about it anyway.

"Chloe, have you been reading the subject reports?" Sabastian asked his wife. "You know you are not to have access to those reports. Are you trying to get me in trouble or get rid of me for one of the younger, new arrivals?"

"You can't get rid of me so easily, babe," she said as she exited the shower and grabbed a towel. "If you don't want me reading them, then you shouldn't be printing them out and leaving them lying around. One thing I remember about my past life is that I was always curious. Warren sounds like a fascinating individual, and yes, I read light blue was his favorite color. I read he had been a music teacher and played the piano. He also made wooden furniture and knows Latin. He would be a good catch for a biologist. Too bad I'm already married. I hope he remembers how to play; I would love to hear some live music."

Sabastian was finally able to squeeze in a word. Chloe did like to talk.

"You know my routines as well as I do. Before you ask, yes, it does help unconsciously put people at ease when seeing something familiar, like their favorite color. We went through a different experience since we were both part of the early groups awakened. Meeting people for the first time after the lone adjustment period can be intimidating to many, causing them not to adjust fully."

"Yes, yes, Sabastian, I know. Why so many secrets, though? Why can't I see the reports? It's not like I'm going to run around telling anybody. There aren't many people around yet to tell."

"Because they say so, and we should leave it at that. You know Chloe, in a way, we're their guests; even though this will all be ours someday, we should respect their wishes."

"So many rules! I long for the day they have less involvement in our lives. I want to be able to spend more time with you, and I want to start our family."

"Me too, honey, but we must be patient. We can't start a family until all the others are awake, which will not happen for a few more years. But don't worry, we will have plenty of time to have two or three children if you like. In the meantime, I have my work, and you have yours. Speaking of your work, Chloe, how's it going?"

"The expanded stations are coming along very well. I have to go over there again on Gealday for two to three days to oversee the observation paddock opening. It's good the Jonton moved all the natural predators over there; some of them are extremely hostile and powerful. It'll be exhilarating to observe them closer without any danger. I'm also looking forward to working more hands-on with a wider variety of the smaller, friendlier animals."

"Sounds like you're enjoying your work. When will you be done with your basic biology education?"

"My education should be complete in a couple of months, and then I will be fully able to add to what we know about the biology of the native species."

Chloe walked over to adjust Sabastian's hair and kiss him.

"You look handsome today. You had better watch it, or Laura will be interested in you more than Warren."

Sabastian sighed as he finished buttoning the shirt and gave Chloe the look of irritation, she knew to be fake.

"You read a lot of the file, didn't you?" Sabastian asked. "Please tell me you didn't read the confidential subfolder. The folder is personal and sensitive information about both of them which cannot and should not be disclosed to them or anyone else at this point."

"Well yes, I read a lot, but no, I didn't read the confidential part. Although tempted, I do understand some need for secrecy and privacy, but I find it all interesting. Does she even know she has been computer matched to him?"

"Yes, she knows. And she knows it doesn't mean anyone will force her to marry him. The chance meeting is merely an introduction, the first of many if needed. However, Warren does not know, since he's still in the adjustment phase of his new life."

"Well, I hope it works out for them. Warren appears to be a well-rounded person. Will he remember how to swim, play the piano, and make furniture?"

"I don't know, Chloe. The process, as Lan would tell you, isn't a perfect science. I'm sure they would prefer Warren still swims like the competitive swimmer he was in college, and I'm sure they hope he still has the desire to build furniture from scratch. Every skill we bring with us is a bit of the past we have the opportunity to preserve."

Chloe twisted her hair with her fingers, something she always did when she had a difficult question to ask. She often wondered if the habit was something she did in her past life back on Earth.

"Sabastian . . . were we computer matched?" she asked as she stared into her vanity mirror, afraid of the answer.

"No, my love," he responded as he walked over and gave her a tender embrace. "I fell in love with you all on my own and you with me, I hope. Our meeting and eventual life together were the natural chemistry called love. The computer match program didn't start until two years ago.

"When Earth was near its end, most people met and fell in love all by chance, but computer dating was a big thing because many people liked the idea of being able to meet others who shared their interests. A small number of cultures still had arranged marriages, neither of ours, by the way, and sometimes you didn't meet your spouse until the wedding day. Centuries before the end, many cultures arranged marriages; love didn't matter."

"Doesn't sound very romantic. I can't imagine forcibly having to marry someone I didn't know. Why was it done that way?"

"In many old Earth cultures, it was the way families preserved traditions and wealth. It brought warring factions or countries together. In others, it was for religious reasons, and it was a way for families to support themselves by marrying off their children.

"History lesson over, I have to go or I will be late. I love you!"

Sabastian

As he headed to the life center to meet Warren, Sabastian thought about how so much had changed in a short period. He had been among the first group of Humans the Jonton successfully awakened to begin their new life. Unlike the rest of that first group, Sabastian knew what had happened to him, and he didn't need to have his memories wiped before beginning his new life. The Jonton only enhanced his body and mind as necessary.

Lan did allow him to remember the two times they met aboard one of the Jonton ships close to the Earth's end. Over the years, they had become friends, and Sabastian helped the Jonton determine which parts of Earth's history should be preserved for future Humanity when they were ready to learn the truth. At twenty-nine Earth years old, he was the oldest taken and he wondered if he even would have been chosen if he didn't have a background in history.

Sabastian often wished Lan had removed the memories of his home. He had been born in Galway, Ireland, a town that existed on the country's western coast situated along the Oranmore Bay. He assumed something of the city remained, but all life was long gone.

The Jonton had removed most of his childhood memories, but he did remember his time at university and his trips to America. He loved the time of the American Revolution against the British, and he traveled to the United States more than once. He visited many cities, but his favorite had been Philadelphia. He loved the heritage and the food. He often thought of the sandwiches he had there and was happy when he found out he could have a Philly steak sandwich at one of the new Life Center eateries. He planned to take his new mentee there since Warren had been a Philadelphia native, and Sabastian wondered if the man would remember.

Sabastian was surprised when he found out his Jonton mentor would be an individual named Tar, not Lan; however, he did know Lan had many other responsibilities on the Earth Project Planet and a few special projects. He believed one of Lan's special projects was Warren, based solely on the confidential subfolder's information.

Sabastian felt some concern and anxiety regarding the situation. He didn't understand Lan's motivation, and he had no right to question, but having to lie to Warren or hold back some truths bothered him. He felt things would not end well for Warren or Laura.

THE NATURE OF HUMANITY II

A life, Human or otherwise, is full of wonder, pain, joy, and sorrow, all stored in the essence that makes each being unique. Does the original individual remain if they lose forever, all the experiences of their life?

If each individual Human is the product of their environment, can the person still survive unchanged in a new ecosystem, removed from the soil of their homeworld? If the new environment and reality are all the mind knows, does it matter?

How deep into the genetic code can be explored, changed, and enhanced before a Human being is no longer Human, but something new, something different? Does a Human's soul change if the structure of the Human is changed?

GRADUATION

Travel Day

Warren woke the morning of graduation day, as he decided to call it, after a restless night's sleep. Graduation day wasn't what Lan called it, but that's what the day felt like to him. After months of education and being under Lan's and the CA's watchful eyes, it was finally time for him to meet some of his fellow citizens.

He had studied many things about his new world in the last few months but not much about his old world or old life. He didn't care about his past, but Warren was curious about Earth. How could he not be? He had listened to wonderful music from Earth and had been able to teach himself some of it on the piano, along with melodies he could remember. There was much more music from Beethoven, referred to as classical music, and from Yanni and Vangelis, both of whom the CA said composed new-age music.

Warren wondered if it was correct to say he taught himself the music. He probably knew it before they took him from Earth, and most likely, he only refreshed what he already carried in his mind.

As he lay in bed, he thought of all he had discovered about this new life since Lan's last visit. The final Learnings taught him more about the regions of the planet. He had viewed images of ships taking off and landing at the spaceports on the other continent and the smaller moon. Most exciting had been the information about the galaxy and universe that reminded him of how insignificant life in the universe remained.

Even though he hadn't slept well, he jumped up, completed all his morning routines, and was ready to go well before the time Lan told him. He wasn't going to bother, but the

CA would not let him get by without having at least some toast for breakfast.

"Good morning again, Warren; how are you feeling after your workout?"

"I'm well this morning and extremely excited to be meeting some of the other Humans on this world. You're okay to talk to, but a man needs more than a voice."

"I can tell by your accelerated heartbeat, and i see; you have not made breakfast this morning."

"I wasn't going to bother."

"I must insist you have breakfast. You have another half hour before it is time to leave."

Warren knew there was no sense trying to argue, so he had toast and jam. As he waited for the time to leave, he wondered where he was going and how he would get there. Lan wasn't forthcoming with information or details. He told him only to be ready today at 7:00 to meet some of his fellow citizens.

"Warren, it is time to leave. Please proceed to the lower level."

"Excuse me, nag, did I hear you correctly?"

"Yes, please proceed to the lower level and go to the door at the left end of the hallway."

"There is no door there."

"There is now, i assure you."

Warren did as instructed and went downstairs to see an open door where there wasn't one before. To the right side were some controls.

"Nag, what are these controls for?"

"I can give you instructions when you return. Please step into the elevator."

Until the CA pointed it out, he didn't realize the door was to an elevator. He stepped inside and noticed what looked like another door on the far side.

"Nag, where does the other door go?"

"It goes to the outside at this level, what you called the shed, and at the lower level, it is the entrance to the platform."

Warren was about to ask what platform when the door closed, and he could feel the elevator descending. The elevator looked large enough to hold five to six people and was rather non-descript with nothing on the white metal walls. It didn't feel like it went down very far, and the trip lasted less than ten seconds.

The door opened, and he stepped out onto a platform about twice the size of the elevator in length and a few cux wider. To the right, a trench about ten cux wide and four cux deep went the platform's full distance. At the bottom of the trench, a bumped-up section, which looked metal, ran down the middle.

He noticed a door on each end of the trench. As he watched, the door to his left quickly opened sideways, and a vehicle silently pulled next to the platform. The transport was a cux or so shorter in length than the platform. There were no windows or signs of a door, but as it stopped, a hatch appeared and opened. The words "maglev train" came to mind.

"Nag, does this vehicle run by magnetic levitation?"

"Yes, it does. Please enter and take a seat."

There were two rows of fabric-covered, high-backed seats facing the direction of travel as it entered the station, as Warren now thought of it. He sat in the closest seat and appreciated its comfort. A display screen on the back of the chair in front of him flashed, "Prepare to depart."

The door closed with a hiss of air, the lighting dimmed, and the vehicle accelerated. There was no sound other than a low hum, and he wondered how fast it would go and how quickly it would get to his destination.

The only other thing in the vehicle was a monitor at the top front that showed a pulsing red line. He noticed other lines, so he assumed the display was a sort of map. A dot on the map slowly moved along one marked in red.

As the vehicle accelerated, his CA spoke in his head, startling him. He was still not used to having conversations start in his head without any warning.

"Warren, would you like to listen to some music as you travel?"

"Yes, how about some Beethoven?" he silently replied. Immediately the vehicle filled with the sounds of Beethoven's Ninth Symphony.

"Nag, how are we still able to communicate?"

"I can communicate with you anytime you are within one hundred cuselts of any common structure or transportation device."

The screen in front of him showed a view of a landscape he assumed was a view of the land above as he traveled. He noticed another house go quickly past as the vehicle continued to accelerate.

"It will take twenty-two minutes to reach your destination."

"What is my destination, and what will I find when I get there?"

"You are going to the Life Center. It is located approximately in the middle of this continent."

He waited.

"Nag, after all our time together, I still have to prod you for full details? Please explain to me what the Life Center is and the purpose of my going there today."

"The Life Center is many things. It is a place for the citizens of this world to gather, socialize, hold Council meetings, and meet with others from off-planet. As I informed you before, it is approximately in the center of the continent to make it a hub for transportation. The purpose of your travel there today is to meet your mentor and fellow citizens, as Lan has told you. It is time for you to learn more about the workings of your society and world."

"So, it is kind of like a capital city of sorts."

"It is not considered a city, but it is not out of the realm of possibility for the future. If you touch the screen, you will see a menu of topics available to you. One topic will be information about the Life Center."

He touched the screen, and a menu came up offering information about the Life Center, the Spaceport, Moonport, and something called the Observation Research Station.

Warren was going to ask his CA about the Research Station but decided to do some discovery on his own.

The Observation Research Station was a combination research facility and a place for citizens to observe the natural inhabitants of the planet. In addition to areas where animals could be studied, there were several observation areas accessible by underground transport in which to see the different habitats preserved or created for the animals.

He was surprised they hadn't included information about the Research Station in his studies, he figured there was so much to learn it wasn't considered important. His inclination anyway, was to discover more about the larger universe, instead of the smaller world around him.

He moved back to the main screen and selected Life Center to review next.

There wasn't much more information beyond what the CA had already told him. The center had meeting rooms, a community pool, and gym, as well as areas for team and other competitive sports. There was also a banquet hall, a few bars, some restaurants, a nightclub, and a hotel.

He noticed the transport slowing and he suddenly became nervous, realizing he was about to meet the first Human since being awakened. There were additional selections in the Life Center submenu, but they appeared grayed out.

He guessed he had not yet graduated enough to have full access. When he selected Spaceport, it provided even less information with not even a grayed-out submenu, and when he selected Moonport, nothing happened at all.

"Warren, you will arrive in five minutes."

"Am I to go anywhere in particular when I arrive?" he asked. *"Lan didn't give me much information."*

"You will be greeted by your mentor, Sabastian McCormick."

"You answer like I know who he is. Can you be a little more forthcoming with some information?"

"What do you want to know?"

"Well let's see—how old is he, why him, what does he do?"

"He is thirty-five Earth years old. I do not know why Lan picked him to be your mentor. I do not understand the last question."

"Lan mentioned eventually doing something with my life, like an occupation or field of study. Does that help?"

"Sabastian is a historian specializing in Earth history."

"I thought we were all restricted regarding what we can know about Earth."

"Sabastian was one of the first to be settled here, so he has had longer to adapt. He had been a historian on Earth as well, so the Jonton granted him special access."

Warren was about to ask for more information when the CA announced he had arrived. He was so into his discussion with the CA he had not even realized the vehicle had stopped.

"When you are ready, Warren, i will open the door."

He stood, a little nervous, and walked to the door.

"Okay, I'm ready; you can open the door."

Warren Meets Sabastian

The door opened, revealing a platform much longer than the one at his house. About fifteen cux in front of him, a group of glass doors led into what he assumed to be the Life Center. He walked away from the vehicle and watched it depart back into the tunnel.

He passed through one of the glass doors and stopped, transfixed by the remarkable sight. The immediate area in front of him was huge, with windows curving high overhead and to both sides. In the center, directly in front of him, was a large garden filled with an abundance of flowers of varying sizes and colors mixed in among trees and rolling grass hills. A few people sat on benches lining the garden's stone and pebble walkways as others strolled around the impressive space.

A clear glass dome many stories above revealed a bright, sunny day. To his right were four upper floors on which he could see people standing together talking. A glass wall to his left gave a view of a few buildings outside standing before hills and mountains rising in the distance. The area was bright, with large lights filling in where the sunshine couldn't reach. The air was comfortable and had a slight smell of an evergreen forest.

Warren stood transfixed—so into looking around at everything, he didn't realize he had only moved one step through the doorway until nag said, *"Warren, please move away from the doors so they can close properly."* Feeling foolish, he moved a few more steps into the building when a man approached from the right with his hand extended.

"Hello, Warren; it's a pleasure to meet you. My name is Sabastian, Sabastian Wilson McCormick. Welcome to the Life Center, and congratulations."

The man had medium-length, reddish-brown hair, and a roundish face with a few freckles. He was slightly shorter than Warren, with large forearms and a firm handshake.

"Thank you, Sabastian. It's good to meet you and finally be away from my home."

"I'm sure you have many questions for me. Lan doesn't usually divulge much information unless you bug him . . . a lot. He prefers the individual to discover their own way of learning and exploring."

"He can be very frustrating to talk too; I'll admit," Warren answered.

Sabastian pointed off to the right and suggested they go sit. "Let's head over to the coffee bar and find a place to sit and talk over some coffee or other beverage if you prefer. They have an excellent menu."

"I skipped my normal morning coffee, so your suggestion sounds good."

They proceeded around the park while Warren enjoyed the variety of blooms. As they walked, he felt a familiar sensation and he checked over his shoulder, though he was unsure why. It wasn't until Sabastian spoke that Warren shook off the feeling of being watched. If Sabastian noticed he didn't let on as he proceeded to tell Warren about himself.

"I was one of the first inhabitants of this new world. Our group consisted of myself and fourteen others. Of those other original fourteen, ten managed to adjust appropriately. Three made it through the first month, but they became unstable. The other person never made it past the first day. Thankfully, the Jonton have learned a lot since those days and now have an excellent success rate.

"I was twenty-nine Earth years old when they woke me from stasis. I was the oldest of the fifteen, though not by much. They brought to this planet, no one younger than twenty-two or older than thirty-five.

"My Jonton mentor, Tar told me, I had been a student of world history and a professor on Earth. I had been interested in history since I was a child. Because of my background and age, I eventually became the unofficial head of our new community. Almost three years ago, my position was made official by a voice vote in our first community meeting. I'm still a member of the Council, but no longer the head."

They arrived at the coffee bar which was named Rembrandt and sat at a booth by the front so Warren could see other people as they passed. Sabastian found the view helped the adjustment, especially when a non-Human happened to walk past. He ordered them both an espresso, which he told Warren was a particular type of coffee drink popular in Italy. The name of the beverage was familiar to Warren, but he wasn't sure what Italy was although the drink was potent and delicious.

"Before we continue," Warren said, "I have a question about the paintings on the walls. They look . . . ancient, I think, is the word; sometimes my mind floods with words I don't comprehend."

"They're original works of art saved from Earth, painted by an artist known as Rembrandt, hence the shop's name. There are other restaurants in this complex named for other Earth artists. Rembrandt was a Dutch painter who lived and worked three centuries before we were born. The painting by the door is one of his self-portraits."

Warren admired the portrait before questioning his mentor.

"One of my frustrations is the fact I'm still permitted to know so little about Earth. After all these months, it shouldn't be a problem for me to know more."

"That's mostly true, and today starts your learning about Earth. Nothing structured, but much more will be available to you for self-study. I can tell you Italy was a country on a continent called Europe, as was Holland, the country in which Rembrandt lived. I was also born in Europe, in the country called Ireland, and you were born on a different continent in a country called the United States of America, or the U.S., for short."

"You know more about me than I know myself," he said to Sabastian as he caught sight of what looked like a man with purple skin walking by the shop.

"You are correct, Warren, and that also will change now. Although Lan has probably not informed you, they gave us information about your past when you were awakened. The Jonton provides our Council with information about all new citizens.

"We know you were born in the city of Philadelphia, in the state of Pennsylvania. You studied music and religion at college. Your favorite instrument was the piano, which I'm sure you have figured out by now. You were working as a music teacher and on your Ph.D. before the gathering. I neglected to mention it is the term our Council prefers, and I always forget.

"In addition to music, one of your hobbies was woodworking. You belonged to a club in college, which worked to keep alive the old ways of furniture making popular with the people who had initially settled in that part of your country. They were sometimes referred to as Pennsylvania Dutch; however, they were settlers from another country in Europe called Germany.

"You liked to swim and were on a swim team in high school and in college, where you won a few competitions. You liked to go hiking in the mountains and jogging around the parks in and about Philadelphia when stressed."

"Yes," Warren said, "I figured, based on the pool in my house and my ability, I must have swum a lot, and Lan had mentioned I liked to run in the parks. Unfortunately, there are no parks by my home, although Lan arranged to have a manicured path made around the house so I could jog outside instead of always being stuck on the treadmill."

Sabastian laughed at Warren's comment. "There won't be much around your house for a while. It was nice he could arrange for an area outside for you to run. They can be accommodating at times and very mysterious at others."

"What about my parents? Did I have any brothers or sisters?"

"Warren, I'm afraid I don't have that information. I don't know if they even have information about your parents. They must for some, as Tar told me they tried to pick people who didn't have any strong relationships or connections, so there wouldn't be as much notice when they went missing."

Warren slumped a bit in his chair, saddened by what Sabastian was telling him, which his mentor noticed as he quickly changed topics.

"Have you thought about what you'd like to do with your life now that you're ready to join the community?" Sabastian inquired.

"To be honest, sometimes I wonder how I'll fit in and why they even chose me. I have the talent to play the piano from memory and read sheet music, but do I want to be an entertainer for the rest of my life? I'm not sure it's a career I would enjoy."

"Why they chose you, I wouldn't know, but I do know you have much to offer the community. We will all have to develop a career and some form of commerce so we can one day become a fully independent society; however, most of the responsibility for forming an economy will fall to our future generations.

"What you choose to do with your future Warren, will be one hundred percent your choice, but I know you could make a career with your music as an entertainer or as a teacher. You could also go back to woodworking and sell your furniture and someday make it a full-fledged business while educating others in your craft. We have a few other artisans here, which is useful for preserving the knowledge of how to do, instead of merely filling our new world with relics from Earth.

"You may also decide to do something new. The Jonton have a deep understanding of our minds and have introduced people to things they didn't even realize interested them for career or pleasure. This new life and new world have much to offer."

Warren sat still as he mulled over this new information. After a moment, he perked up and frowned. "What about God," he asked. "I hadn't thought about religion at all since my rebirth, but now since you told me I studied religion, I feel like a new part of my memory has opened."

"Our religious background isn't something routinely disclosed. I believe the Jonton erased details such as religious dogmas from our minds. I have a historical reference to religion, and how it caused wars and shaped lives. Some of those awakened haven't even recalled the concept of a God; maybe they were never believers in the idea of a creator or supreme being. Religion back on Earth caused much hardship and much happiness, much good, and much cruelty. The religion itself wasn't the problem—throughout history, people were the problem. Hopefully, our new civilization will do a better job respecting and accepting any beliefs that may, over time, develop.

"The other spacefaring civilizations of the galaxy have no new great revelations about God. Most advanced civilizations have no faith in regards to a supreme being, but almost all believe there is more after this life.

"The principles we use to guide our new civilization are founded on religious philosophies and the belief of and in the individual. The rights of liberty and property were fundamental to most of Humanity. Our new civilization will not be as concerned with property rights, but will stress individual freedom and responsibility."

"You appear to know many things about our life on Earth. Do you spend your time studying our past?"

"Tar told me I adjusted exceptionally well to my new life. He believes my study of history helped me adjust, so they allowed me to remember more Earth history and gave me unrestricted access to the archives. Everyone will have full access in the future, and as I said, you will now have access to some Earth records but not in a lot of detail." He paused and smiled. "Now, I don't know about you, but I'm hungry. Should we order some food?"

"Actually, yes. I'm curious to see what kind of food they have here."

Sabastian called over a waiter and asked for menus. Since this was primarily a coffee bar, the selection was mostly breakfast items and some small lunch sandwiches. Warren ordered a BLT since he recognized the name, and Sabastian ordered a Philly cheesesteak sandwich and watched to see Warren's reaction. Warren noticed the look, so after the waiter departed, he had to ask.

"Should I know what a Philly cheesesteak is? It sounds familiar, and I believe they named the sandwich after the city where you say I was born, but . . . ugh this half knowing is driving me crazy."

Sabastian laughed and said, "Yes, Warren, I ordered it deliberately to see if you had any memory of them from before; I didn't intend to frustrate you. I'm sure you grew up eating them all the time. They're fantastic. I fell in love with them when I visited Philadelphia as an exchange student while in college. I think they erased your memory of them because of the close association of where you grew up and lived. You will love them once more, I'm sure since I know you weren't a vegetarian."

Warren began to drift off until he sensed yet again someone watching him. Not casually, but intently, and he could almost hear thoughts in the person's mind. This new experience would have freaked him out and caused him to doubt his sanity if alone at home.

"Warren, are you okay? You looked lost in thought."

"I'm sorry, I drifted off a moment," he said as he casually looked around the plaza.

While waiting for Warren to collect his thoughts, Sabastian became lost in his. He hoped Warren was okay; there was something he could tell wasn't right. His mentee wasn't asking the usual questions others had brought forth. Warren's questions were more specific to himself and his past life.

"As you know," Warren started, "you're the first Human person I have talked to since . . . the beginning, and . . . I . . . I don't know why, but I feel I can trust you. I keep feeling as if someone is watching me. It started at my house months ago. I had even thought I saw someone in the woods outside my house a few times."

"Have you told Lan?"

"Yes, and he says it's not possible, but at the same time, I sensed he was concerned."

"But there's more, am I correct?"

"Yes, one time, I even saw myself sitting in my house, through the eyes of the person. I know this is nuts, but I'm sure it happened. Lan said they had altered our minds to use more of our brain than we could use on Earth; maybe this is part of it. Have you had any similar experiences?"

"No, I haven't. Not like that anyway. I know I can sense danger. I have, in the past, moved at the last second to avoid being hit by a tree and even a bolt of lightning when I was stupid enough to be outside during a storm. I know it is an ability they gave us for protection. This planet isn't one hundred percent safe, and we are a distance away from each other."

"I'd like to talk more about transportation with you, Sabastian. The mode of transport to get here was unexpected. How else can we get around? I had asked Lan about an ATV, but he avoided the question and stressed I should be more concerned with my Learnings."

Before Sabastian could respond, the waiter arrived with their food. He handed Sabastian a slip of paper, which he signed, placed his thumb against, and returned to the waiter.

Warren raised his eyebrows. "Do things like food get billed back to you by your name and thumbprint?"

"Maybe someday, but not now. Everything is free. The purpose of the signing and thumbprint is to track the usage of resources and habits. If someone were to abuse the system and take too much, they would be talked to and receive counseling. It hasn't happened; everyone has been content only to have what they need. In the future, after everyone is awakened and placed, we'll begin to establish an economy and monetary system. The inhabitants' habits, likes, and dislikes will help us plan. One day we'll become a full member of the Galactic community, with other races coming here for commerce and tourism, but the day is many years away."

Sabastian cut off a piece of his sandwich and gave it to Warren. Eager to see if Warren would remember.

"Try a piece of my sandwich."

Warren took the piece offered and knew as the smell reached his nose that he would like the sandwich. As he ate, the taste was familiar, and the name 'Jim's' came to mind, but without any context of actually having one in the past. They ate for a few minutes in silence before Sabastian restarted the conversation with an invitation.

"We have a lot to talk about, including more about your possible extra ability. I haven't forgotten what you said, and I feel we need to talk more about what's happening, whether it's real or not. This facility has hotel rooms available to anyone at any time as long as they aren't full. I always reserve a room in case my mentoring session goes longer than planned, so please stay the night so we can further our conversations. I have much more to tell you, and I feel you have more to tell me."

"I wasn't expecting to stay; I have no clothes with me and . . . Oh, I don't know."

"Clothes aren't a problem. Everything you need will be made available in the room."

Warren thought about it for a couple of seconds and decided it would probably be good to spend more time exploring his new life outside his home. It wasn't as if he had anything to get back to except nag.

"All right, Sabastian sounds good to me."

"Great, we can walk—hey, hi, Laura, come on over."

Sabastian stood, and as Warren also stood, a woman with long, black hair and beautiful blue eyes walked toward the table. She was slightly shorter than Warren and nicely built—slender and full-bodied like . . . the image faded from his mind; however, he experienced an instant attraction as if he were meeting a long-lost friend.

"Laura, this is Warren Estridge. Today is his first day."

"Hello, Warren; it's a pleasure to meet you. I hope Sabastian hasn't been boring you with his talk of Earth. Sometimes he goes on a tad too much," she said with a wide grin.

"Hi . . . ah, Laura," he replied as he almost stumbled over his words. "Our conversation has been interesting. Sabastian knows more about me than I do myself."

"Don't worry about it. I experienced the same thing with my mentor. It bothered me for a while, but I got over it. They give our mentors information about our past life they can impart to us or not, depending on how well we are dealing with our new life. I found out I was working as a fashion designer before the gathering, as they prefer us to say. They gave me access to some information about fashion, which brought back my memory and abilities. I design and make clothes with our hosts' help, and I have a little stand over in the market square."

"What is the market square?" Warren asked.

"It's an area for citizens to display the things they bake, create, make, or to trade things they are given access to like old books from Earth. You can give or trade them and offer services to other citizens. We'll walk through on our way to the hotel."

"Warren has decided to stay the night," he told Laura. "If you're free, how about you meet us for dinner tonight? I'll bring Chloe, and we can introduce Warren to more of what the center has to offer; we can do as they used to say, 'dinner and a movie.'"

Warren noticed odd looks between Sabastian and Laura, and he knew for sure something was going on between them he didn't understand. His heartbeat quickened, and his hands were again sweating, but it wasn't from fear or anxiety. He listened to their conversation while feeling like the experience was part of a dream.

"I would love to; tell me where and the time."

"I know Warren loved authentic Chinese food, so how about the Panda at 15:00?"

"Sounds great to me. I'll meet you there, but now I have to run to a meeting about starting classes to teach sewing skills. See you tonight, Warren."

Hearing his name brought Warren out of his daydream as Laura hurried off before he could even push out a goodbye. His throat was dry, and he needed to sit and finish his drink. Sabastian talked some more about the facility, but Warren wasn't listening. All he could think about was Laura. After they finished the sandwiches, they headed over to the hotel.

Life Center Market Square

"So, Sabastian, is Chloe, your girlfriend?" Warren inquired.

"No, she is my beautiful wife. I met her at a Council meeting about three years ago, and we have been married for almost two years."

"What does she do? If you don't mind me asking."

"I don't mind. I'm glad you are being interested; it's a good sign. She works at the Observation Research Station located on the other large continent, which we just yesterday decided to call Sanctuary.

"She is a student of biology, the head of her department, and the head of the tourism board for the facility. She is busy, and we don't see enough of each other, and now she has been asked to lead a project to catalog the native wildlife of this planet. Tonight will be a treat for both of us."

"Oh yes, I was reading about that on my way here on the . . . ah, what do we call the vehicle I rode?"

"Some call it the tube, which sounds odd to me, but some refer to it as the transport."

"Anyway, the station sounded interesting. How would I get there, assuming I'm allowed to go there?"

"You now have full access to all the common areas. However, you cannot visit any residence unless you have been invited and given authorization by the owner. The transport can take you to the airport where you can get a flight to the spaceport or the airport on Sanctuary. You can then take the transport to the Research Station from either location.

"The station does have restricted areas but will shortly be opening new areas specifically for visitors. It is one of the things Chloe is most proud of and never stops talking about."

"Speaking of access, I would like better access to my land. We were interrupted at lunch before you could answer. Is there a chance you could hook me up with an ATV or something so I can get around my property a bit easier?"

"Maybe. I know some who have them, but a couple of accidents have caused the Jonton to reconsider letting people have ATVs. They say there is no reason to access all your property."

"Well, then why have so much property? Why not put us closer together?"

"The plan is to divide the land to allow for more houses as necessary. When we have children and they get to adulthood, they would occupy a house or two built on the parents' land. Eventually, we will divide the land into much smaller estates. I envision a time; long after we are gone, there will probably be cities filled with apartments."

"That does make sense. We need room to grow if Humanity is to survive and prosper. You can't have a civilization with only one thousand people."

As they walked, Sabastian pulled out his communication device and made reservations at the Panda for the evening. He then called Chloe to let her know about the dinner plans. After a few minutes of conversation, they meandered through another beautiful park and approached what looked to Warren like the market square. There were booths with brightly colored tents lining a few walkways. He saw people selling books, and various objects like Sabastian had told him.

"So," Warren continued, "getting back to our prior conversation, you mentioned children. Are there any children here?"

"No, we are temporarily prevented from having children. After everyone has been awakened and settled, they will remove the pregnancy prevention and allow nature to take its course. It's something Chloe and I are looking forward to very much. We both want to have children, and sometimes the wait is frustrating. If all goes as planned, we should have a child in about three years."

The idea of being manipulated in such a way brought out Warren's feelings of anger. He hadn't experienced them for some time, but the idea of someone else controlling their lives bothered him a great deal. He was going to tell Sabastian how it affected him when he heard someone calling his name.

"Hello, guys come on over to see my clothes."

Warren looked toward the familiar voice and saw Laura standing next to a booth with brilliantly colored clothes, hats, and scarves. He felt drawn to Laura and started walking over, not caring if Sabastian followed behind.

"Long time no see," Warren said, and his blood rushed to his face. *What a lame thing to say.*

He wasn't sure what to say next. Luckily, Sabastian spoke up.

"So, Laura, how is the product moving?"

"Good, I traded a few things, including a scarf for this book about meditation and exercise. My routine is getting a tad boring."

"So, you don't sell your clothes?" Warren asked.

"No," Sabastian answered. "Everything here is traded. For now, we have no currency, and nothing is bought or sold. It will not be until everyone has been awakened and educated that we will form an economy with money and commerce."

"Laura, where is the person you traded with for the book? I would love to see what they have to offer, even though I have nothing to trade."

"I'm sure it being your first day, he'll offer you a gift. Tell him I sent you. He's right around the corner and down two rows."

"Great, thanks."

"I made reservations at the Panda and spoke to Chloe." Sabastian cut in. "We're all set for dinner this evening. She'll meet you at your place and then meet us at the Panda Bar."

"I'm looking forward to it. See you later, boys"

They walked toward the book trader in silence. Warren thought about Laura as he mindlessly brushed his fingers along some of the more interesting items available for trade and took a deep breath, "So, Laura."

"What about her?" Sabastian asked.

"Is she married or, you know, dating anyone?" He began to fidget with his hands while hoping he sounded natural.

Sabastian smirked. "Why do you ask?"

"No reason," Warren said.

Much to Warren's relief, Sabastian dropped the interrogation and shrugged. 'Not married; I know that much for sure. I don't know about dating. You're interested in Laura, I think?"

I hope Warren's possible abilities don't extend to mind reading. I don't need him, knowing more about Laura than necessary.

"I feel drawn to her. She even looks familiar to me."

"Maybe you can ask her for a date tonight."

"I think I should get my bearings first. I don't even know what we would do. I might ask Laura for her communication information. At least she doesn't have any family to worry about impressing."

As soon as he said it, Warren realized the statement might be considered cruel humor or insensitive.

"Sorry, Sabastian, not the right time for dark humor."

"It's okay. We all have to come to grips with the new normal."

They passed booths displaying everything from paintings, pottery, cooking sauces, and herbal medicines. After a minute, they came to the book trader, who was busy conversing with another patron. While waiting, Warren looked at some of the books and was surprised to find fiction among the selections. He picked up one book that caught his eye, *The Foundation Trilogy* by Isaac Asimov. The words 'Trantor' and 'Mule' flashed into his mind, yet he had no idea why.

A voice came from behind him. "Are you an Asimov fan?"

Warren turned to find a tall young man standing behind him with a pile of books in his arms. Warren looked to the book he was holding and raised a shoulder.

"I don't know. Is—was he a good author?"

"Asimov was one of the greatest science fiction authors of his time as well as a professor and scientist."

"I'm surprised to see Earth fiction. I thought it wouldn't be allowed."

"I'm allowed to reprint science fiction as long as it takes place off Earth. I had asked about future Earth fiction, but they told me I wouldn't be allowed at this time. I also have some horror, which has been deemed acceptable. Some of the horror books have covers with art I created myself."

He handed Warren a book called *Frankenstein*, which had a drawing of a disfigured creature a mad scientist had sewn together.

At that moment, Sabastian spoke up. "Excuse me for not making a formal introduction. This is Warren. It's his first day."

"Well, congratulations, Warren, and welcome back to life, as I like to say. In honor of your first day, please have the *Frankenstein* book as a gift."

"Wow, thank you, ah . . ."

"Robert. My name is Robert Spencer, and you're welcome."

Warren turned to Sabastian. "You know, Laura was right!"

"Oh, you know Laura already. She is a beautiful woman and unfortunately, only a friend."

"Yes," Warren replied, "I met her earlier. We were looking at her clothes when she suggested we come over to see you. She was certain you would offer me a gift."

"Well, since you are a friend of Laura's, I will give you the *Foundation* book as well, and when you see her again, put in a good word for me."

Warren thanked him once more as the book trader put the gifts in a carry bag, and he told Robert he would, even though he thought Laura was too good for him. The thought caught Warren by surprise as he recognized the emotion of jealousy. Sure, he was attracted to Laura, but he had no right to judge who was good for her.

"Are you okay?" Sabastian asked.

"Yes, I momentarily had the strangest feeling and a flash of what I think was a memory of a woman I knew back on Earth."

"Odd; has it happened before?"

"Yes, a few times. I mentioned it to Lan; he seemed unconcerned and thought it unusual and remarkable. An odd response, but I'm coming to understand; that is Lan."

"Well, if it doesn't bother him, then it's nothing I think we need to worry about."

Sabastian wasn't entirely truthful, and he regretted it, even though he knew it was for the best. Things needed to play out naturally.

Life Center Hotel

As Warren and Sabastian walked to the hotel, Sabastian stopped multiple times to introduce Warren to a friend of his or point out a Center feature. The enormity of the place surprised Warren, though some areas looked to be vacant. A sign in a fancier area of the Center said, "Life Center Hotel." A large brass door opened to the entrance and lobby. To one side was a bar displaying a wide variety of bottles, and there were a few tables and chairs by a fireplace in which to relax. On the other side of the lobby, he saw a few people sitting in front of a small café. The glass ceiling over the two-story lobby revealed the hotel was six stories tall with various facade styles.

Sabastian took Warren directly to the front desk, where the clerk's appearance caught him by surprise. The being was utterly bald with pinkish-colored skin and oval eyes, a mixture of bright green and gold. The most jarring of all, Warren couldn't tell by the body or the traditional hotel staff uniform if the clerk was male or female.

"Hello, Brother Bantor," Sabastian said. "This is Warren Estridge. Today is his first time at the Life Center, and he'll be staying in the room I reserved."

"Hello, Brother Sabastian, and hello, Brother Warren," Bantor replied. "Your room is ready for you. It is room 620 on the sixth floor, of course. Touch your thumb to the door, and it will open. The elevators are to your right. Please do not hesitate to call the front desk if you need anything."

"Thank you, Ban—Brother Bantor," Warren said as they headed to the elevators. Warren was about to ask Sabastian about Bantor when he indicated he had to go.

"I have a meeting I must get to in a few minutes. Take some time to relax or use the facilities in the hotel. I'll meet you at the Panda Bar at 14:50. It's only a couple of minutes away, and you'll be able to view a map in your room. We'll talk more at the Panda before the ladies get there. See you tonight, Warren."

Sabastian left the lobby before his mentee could ask any questions. Warren hoped they did shave some time before dinner for additional conversation.

Curious about what the guestrooms would look like, Warren went to his room, which he found at the end of the sixth-floor hallway. The walls were adorned with off-colored landscapes and decorated with a pattern that looked old to him, not worn but old . . . fashioned, he believed to be the word. A window faced out the side of the hallway toward a view of a low mountain range. Distant storm clouds appeared to drop more snow on the sloping sides of the mountain as he admired the view.

When Warren tired of watching the distant storm, he placed his thumb on the door handle of his room, and it immediately opened. He walked inside to a spacious area that was more like a suite. Off to one side stood a small bar area stocked with various refreshments, and across from the bar, a window looked out to another breathtaking view of the approaching storm.

A plus red sofa faced a wall straight ahead, which extended three-quarters across the room and held a video screen. Warren walked around the wall to look at what he assumed was the sleeping area when a voice startled him.

"Hello, Warren, is your day going well?"

"Nag, is that you? What are you doing here? Well, not here exactly, you know what I mean. How did you know I decided to spend the night at the hotel?"

"I was alerted when you registered. Everything you need should be inside. Is there anything i can do for you at the moment?"

"No, not at the moment, other than not startling me. I guess I'll eventually get used to the fact you are everywhere."

Warren walked around the wall to find an oversized bed with a mint sitting on one of the many pillows. He recalled they always provided a mint when he went to . . . as quickly as the thought entered his mind, it was gone.

Another large window overlooked the airport in the distance, and beyond was another impressive mountain range covered in snow. To Warren's right hung another viewscreen over a chest of drawers. In the drawers, he found fresh clothes, enough for a couple of days, and he wondered how long Sabastian expected him to stay. Upon further inspection, he found workout clothing and a bathing suit.

"Nag, can you bring up a hotel map on the bedroom viewscreen?"

"Is there anything, in particular, you are looking to find?"

"Yes, I'm looking to see what kind of activity areas they have, such as a workout room and pool."

A map displayed a large area marked as Gym and Pool. The image also indicated a game room, various sized meeting rooms, a few bars, coffee shops, and restaurants.

"Nag, is there a locker room in the gym?"

"Yes. It is complete with towel service, dry and wet saunas, a whirlpool tub, and attendants offering massages. If you are going down to the gym, i will reserve a locker you can access with your thumbprint."

"Yes, please reserve a locker. I will be going as soon as I grab my bathing suit."

He looked at the map again to verify where he needed to go and asked nag to turn off the display. The CA told him the locker number, and he headed out, looking forward to some relaxation.

<<<>>>

Warren was greeted by an attendant waiting for him at the entrance. "Hello, Brother Warren; my name is Brother Arman. I will show you around our facility and then direct you to your locker."

Arman began by walking Warren through the gym, showing him the various equipment and exercise areas. He explained that attendants were available to help with equipment or act as spotters. Arman next escorted him to the impressive pool area, complete with hot tubs and an Olympic-sized pool, with swimming lanes and a free swim area. During the tour, Warren noticed all the attendants in the facility were of the same alien species.

Arman took him to the locker room, which contained a juice bar, saunas, two more hot tubs, and an area for massage and aromatherapy. He showed Warren his locker, verified he could open it with his thumb, and bid him a productive and relaxing afternoon.

Warren wanted to stop Arman, to inquire about his species, but he figured it wasn't the right place and even maybe not polite. Lan confirmed months ago, Humans on Earth were not routinely sending ships to outer space, so they certainly had never met races from another solar system. Warren wondered what he would think and how much more amazed he would be if he could recall the things he never before realized were possible. Warren was beginning to understand why suppressing memories of the past and the adjustment period were necessary.

Warren changed and proceeded to spend the next hour in the pool doing various laps. It was great to have such a large area to swim. No other being was in his way, but knowing others were around and nearby after months of being alone was comforting.

After swimming, he picked up an energy drink at the juice bar and took it to one of the hot tubs. He enjoyed the drink while he relaxed in the soothing waters and afterward spent a few minutes in the wet sauna until the heat became too much. As he headed to the showers, one of the attendants asked if he would be interested in a massage. He didn't remember if he ever had one in his previous life, but he decided to go ahead and give it a try.

After a few minutes, Warren was glad he had taken the offer. It was an extremely relaxing experience, which caused him to drift off . . .

Don't stop, Samantha. Your touch on my shoulders feels so good after the long day. Hey, don't be starting something we don't have time to finish . . .

"Brother Warren—Brother Warren, please roll over onto your back."

As Warren rolled over, the vision or memory quickly faded, but the name Samantha still filled his mind, along with an image of a woman with medium-length blond hair and blue eyes. As he lay there enjoying the massage, he realized this was the first time since being awakened; another . . . being had touched him, at least that he remembered. The hands were not Human, but the touch was comforting, and he began to understand loneliness.

After the massage, Warren used the facilities to shave and shower. He thought more about the woman in his vision and became aroused as if she were standing there naked in front of him. Thankfully no one was around to see what he believed was his first experience of arousal since they woke him. He wondered as he stood there embarrassed if the Jonton had done something to lessen his sex drive.

When Warren returned to his room, he still had two hours before he had arranged to meet Sabastian. He told his CA he was going to take a nap and to wake him in time to get dressed and be at the Panda a little early, in case he got lost.

He pulled down the covers, closed the curtains, and asked the CA to play 'One Man's Dream.' He began to drift off to sleep as he drifted back into his earlier vision . . .

"Samantha, will you marry me?"

Panda Bar

Warren found his way to the Panda without difficulty. The CA had provided him with directions and said he could use the direct internal link to contact him if needed. He still didn't like the feeling, but Warren had to admit he appreciated the convenience of nag communicating in his head whenever he needed or wanted information.

Warren arrived early at the restaurant, so he sat at a table next to a window and watched the snow falling and the sky darken. Pictures he immediately recalled as being of pandas and bamboo trees decorated the restaurant. He also recognized symbols on the walls as Chinese words. He couldn't read them but wondered if he should even remember they were Chinese or the fact China was a country on Earth. Try as he might, he couldn't remember anything specific about the country but did know it was the location of the pandas' habitat. He thought maybe he had a thing for pandas.

"Hello," Sabastian said as Warren watched him approach the table. "I trust everything was satisfactory with your room."

"Yes, the room is wonderful, as is the entire facility. I enjoyed time in the pool and sauna, plus took time for a relaxing massage. The experience was quite tranquil."

"Good, I'm glad you enjoyed the facilities. The ladies are running a little late, but that's good since it will give us more time to talk. I see you haven't ordered a drink. May I suggest a gin martini?"

"Sounds good, I guess. I don't remember if I ever had one or if I was even much of a drinker, and I'm getting tired of saying the same thing all the time."

Sabastian laughed while confirming Warren had a preference toward gin and called over the waiter—also of the same species as Bantor and Arman. Order placed, Warren asked about their species.

"They are known as the Tranlay," Sabastian explained. They work at most of the hospitality jobs in the center."

"Why do they put 'Brother' in front of everyone's name?" Warren asked.

"Brother is an honorary title of friendship they also use to show comradeship and respect. In their culture, being stripped of your right to be called Brother or speak the word is considered the worst possible punishment. They reserve it for the worst offenses. In addition to other penalties."

"Do they get paid to work here?"

"Yes, they do. Working on this planet is a great honor for them, but they also get paid nicely in Galactic credits. At some point in our future, when we have a larger population, we will be able to take on some of the jobs they do if we desire."

"Sabastian . . . this next question sounds vaguely familiar to me in an uncomfortable way," Warren said. "But how do you tell them apart when they all look alike? I couldn't tell if they were male or female."

Sabastian laughed and then apologized. "Your uneasiness with the question is probably because back on Earth, there was a time when many people often said the same thing about various ethnicities. For instance, the woman over at the bar with dark-colored skin and the people who lived in the country this restaurant represents. People who were not comfortable with their differences said the statement often about them and some others.

"Those days were mostly behind us when the Jonton began to gather us, but prejudice did remain. The Jonton made sure to choose representatives of all ethnicities when they started the process. I'm sure someday we'll be so blended together we will finally realize we're all one Human race. The bigger problem in this expanded world we now live in is species prejudice. It does not happen or rear its head often, but it's out there.

"In time, you'll find it easy to tell one Tranlay from another. As far as sex, well, they are neither and both. The Tranlay are an old species and have moved far beyond the traditional concepts of male and female. To reproduce, they have a small piece of what was once a sex organ removed from their bodies and joined in a birthing facility. There the offspring grows until it is time for it to be born taken home and raised in the same way you would be used to back on Earth and eventually here as well."

"Wow, I still have so much to learn. I noticed when I visited the gym, there were only Humans using the facilities, and all the Tranlay were working. Are there any other species here in the center or hotel?"

"There are no laws forbidding aliens from visiting or staying at the hotel, when necessary, but they are discouraged from coming to this facility. It's not because of any animosity or prejudice. The purpose is to give Humanity time to adjust and flourish independently without too much alien influence.

"There is another hotel at the spaceport which caters to all the various species which could be here visiting. We are encouraged to hold any meetings with them at those facilities for the time being, so they can be more comfortable and have less influence on our day-to-day lives.

The waiter returned with the drinks, and Warren took a sip. He found the taste pleasant and refreshing. He could get used to eating and drinking anything he wanted without having to worry about paying. The concept of trade bothered him because he had no idea what he would have to trade.

"So, I think it's time we talk more about you and your progress," Sabastian said, tearing him from his thoughts. I know you spoke to Lan about your ability to remember certain things, but I'm still concerned. I'm not worried about the process or what you might remember; I'm more concerned with how you feel about it and how the memories affect your mental health.

"I'm also interested in your abilities to sense being watched and even seeing through someone else's eyes. I'm worried maybe it's your imagination or insecurities coming through, possibly because of the memories. Your uneasiness with the question about race is an example of a negative memory that could be causing some of these things."

Warren took another sip of his drink. He found the alcohol comforting.

"I don't know what to think. I feel fine. I'm happy, and I don't feel afraid. Until earlier today while walking and at the coffee shop, I hadn't had the feeling of being watched for many months."

"Tell me, Warren, was it before Laura came over?"

"It was."

"Interesting."

"Why?"

"I'm not at liberty to say at the moment. You asked earlier if Laura were married; was there a reason other than the fact you are attracted to her?"

Sabastian waited, knowing Warren was struggling with what to say.

"She's familiar to me, Sabastian as if I've known her before. I don't feel like this is the first time we have met. While I had my massage, I drifted off and had a vision or dream of being with a woman sexually who might or might not have been Laura. And then later, as I was taking a nap, I had a dream about asking this person to marry me."

"Yet you say these visions and memories don't bother you."

"They don't bother me!" Warren snapped, immediately regretting his outburst. He took a deep breath to calm himself. "Sorry. It's just that I find it all strange. Strange, I should be so attracted to someone I don't know and strange you can't tell me something you know. Why all the secrecy, what are you and Lan not telling me about my life?"

Warren continued without waiting for Sabastian to answer, as he clenched the glass hard enough to turn his knuckles white before he relaxed.

"What I'm more concerned about, is something I haven't mentioned to you, but think I should. There were times when I first awoke, I had feelings of anger, directed mostly at Lan and the Jonton, that they took liberties with our lives and did whatever they wanted to with us as if they owned us. Even now, talking about it brings back some of those feelings. I'm not sure if Lan noticed—"

"Oh, believe me," Sabastian cut in. "He could tell, same as I can. That's something they monitor very closely."

"Then again today," Warren resumed "I was feeling anger or maybe jealousy toward Robert when he spoke about Laura. And even earlier, when you were talking about being prevented from having children. I understand the reasons for everything they have done and continue to do, and we should all be so grateful to them, but these feelings don't appear to be going away."

Sabastian noticed how Warren played with his hands when he became agitated and wasn't unconsciously trying to crush his glass.

Are Warren's ongoing anger and behavior something I should discuss with Lan? I need to try and calm Warren so they don't decide to start another time.

"I'm sure the feelings are connected with your ability to remember your past life. Humans have always had an aversion to being held captive, having their lives controlled by another, or anyone telling them what to do. The country in which you were born originated on the idea of personal freedom, so these feelings aren't unusual outside of the context of your abilities. Lan didn't find them a reason to hold you back, and I don't think they will hurt you in the long run. You are not the first person to experience some anger and you probably won't be the last.

"It's something to talk about, but I think they will go away in time like it has for others. You are a remarkable person, and I'm glad to be able to help you if needed. I hope we will be more than a mentor and mentee. I hope I can call you, my friend."

"As do I, Sabastian."

"Oh, here come the ladies."

Dinner and a Movie

Sabastian rose from his chair to introduce his wife, Chloe, and give her a big kiss. Warren was feeling strangely out of place as his attention drifted to Laura. She wore a beautiful blue dress with her long hair flowing over her shoulders. He looked at her, and the image of Samantha, whomever she had been, came back to him as clearly as in the dream.

"Warren, I would like you to meet my wife, Chloe!"

Sabastian's voice woke him from his thoughts, he said hello to Chloe, and they exchanged a few pleasantries. He then directed his attention back to Laura and told her it was a pleasure to see her again. Sabastian went to inform the maître d' everyone was there as Warren and the women sat.

Chloe was the first to speak.

"How does it feel, Warren, to be out of your house and among other people for the first time? It drove me crazy being in the house for so many months."

"It's a bit strange in a way," he answered, "but it's also exciting and familiar, like a lost friend you had almost forgotten about from childhood. I have learned so many new things already today, which is surprising considering how much I had to learn before I was allowed to venture forth from my cocoon."

"That's beautiful," Chloe said. "It's so poetic, the way you describe the beginning of your new life."

"It does actually. Maybe I was poetic in my old life? I'm sure I'll never know."

Be careful, Warren, he thought to himself as the anger began to rise. Thankfully, Sabastian was coming back to the table.

"What did I miss?" he said as he sat.

Chloe gestured to Warren. "Warren was waxing almost poetic about his emergence from his cocoon to join civilization."

"I never actually thought about it in that way, but I guess it is a good analogy," Sabastian said. "Our table should be ready in a few minutes."

"So, what were the two of you discussing before we arrived?" asked Chloe.

"Warren was telling me about his afternoon at the hotel. He spent some time at the health club and spa there. Afterward, when resting, he had a dream which might have been about his past life."

Warren sat stunned when Sabastian mentioned his experiences to the women. Even though he didn't go into detail, Warren thought it odd and humiliating.

Laura asked, "Is that even possible, or maybe I should say, should it be possible? I know the only dreams I've ever been able to remember are all about my new life."

"The same for me as well," Chloe said. "And most of my dreams are now about this wonderful man sitting there with the red face."

Sabastian went to speak and defend his blushing when the maître d' came over to escort them to the table.

The ambient light in the main dining room appeared to come from an evening sky on the ceiling and the lights shining on trees scattered in front of the dark wooden walls. The lighting, as well as the candles on the tables, created a relaxing and romantic environment.

Warren had sought to take Sabastian aside to ask why he mentioned the dream, but there wasn't an opportunity. When they arrived at the table, Warren was seated across from Laura, who smiled at him as their eyes met. He remained so attracted to her that it was almost scary.

They spent some time with idle chitchat as they read the menu, talked about what they had tried before, and placed their orders. When the waiter left the table, Sabastian folded his hands in front of him and smiled at the group.

"I had a meeting with the Council this afternoon, and we talked about the long-term future of our world. The Jonton expect to finish the reintroduction process in less than three years. At that time, the restrictions on having children will end. I'm sure we can expect our first baby boom, of which I plan to be a part."

Chloe laughed. "Oh, I don't know, babe, if I'm willing to give up this slim, trim body for a child."

"Yeah, right," Sabastian joked. "Then who is that woman who has been complaining about not being able to start a family? I could have sworn it was you! You know I'll love you no matter how large you get, my dear."

"And I'll try to love you still on that day in the future when I'm lying there in agony delivering your child."

"Oh, my child, now. I see how it will be."

Warren sat listening while feeling the anger again, which he quickly put down as he moved his hands to his lap so no one would notice his fidgeting. He didn't want to look like a nut case destined for failure. Why did he have such a problem with the Jonton controlling their lives? Was it only because of his beliefs and expectations from his previous life?

"Well, getting back to my point," Sabastian said, "as part of our discussions, we talked about the eventual need for schools and teachers. There will be so much more for the children to learn. The goal and responsibility of becoming a full independent society someday will fall mostly to our children and grandchildren."

"Well, they won't need to learn about history," said Laura. "After all, what good is it to learn the history of a planet that doesn't exist?"

"The planet still exists, Laura," Sabastian said, "However, it no longer supports life. Someday though, I'm sure there will be expeditions back to Earth to retrieve more of the art and culture which had to be left behind. As a historian, I certainly hope so, anyway. Maybe my child or grandchild could go back someday. I don't expect it'll be in my lifetime."

Sabastian continued after a brief pause in which his eyes glassed over while lost in his thoughts.

"We will still need to teach history," he said. "Not the dates and places so much as the problems, which plagued Earth. Our children will need to learn from past mistakes to avoid the things that caused wars and violence. We have received a new world, and our children must be taught not to spoil it the way Humanity ruined the Earth with war, pollution, and overpopulation. It will be easier to avoid those mistakes with the knowledge of the past and the assistance of the greater Galactic community.

"It'll probably be some time before we have our own teachers, so the Jonton have offered to act as teachers until we can develop our education infrastructure and programs. They are responsible for creating the Learnings programs we all went through so they would appear perfect for the task."

The appetizers arrived before Sabastian could continue his lecture—much to Chloe's relief. They spent the rest of the dinner talking about Laura's designs, Chloe's work at the Research Station, and Sabastian's love of history. Chloe invited Warren to a tour of the Research Station, which they scheduled to do in a couple of weeks. After dinner, they started talking about their new homeworld as they waited for dessert.

"I would love the opportunity to see more of this planet," Warren said. "I'm close to the ocean but have not yet had the opportunity to hike that far to see it for myself. Hopefully, now, with the majority of my education out of the way, I can make it there."

"It's not safe to go wandering about everywhere," Sabastian said, "however, there are tours the Jonton have set up you can take. They offer exploratory tours of the smaller continents and islands, as well as overnight camping trips. There's a requirement you go through survival training first. If you're going to be out in the wilderness, you need to be well prepared."

"I would love to see the oceans," Laura said. "Maybe you can take me some time, Warren?"

"It would be my pleasure!" he said as his heart practically jumped out of his chest with excitement.

"Is there a beach near your property?"

"No, Laura, not according to nag," Warren said, then quickly added, "that's what I call my computer. It's a sheer cliff in the area with no beach along the water. When I spoke to Lan about the ocean, he told me going in the water isn't safe. The waters contain many large creatures that come close to the shore, and he said some would put an Earth shark to shame."

"Hey, Sabastian, didn't you tell me there was a long-range plan to develop a seaside retreat?"

"Yes, my dear, that's correct. The Jonton can create a force shield in the water to keep out the harmful predators so we'll be able to develop a beach resort where people can vacation and enjoy the sand and surf. And the Jonton tell me the alterations they made to our bodies will allow us to get a tan but not allow us to burn or develop skin cancer from the sun."

"The wonders of alien science," Warren said. "Cheers to the Jonton." It came out a bit more negatively than he intended, and Sabastian raised his eyebrows at him.

"So, what else is there to do for entertainment?" Warren asked as he began to pick at his dessert.

"We have many activities available to us at the center, all of which I'll show you tomorrow," Sabastian answered. "One of the things we have are movies, and we will go to one tonight. In fact, we only have about twenty more minutes. We're limited in what we can show because we can't have direct references to Earth, but there are some good science fiction and fantasy movies available to us."

<<<>>>

Warren arrived back at his room around midnight, and his CA greeted him.

"Hello, Warren, i hope you had an enjoyable evening."

"I did, nag, thank you. It was a sensational evening, but I won't bother you with the details since you probably know them already."

"Did you enjoy the movie?"

"I thought it to be an odd choice under the circumstances."

Although there was mention of Earth, you never saw it in the movie, and the story was to have taken place over one hundred years in the future—a future the Earth would never realize. Warren expected his new world to have a great future in space, as long as they didn't happen upon aliens who wanted to use them as food or incubators. After that movie, he anticipated having nightmares instead of a dream about a mysterious woman. As he prepared for bed, he started thinking about Laura.

The best thing about the evening was Laura giving him her communication number and asking him to contact her after returning to his home and genuinely settling into his new life. Warren was excited but also exhausted. He fell asleep quickly, with no dreams.

Morning with Sabastian

"Good morning, Warren, it is time for you to prepare so you are not late for your breakfast meeting with Sabastian."

"Do you know everything? I didn't mention my meeting. Please switch to the room system for communication."

"Sabastian requested i add it to your calendar."

"What time is it?"

"It is 6:00, and, your meeting is in an hour."

In less than an hour, Warren was ready and left the room wearing new jeans and a light blue button-down shirt. Wearing clothes, someone else picked still bothered him. At some point, he hoped to be able to choose his wardrobe. The selections weren't bad; they only weren't his, although he liked the shirt's color.

They were to meet in the hotel coffee shop for a light breakfast before venturing off. Sabastian hadn't said where they were going before they parted the previous evening. When Warren arrived at the coffee shop, Sabastian was entering as well. They sat in one of the corners, and after they both ordered, Sabastian asked Warren if he had enjoyed last evening.

"Yes, I enjoyed it a great deal. The movie was a bit bloody and wild, but since it didn't seem familiar, I either never saw it on Earth, or my memory of things I shouldn't be remembering has its limits."

"I suspect even if you did see the movie before, unless it was important to you, or scared the shit out of you, it wouldn't have an impact. The books you received yesterday are probably ones you read and enjoyed in the past since they did seem familiar.

"What about Laura?" Sabastian asked.

The mention of Laura made his pulse quicken.

"That was a quick change of subjects. What about her?" Warren asked.

"Well, yesterday you were very interested in knowing more about her. Are you still interested? I know she gave you her number, and you did say you would show her the ocean."

"Okay, yes, I'm still interested, as I'm sure you already knew. Laura is like an old friend or—"

"Lover? Did you dream about Laura last night, Warren?"

"No," he said sharply. "And why did you say, Laura? I never said I dreamt about Laura before, only it was someone who looked like her. She is not Saman—"

"Why did you stop Warren, and why are you angry?"

Warren ran his hands through his hair. He had done it twice before, and both times were when aggravated. He put his hands down and looked at Sabastian with a tempered appearance.

"I stopped because I don't want to appear crazy," he said. "I don't know who Samantha is, or was, or why I can't forget her, and I'm angry because I feel like you are interrogating me, and why did you mention my experience at the health club to the ladies?"

"Slow down, Warren, take a breath. You just mentioned a woman's name, possibly from your past."

"Yes, Sabastian, the girl's name in my dream, I'm sure, is Samantha. Now please answer my question; stop stalling."

"I'm sorry, it's not my intention to interrogate you. I'm trying to help you adjust. I noticed some anger last night when we talked about the Jonton altering our DNA, and I worry it might get out of hand. As far as mentioning your experience, I did that to get you more comfortable talking about them. They may not be as unusual as you think. I found out yesterday from Lan some similar things are happening to others. If you would feel more comfortable talking to a professional, I can make the arrangements."

"They have shrinks here?"

Sabastian laughed at the old term Warren recollected. "Yes, two people, a man, and a woman, who were psychologists back on Earth, were allowed to keep their knowledge of psychology so they would be available to help others if needed."

"That's interesting but not necessary. I don't need another person judging my thoughts and actions. I have no problem talking with you, and I'm sorry. I trust you and enjoy our conversations."

"Good. Here comes our breakfast. Let's enjoy, and then there are some things I want to show you."

A half an hour later, Sabastian and Warren walked to a section of the center devoted to recreation. A short elevator ride to a lower level brought them to an area bright with artificial daylight and a high ceiling, which looked like a clear blue sky. In front of them, Warren recognized a baseball diamond, and to the side were fields for soccer and rugby.

Sabastian told Warren the area was for the citizens of the planet who were not staying at the hotel. In addition to the fields, it also included a complete gym, Olympic-sized swimming pool, basketball, racquetball, and bocce courts. There was a billiards room and various rooms for cards and other games for the less athletic. Next to the registration and information desk at the front of the facility stood a juice bar and refreshment stand serving light lunches and snacks.

"What do you think of everything the facility has to offer?" Sabastian asked.

"It looks and sounds great. What about equipment? I remember I had a baseball glove and bats when I played the game at some point in my past. It's odd; I can see the glove in my mind and smell the leather, almost as if I wore it ready to play, but there is no background context and no memory of using them. Will I remember how to play, and will I have retained any skills I might have possessed?"

"It's peculiar the things you remember, but yes, you should have retained any skill and knowledge of the games. Anyway, everything you need is available here, and to make it even more convenient, you can request to be assigned one or two lockers. One in the main locker room for changing and showering plus a storage locker in which you can keep any personal equipment you may acquire."

"That could end up being a lot of lockers. What happens as the population grows?"

"Only about half our citizens have lockers here, and there are plans to build other facilities for the future. Access to this facility isn't something that will remain free forever, but it's great for now. It would help your adjustment if you looked into joining a team or two. It might help resolve some of your anger that surfaces from time to time. Smashing a ball out of the park and throwing a runner out at third are better things to do with your hands than run them through your hair.

"Since I remember bats and gloves and I recognize the field, I guess I know how to play baseball, but I'm not so sure about some of the others. I'm familiar with the names soccer and rugby, but that's about—football—the term sprang into my head."

"I know you never played football, except possibly as a youth, and they don't have football here; however, there are instructors for anything you might like to try. The Tranlay are outstanding players of our sports and also exceptional instructors. Although their bodies look different, they move in much the same ways as Humans."

A few minutes later, when back on the main level, Sabastian walked back to the hotel with Warren; he showed him the transport stations that would take him to the airport. "From there, you can board a jet to the spaceport and research facility on Sanctuary. You have to take the general transport here first and then walk to this transport station," Sabastian told him. "I have another meeting in a few minutes, so I'll leave you here. You can stay at the hotel as long as you like, but please let the desk know when you're leaving. Remember, I'm available at any time if you need me or need to talk."

"Thank you, Sabastian; I'll call if I need you or maybe only to say hello. The tours and conversation have been great, but I still feel uneasy and feel like you're keeping something from me."

Sabastian reached out and put his hand on Warren's shoulder. "You mentioned earlier about trusting me. I promise always to tell you as much truth as I'm allowed. You're correct. I possess additional knowledge of your life; I'm keeping the details from you for now. And the reason is, you're not ready."

Sabastian nodded a subtle goodbye and quickly headed to his meeting before Warren could say anything in response. Warren stood there dumbfounded, not sure what to think.

After walking around the Life Center, taking it all in, he headed back to the hotel to check out. There was a suitcase in his room now, and the CA instructed him to take home all the clothes provided. An hour later, Warren was on the transport, where he spent the entire ride wondering what it was Sabastian wasn't telling him.

What does Sabastian know, and will I care when I find out?

WARREN AND LAURA

A First Date

Days passed since Warren had come back home from the Life Center. He spent those days getting back to his regular workout routine, checking on and ordering supplies, and doing other things to avoid thinking about what Sabastian said to him. He had spoken to Sabastian a couple of times since then, but he didn't mention the subject, nor did Sabastian.

With no set Learnings routine, he had time to browse through the available information and learn more about whatever he found interesting. Music interested him most. He spent hours digging through the computer archives for music he desired to play, and he asked the CA to find obscure, challenging pieces. Warren could read the sheet music, hear it in his head and play almost anything the CA printed for him.

When not busy with his new life's daily routines or delving through all the available music, he spent his time wondering about his future. Were there other musicians the Jonton saved, soon to be awakened, or already living their new lives? If so, could they form a band, a quartet, or an orchestra? Should he pursue his passion for old-style woodworking? He planned to ask Lan or Sabastian about the possibility of getting the tools and raw materials.

Trading was on his mind as well, and he thought, if he made furniture, he would have something to trade. He could also offer music lessons. He had been a teacher in his old life, so undoubtedly, he could be again. He wondered where his pupils would get the instruments. Did the Jonton save any, and if not, could they recreate them? The piano sitting across the room would indicate anything to be possible.

Warren had a lot of new information to absorb and process, plus he wanted to learn more about the customs of the other species. He didn't want to look like a fool or an ignorant idiot if he ran into someone other than a Human or Tranlay.

Three days after returning home, Warren finally accomplished his goal of making his way to the coast. He sat there on the edge of a rocky cliff and stared at the vast and beautiful blue ocean. He hoped next time to find a pathway down to the tiny beach below, covered in pink-white sand.

Warren was ready to call on the morning of the fourth day home. He had been procrastinating, doing everything but getting up the nerve to make contact. He didn't want to appear too anxious or wait too long and not seem interested. Warren desired to be with Laura so much that he hadn't slept well the night before, from thinking about her while tossing and turning, with images in his mind he didn't comprehend.

When she answered, he stumbled over his words like a nervous child. After a few minutes of bantering back and forth, he found the courage to ask her to meet him the following evening for dinner. She sounded excited and immediately said yes.

Warren spent the rest of the day doing anything he could to take his mind off her, but he found it difficult, so he went to sleep early, and as usual, he dreamt.

Don't stop Sam . . . feels so good . . . I want you more than I ever have . . . Laura, oh Laura . . .

"Warren, your blood pressure, and respiration are above normal range? Is everything okay with you? Was your earlier workout too strenuous?"

The worrisome greeting from his CA was not the way he wanted to awake from his nap. He had performed a more intense workout in the morning, partially to get his mind off the coming evening. It hadn't worked.

After cleaning, he had taken a nap to pass the time so he wouldn't be tired later. He hadn't slept well again the previous night, so he knew he needed the rest. He had dreamt further about Samantha. This dream was more intense than previously. He imagined, or recalled in the dream, making love with her. When he awoke from the nap, his body was still ready for action, and as the CA had indicated, his blood pressure and breathing were at higher rates than normal. He wished he knew who Samantha was and how or why he could remember her so well.

Before the CA asked him again, he said he was excited about his first date with Laura tonight. An actual person would have made a snide comment about his excitement being obvious. Thankfully, nag was not a person.

As he lay in bed waiting for his body to calm down, he realized how much he desired the touch of another. Since the dreams had started getting more realistic and sexual, Warren was having trouble getting thoughts of sex out of his mind. He never was one for self-gratification; at least he didn't think so. Who knew? He certainly wasn't going to ask Lan.

Laura giving him her contact information surprised him. He expected she might be as lonely as he, living alone in her home. He had asked her to meet him at Michelangelo's, a restaurant that featured food from the Earth country of Italy. Michelangelo was an artist from an earlier Earth period. Some of his work and copies of work not salvaged were part of the restaurant's décor.

More upscale than some of the other options available, Michelangelo's restaurant had a dress code. Looking through his closet, Warren found a charcoal gray suit he thought appropriate. He picked a light blue dress shirt and a dark blue and gray tie to match. He wasn't sure if he knew how to put on a tie, but once he started, it all came back as if he had been doing it all the time.

For the first time, he looked at and paid attention to the nicer clothes provided; as expected, he also found a pair of black dress socks and shoes. After combing his hair, brushing his teeth, and experiencing butterflies like a teenager, Warren was ready to go—physically anyway.

Now, if he only could lose the nervous feeling so his stomach could calm. He didn't know why he should be so nervous; it wasn't their first . . . date. As soon as the word date came to mind, an image of another woman popped into his head. It was his first date with Laura, and hopefully not his last. What was he thinking? Why did he feel as if he knew Laura? He pushed the crazy thoughts out of his head, went downstairs, and was on his way to the Life Center in a few minutes. The trip seemed to take longer than before, and he sat there playing with his fingers, interlacing them together and twisting them like a game. Maybe it was because of his eagerness to see her again. The situation was crazy. How could he be so in love with someone he didn't know?

Warren arrived at the restaurant a few minutes early. As he sat, he had the familiar feeling of someone watching his every move. He looked around but didn't see anyone or anything out of the ordinary.

He should have a flower or something, but where would he get a flower at this point, unless he picked one from the plaza garden?

Sure, get arrested before our first date. Do they even have anything like police?

He sat nervously for about five minutes before Laura arrived. She looked even more stunning than the last time he saw her. He stood as she approached and was a little surprised when she gave him a big hug.

"It's so good to see you again, Warren!"

Laura sat on the sofa and when Warren sat, next to her, she smiled and continued talking. "Sabastian and Chloe are close friends, but everyone else I know is nothing more than an acquaintance. Getting to go out with someone special is wonderful and makes me happy."

He knew his face was now flush, partially out of excitement, and also some embarrassment. He didn't know what to say. Thankfully, Laura didn't give him a chance.

"Oh, so sorry, I embarrassed you with my crazy forwardness," she said. "I assure you I'm not always like this; I feel so . . . oh, shut up Laura, before you put your foot in your mouth. So, Warren, how have you been?"

"Well first, now that I can talk," he said, laughing, "let me say how great it is to see you again too, and how beautiful you look this evening."

Now it was her turn to blush.

Warren motioned to let the maître d' know they were ready, and he immediately escorted the couple to their table. The restaurant, decorated with statues scattered about and paintings on the ivory-colored stone walls, looked to be popular. The chairs, upholstered with plush red velvet, were made of polished dark wood. An old wine bottle on each table had a candle stuck in the neck, with wax from previous candles remaining down the sides of the various shaped bottles.

He pulled out Laura's chair for her and sat across the table, hoping she would not see how nervous he still was around her. After some small talk, she asked if he had given any thought to what he would do with his new life.

"Sort of," he said. "As I mentioned the other day, I appear to be well trained and talented on the piano. I plan on asking Lan if I can offer concerts or lessons. According to Sabastian, I taught music in a school and gave individual lessons. The problem is, I don't know if I know how to teach still. If there are other musicians with us, starting a band has also crossed my mind."

"I would love to be able to play the piano," Laura responded. You could experiment on me. It would be fun. And it would give me an excuse to see you more."

"I may take you up on your offer," he said with a huge smile.

The waiter brought the wine selection Warren had pre-ordered. After Warren's approval, he opened the bottle, poured the wine, and took their appetizer and entrée order. After the waiter left, Warren continued the conversation.

"Sabastian told me in my past life that I was part of a club that built wooden furniture as a hobby. I've been able to access some non-restricted information about Shaker-style furniture, which seems to appeal to me. When I researched how to make furniture, all the knowledge came back like it was inside, waiting to be re-discovered. So, maybe I'll make furniture to bring an old tradition to a new world and give me something to trade." He paused to take a sip of wine.

"What about you, Laura? That's a beautiful dress you're wearing, and I assume it is one of your creations? I noticed you had many nice-looking clothes at your booth last week. Is that what you would like to do?"

"It is, thank you! I finished it last week. When they brought me the fabric, I fell in love with it and had to make something. I think designing clothes will be part of my future, but I also want to know more about fabrics. I want to know where they get it, how to make it, and someday I would like to make some of my own unique fabrics. My mentor says it's something that may be possible in the future.

"But my main goal in my life is . . . well actually . . . I want to be a mom. I want to have children. I mentioned last week the only dreams I have had here are dreams about this life, but the other night I dreamt about children playing in a playground in a park. It appeared like a memory, but I know they would not have taken me if I had children back on Earth."

"Have you ever thought about having children, Warren?"

Warren's eyebrows raised. "I don't know, it isn't something I've thought about, but I bet we would have beautiful children." His mouth snapped shut and his palms grew sweaty. "Oh my, I can't believe those words came out of my mouth. The thought popped into my mind and didn't stop."

"It's okay, Warren," she said while laughing at him. "It's a beautiful thought, but maybe we should get to know each other first."

She laughed it off, but he sat there, embarrassed, not knowing what to say, so he offered a toast.

"Well, let's toast to a future filled with happiness for both of us no matter where our paths may lead."

"Cheers!" they said in unison.

They spent the rest of the dinner discussing other people they had met and their new world in general. They were both trying to stay away from getting too personal. After dinner was over, they went for a walk around the Life Center complex, and Laura suggested they take a walk outside, around the little lake.

"It's not a cold evening, and I believe it is a good night for stargazing. You have your jacket, and I have my shawl; if need be, you can keep me warm by holding my hand."

"I would be honored to escort you around the lake."

She led the way since he wasn't familiar with the spaces outside the buildings. The evening was beautiful and calm, with many bright stars showing in the clear sky. The moons were behind the planet, so the stars and distant galaxies shined alone. The only thing fighting the starlight came from lamps along the walkway meandering around the lake. They sat on a bench, looking at the stars, enjoying each other's company, until the cool air became a chill. When they continued their walk, they held hands, and Laura told him how much she was enjoying the evening.

They didn't talk much other than to point out a particular star or faint galaxy in the sky. Warren could feel her grip tightening on him as if she never wanted to let go. Warren was happy about not talking. He was strangely emotional as if this reminded him of something he no longer had in his life.

After the walk around the lake, they went inside, and he escorted Laura to her transport station.

"Thank you for a wonderful evening. I haven't felt so content since . . . I don't even know."

She thanked him once more for a beautiful evening, repeating herself and sounding foolish. As the station door opened, she didn't want to part but hesitated to say more. Before she could enter, he grabbed her and gave her a long, hard kiss.

"I hope that wasn't out of line; I—"

"No, Warren, it wasn't."

They parted awkwardly, and he experienced an ache in his heart as the door closed.

He slowly walked to his transport station for the trip home, so lost in thought about Laura, he almost bumped into a person walking the other way. As he said, excuse me, Warren was about to add the name, Barty. The thought made him laugh for no reason he could comprehend.

Oh great, another mysterious name maybe from my past.

He recalled it wasn't the first time that name or one like it had popped into his head. The Jonton might need to do a better job with their memory suppression. As he walked into the station, he looked back and saw the man standing there watching him. He thought it was strange but then forgot all about it as his mind filled with thoughts of Laura.

He spent the short ride home thinking of nothing but their time by the lake. Was she as drawn to him as he to her? It appeared so, and based on her talk about children, it seemed all but certain. He still sensed he had known her for a long time, and when he looked into her eyes, they were familiar.

I was late when he exited the shuttle. When he went upstairs, he stood by the window looking out into the valley, wondering what his life would become. Shortly after, he went immediately to bed, where he dreamt.

I want you more than ever before . . .

Laura, I missed you . . . Marry me . . .

Sam, I'm sorry . . .

Laura, I miss you . . .

I Think They Should Know

Sabastian arrived home from his last meeting of the day later than he had expected. There was a lot to discuss with the

Jonton, as there were twenty more awakenings planned for the next month, and he had to find Human mentors for all of them.

The Jonton mentors were never a problem as there were over one hundred of them in the vicinity, either at the spaceport, orbital station, or the moon base. The bodies they used as avatars were also plentiful, so they had more than enough resources.

Sabastian remained a little uneasy with the knowledge the Jonton had extracted DNA from those they had taken but later rejected. Lan had explained in addition to growing bodies for their needs; it also allowed extra Human genetic material to be available to the Human civilization if necessary.

As he opened his door, he found Chloe waiting for him with a large glass of wine in her hand and her favorite negligée wrapped around her slender body.

"The computer told me you were on your way home, and I figured you would need some wine and maybe some me. You have been so busy lately, Sabastian; I miss you when you're not here."

"Thank you, my love. You're always thinking of me and my needs."

They took their wine into the bedroom.

Later, Sabastian shared the discussions from the meetings with the Council and the Jonton. When he finished, Chloe filled him in on her day.

"I spoke to Laura today. She and Warren had a wonderful evening together last night. It sounded so romantic. I think she is falling in love. It will be nice if things work out for them. I think Laura could use someone special in her life. Like me, she's looking forward to having children someday."

Chloe took a much-needed sip of wine, knowing the next question could get a mind-your-own-business answer. After a brief pause, she continued. "So, when will you tell them?"

"Tell them what?"

Sabastian's heart quickened as he worried his wife had learned the truth. Did it matter? He didn't know, but he needed to talk to someone other than Lan.

"Don't be coy with me, Sabastian. When will you tell them you and the Jonton are playing matchmaker?

"Don't be blaming me. This is not my plan or process. Why should I tell Warren and Laura anything? Why can't we let nature take its course? We introduced them, and as the matching program predicted, they were attracted to each other when they met. Sometimes it's best to leave well enough alone. This is one of those times."

"I think they should know," Chloe said as she rubbed her hands along his body. "Even though they seem attracted to one another, it might give them the extra push they need. Or maybe they would want to make sure and see other people first. Hopefully, not."

Chloe was trying to manipulate him with her touch, and it worked. "Things aren't as simple as they appear, Sabastian said. "Things aren't as simple as they appear, Sabastian said. "There are circumstances you don't know about Laura, and I'm not sure her knowing too much would be good."

She stopped her ministrations and sat up in the bed. "Now, I am curious!"

"I shouldn't even be discussing this with you, but I need someone to talk to other than the Jonton." He paused as he wrestled with what he knew, his duty to keep it a secret, and his desire for someone else to share the burden. "You understand not everyone makes a smooth adjustment to his or her new life. Laura was one of the ones who had a problem. She and another person were part of the original group, first awakened with me."

"Sabastian, you make no sense. The Jonton woke Laura less than three years ago."

"That's correct. Laura started her new life at that time, but she wasn't always Laura."

"Have you been drinking something other than the wine? What the hell are you talking about, Sabastian?"

He hesitated, knowing he shouldn't say more, but he knew there was no going back now. "The first time didn't go well, and she had to repeat the process. The process went better the second time, but her mind couldn't handle the truth again, so they put her back to sleep."

"I didn't think they ever tried more than twice."

"That's true, Chloe; usually they don't, but this was a special case, so they decided to try something different. Before awakening her the third time, they went deeper into her mind and fully erased her memories. They erased her name and a small part of her original personality. It was something they had never tried before, but Lan considered it warranted."

He lay there a moment as Chloe waited for him to continue. After a loud sigh and mumbling something under his breath Chloe didn't catch; he got out of bed and grabbed a file from his closet. His hand was slightly shaking as he held the file.

"It might be better if I let you read it yourself," he said.

Chloe saw the name on the file as Sabastian held it in his and was taken aback.

"Why do you have Laura's file? You're not her mentor."

"It's a copy. Other than their matching, there's a reason; I need Laura's information."

He handed her the file, opened to the appropriate page. After a few minutes, she slowly put the file aside, letting what she read sink in.

LAURA

Dream a Little Dream

Don't hold back Warren, take me in your arms, you feel so good. I want you more than ever before . . .

I missed you so much, yes, I will marry you . . .

Laura woke from the strangest dream she ever remembered having and experienced a deep sense of loss as it faded away. She knew the dream was about being with Warren in multiple places she couldn't recognize. They ended up in bed, and though the visions faded, the memory of his touch had not. She knew they were compatible based on the report she had read, but she didn't think one date with him would cause such a reaction. She should have known it would, considering how things went the first time she saw him.

She wondered if she should confess to Chloe and Sabastian that she had discovered Warren's folder sitting on a table at their house several months ago and read it while they were busy in the kitchen. She had picked it up out of curiosity and was startled when she saw her name in the file. The Jonton had been playing matchmaker to help grow the new civilization, which made her a little angry initially, but the anger passed as she realized she had become lonely. It would be nice to meet someone new.

According to the file, Warren had been awakened that day and was beginning his adjustment. She regretted there was no picture in the folder. She made a mental note of his name and his house's location while she planned a way to see him.

His property was next to her friend Trish who worked with Chloe at the Research Station and spent days there instead of going back and forth. Laura knew Trish's frequent absences would give her time to spy on Warren without Trish suspecting anything. Trish had an ATV, and on the pretense, Laura was thinking about requesting one for herself; she asked Trish if she could take it out for a ride. Trish agreed and gave her access to the property and house to try it out whenever she wanted.

Laura visited for the first time a few days after Warren's awakening. She knew she might be pushing it since his Jonton mentor could be around, but she couldn't stop thinking about seeing him. She went to Trish's house early in the morning, pulled out the ATV, rode across Trish's property, and parked the vehicle a few cuselts from his home.

She hid in the woods behind the little barbecue area, hoping he would be outside. As she wondered where in the house he was, she felt someone near her, though no one approached. She became dizzy as an image of a man, a naked man, flashed in her mind. She had no idea who the man could be, but he seemed familiar.

She made herself comfortable in a small folding chair, and finally, her patience paid off when he came out on the patio to eat. She wished she had binoculars. She couldn't see enough of him to make her happy, so she slowly moved closer to the edge of the woods to get a better look.

Laura was shocked when he looked in her direction, stood, and came down the stairs from his patio. She scrambled farther into the woods, jumping into some large bushes and scaring away a few birds. She was too afraid to look up even though she needed desperately to see his face.

When she knew Warren was walking away, she looked but could only catch a glimpse of him. Laura was disappointed, and her heart was beating much faster than usual as she trudged back to the ATV. She sat in the vehicle, ate an early lunch, and drifted off to sleep.

It was late afternoon when she woke, and she knew the sun would soon be setting. She decided to try to see him one more time, even though she knew the idea was risky.

Laura walked back toward his house and stood in the woods. Today was her lucky day; she could see him through the window, and it looked like Warren was sitting. The patio blocked her view, and only the top of his head was visible. She had to get a better look. She didn't know if she had ever done this before, but she climbed a tree as high as possible.

Laura could see him playing a piano, but still couldn't see his face clearly, yet his image at the piano was familiar and comforting. Another wave of dizziness washed over her, and she clutched a nearby branch to keep from falling. When the dizziness passed, she looked at Warren again and saw him looking out the window in her direction. She remained perfectly still. When he walked away and didn't come outside, she started to breathe again. As she climbed down, she realized from what little she could see of him; he resembled the male image which had earlier flashed in her mind.

The next opportunity to try to see him came a few days later. Trish would be away for a few days and hadn't revoked Laura's access rights to her house.

Laura took the ATV and headed to Warren's house and was surprised to see Warren sitting on the patio having lunch with a man she believed she had never seen before, but even he appeared familiar. She didn't get too close because she prepared well with a pair of binoculars this time. She raised them to her eyes and gasped as she focused on Warren and confirmed he was the man whose image had flashed in her mind.

Without warning, Warren jumped up, ran to the patio's edge, and looked in her direction. She froze. She sighed her relief when he returned to his seat with his friend. She knew she had come too close to discovery and vowed never to do it again.

A few months later, Sabastian approached her about Warren, and she acted surprised. She told Sabastian she wasn't sure if she liked the idea of computer arranged dating but agreed to pass by Rembrandt's at the appointed time on Activite ten. She hoped he didn't detect the slight quiver in her voice.

She did more than pass by at the appointed time; she waited at the Life Center and followed Sabastian as he headed to meet Warren. She stood behind one of the trees and waited. When Warren came out of the shuttle door, she froze. Something familiar about him made her feel as if she looked at a long-lost . . . friend, or lover.

She became hooked as soon as she saw him up close and spoke with him. She hoped he couldn't see the nervousness she tried to hide, and as planned, she accepted the dinner invitation from Sabastian.

That night at the Panda, Laura knew she was falling in love. She could not explain or understand the instant attraction and wished she knew why he seemed so familiar and why she fell for him so quickly.

The Date

Laura had decided to take the first step and give him her communication number. When a few days passed, and he hadn't called, she began to worry. Eventually, Warren did call, sounding nervous and unsure of himself, something she found cute. When he asked her to meet him at Michelangelo's, one of the more romantic establishments, she agreed, ended the communication, and giggled like an excited schoolgirl.

Laura arrived outside the restaurant early so she could watch Warren. She didn't understand why he seemed so familiar or why the attraction was so strong. She saw him in her night dreams and daydreams when she relaxed and even when she worked on her clothing designs.

After a few moments of mutual embarrassment caused by their conversation, she steered the discussion to safer topics like his new life and what he desired to do with his future. When Warren mentioned his talent with the piano, she expressed her desire to learn.

While Warren talked, Laura drifted into an erotic fantasy of him leaning over her shoulder, guiding her hands across the keys. She became so lost in her thoughts; she hadn't heard him ask about her clothing designs, and when he asked if it was what she wanted to do, she had started talking about children. His response had startled her, but she desired to take him to the nearest dark corner and start practicing for the day the Jonton lifted the ban against children.

They stayed away from personal issues for the rest of the evening, but when he kissed her at her shuttle station, it stirred up the desire to be with him right then and there. As the shuttle carried her home, she drifted off to sleep and dreamt of having sex with a man who was and was not Warren. She awoke at her stop, disoriented. She desperately hoped for another date. She didn't have too long to wait.

TOUR ON SANCTUARY

A Day of Travel

Warren awoke, feeling exhilarated and refreshed. He had spent the previous day hiking through his property, followed by hours of intense exercise, for he wanted to look his best when he saw Laura again. The exhaustion also guaranteed him a good night's sleep. He didn't want to be anything but his best for his trip to the Research Station, and he didn't want the strange dreams to interfere.

Since his first date with Laura, Warren had dreamt practically every night of him and Laura having sex in places he had never seen before. Some of the dreams were with Laura, and in others, he was with someone who looked like her but wasn't Laura. He always awoke with the name, Samantha in his head, even though he knew no one by that name.

One night his dreams were so intense he awoke to find he had stained his underwear in his sleep, and he wondered if the experience was typical for him. Warren wasn't sure if he should mention it to Sabastian. He liked Sabastian as a friend and mentor but didn't want to have a discussion with him about his wet dreams. They were going to meet tonight for dinner and drinks at the station complex, and he believed Laura was going out with Chloe.

Tomorrow he and Laura would meet Chloe for a private tour of the facility and then have dinner together at the spaceport. He had heard of Un Goût De France, a great place to eat and watch the ships take off and land.

"Nag, what time is my flight to Port Nateria?"

"Your flight leaves this afternoon at 11:70, and your transport to the airport will be here at 10:00."

The time was now 7:15. Warren had slept later than intended, but he was packed and, on the patio, having breakfast by 9:00. The morning was crisp and beautiful, with the sun glistening off the patches of snow. Even though it was cold, the patio heaters kept him comfortable.

"Warren, did you remember it will be warmer at the station, and did you pack accordingly?"

"Yes, nag, I did."

He had packed a short-sleeved shirt, which fit him well and showed off the muscular body he had been working so hard to maintain. The more intense workouts were starting to pay off. He wanted to make sure he looked his best for Sa—Laura. His mind barely registered the slip.

With time to kill after breakfast, he sat at the computer, looking up more information about the animals on this continent and at the Research Station. He recognized some animals from Earth, but those at the Research Station were native to this planet. The Jonton preserved the area as close to pre-terraforming conditions as possible. A few new sections of the station were about to open, and they would be some of the first to have a pre-opening tour. Warren was looking forward to seeing these animals in their native habitat.

The trip to the airport was quick as he anticipated seeing the airplanes the new world utilized. He had memories of traveling, and he knew he had enjoyed it in his past until . . . something happened. An incident he couldn't remember, aside from a quick flash in his mind of a tall building burning. He expected it was another one of those things they didn't want anyone to remember from their past lives or something specific from his past?

He knew from his Learnings these jets were more like space planes. The jet flew to the farthest reaches of the atmosphere before heading down to the Sanctuary continent, where the spaceport and Research Station awaited. The entire trip would take little more than half an hour.

When he arrived at the airport, a Tranlay attendant named Partanra escorted him to the waiting area for his flight. A few other people also waited, and Warren was about to strike up a conversation with another man who looked familiar when they announced, time to board.

The flight crew escorted each person individually to his or her seats. Even the pilots escorted passengers, explaining the jet to them, and offering refreshments. Warren was sure this wasn't the normal procedure on Earth, but he couldn't remember details. The jet was spacious; two seats per row, a space between each, and an aisle down the middle of the row. A padded armrest and pockets on the side provided storage. The seats were large and comfortable, much like traveling first-class back on Earth. For some reason, that detail he could remember.

There were no windows in the jet, but each seat had a fold-up view screen the passengers could direct to any view out of the vehicle they chose. Like the ground transport, the displays could access any information available or also anything stored on computers at home.

Warren was surprised when the Tranlay attendant asked if he wanted anything to eat or drink for the flight.

"Partanra, is there a delay with our departure?"

"No, sir, we are preparing for takeoff."

"Sorry, I'm a little confused. I remember back on Earth when the plane was taking off or landing, everyone, including the attendants, had to be seated, and nothing could be out which could move around."

"The jets are built with gravity adjusters, which make it possible to control all random movement, including acceleration and deceleration. Everything in the jet will be calm and smooth the entire trip. We have taken off while we were talking."

"That's amazing. Not only didn't I feel the acceleration, but the plane also stayed level the entire time."

"Yes, it will be the same for the duration of the flight. Please relax, and we will arrive in thirty-five minutes."

"Thank you. I would like to have some water at the moment."

He had missed the takeoff, which was disappointing, but he switched on the viewscreen and selected a forward and down view. He saw the ground below and realized they were practically in space already. The attendant brought his water as he watched the world spin.

A short time passed as he was mesmerized by the view. When the screen indicated they were beginning their descent, he watched as the planet's surface grew more detailed and eventually showed the coastline of the Sanctuary continent. The landing was as smooth as the takeoff, and he enjoyed the view of the forest and mountains as they glided into the spaceport.

A few minutes after landing, he stood inside Port Nateria in amazement of all the new species of Galactic beings he could see about the area. There were a few Humans here, but most were travelers from the stars. He knew, in another life—his past life—this sight would have had him wondering if he had lost his mind. He didn't remember much of his former life, but he knew the Earth's inhabitants had no knowledge of other civilizations in the galaxy. Many said there had to be life out there among the stars, but most thought even if there were, it would not be intelligent or advanced enough to make contact. Little did they know it was Earth that wasn't advanced and, some might say, not intelligent.

Warren was roused from his thoughts when a short, bald member of a species he hadn't seen before asked him if he needed help finding his way. The being's robe covered most of its body, but Warren could see yellow scale-like skin covering the being's head and hands. There were no scales on the being's face, but its lips were thin and the eyes more oval than a Human's.

"Hello, yes, maybe. I'm looking for the transport station to the Excelsior Hotel."

The unknown being responded in a soft squeaky voice, "The transport station is around the corner behind the Old Earth Foods shop."

"Thank You!"

"Pleasant day!" the being said as it scurried away, while Warren wondered if it was male or female.

Warren was in a hurry to check in to the hotel, but he couldn't resist looking in the shop.

"Greetings, kind sir," said the clerk behind the counter. Warren assumed the being to be a male based on its looks and attire. He stood tall and skinny, with dark skin showing strange markings and tufts of hair. His hands had long fingers and ended with nails like an animal Warren couldn't place. His voice, which didn't match his looks, was deep pitched, intense, and for some reason, disturbing. He experienced a vague recollection of something in the back of his mind.

"Greetings to you," Warren responded. "I was on my way to the transport but wanted to see what you have available."

"We have many items from Earth's past. Some removed from Earth and preserved, but most are replications. Let me know if you have any questions."

Warren wandered around the store and came upon a few items he remembered from his former life. One was a box of Cracker Jack. He recalled it being one of his favorites, and it brought up a memory of a park, a ballpark. He had a memory of attending with someone he couldn't picture, yet he could recall enjoying his box of popcorn and peanuts. The memory made him sad, and he knew Lan would not be happy if he became aware. He browsed a few more shelves and stopped to examine ginger candy from a place called Japan, fruitcake, cheeses, and sausage-like meat called Kielbasa.

Warren moved on before he triggered any more unsettling memories and headed to the transport station. The transport took him directly to the lower-level entrance of the hotel, and an escalator carried him to the main lobby. He stopped for a moment to take in the view around him.

He didn't have much of a memory to go on, but this appeared modern. It was almost too antiseptic, too cold, and uninviting. Art and some objects and decorations he assumed were art adorned the walls. He observed what he would call sculptures and then noticed the different kinds of seating arrangements. He reminded himself, that he stood in a hotel for guests from all over the galaxy, filled with a much different variety of species. "The décor is probably appropriate for the clientele," he thought as he approached the front desk. A Tranlay named Brinally with purple hair and bulky jewelry greeted him. The hair surprised him since all the other Tranlay he had seen were bald.

"Good day and welcome, sir, to the Port Nateria Excelsior Hotel. How may I be of assistance?"

"Hello, Brother Brinally, and good day to you. My name is Warren Estridge. I'm here to check in if my room is ready."

"You honor me, Brother Warren. Your accommodation is ready; you are in room 724. The elevators are to the right. Would you like me to have your bag taken up for you?"

"No, thank you; it's small and not heavy."

"Very good, sir, please have a pleasant stay and be sure to contact the desk if there is anything you require."

After thanking Brinally, he headed to his room. It was spacious with a sitting room and a separate bedroom. The large window overlooked the spaceport, and he stood there a few moments watching a ship take off into the sky and quickly disappear.

"Hello, Warren, how was your trip?"

"Well, nag, as you know, everything was fine."

"Yes, i do know, but i am trying to be more polite."

The process of silently communicating had grown on him, so Warren didn't ask the CA to use the room system.

"You have a video message waiting from Chloe McCormick. Would you like me to play it for you?"

"Yes."

He looked over at the towall monitor and saw Chloe.

"Hello, Warren, I hope you had a pleasant trip. I'll meet you at the station reception desk at 7:00 in the morning. There are plenty of signs to guide you there, but your CA can assist you if you get lost.

"Sabastian asked me to apologize to you as he will not be able to meet you for dinner. He has a special meeting with the Jonton and the Council he is required to attend.

"Laura and I are having a girls' night, or I would have met with you this evening. I suggest you check out Maguire's Table for dinner. It's right outside the hotel; you may have seen it when you arrived. They have delicious food and Irish beer. The bartender told me the name of the beer is from the country of Earth, which had been Sabastian's homeland.

"If you need me before tomorrow, call. Have a good evening, and I look forward to showing you our wonderful creatures."

Maguire's Table

"Nag, show me the menu for Maguire's Table."

The menu appeared on the screen, and some items sounded interesting. They had Irish stew and mutton, as well as fish and chips. He knew what fish and chips were, but he didn't remember ever hearing the word mutton. He knew Irish was a nationality, Sabastian's ethnicity, but could not remember more about the name or the food. Reading the menu made him hungry, but it was too early for dinner, so he decided to research the spaceport.

"Nag, bring up everything you can show me on Port Nateria in categories with menus and submenus."

He reviewed general information about the facility when, on a whim, he asked the CA to play some music.

"Nag, play some Irish music."

He wasn't sure if there was such a thing, but he found it refreshing and familiar when the music began. After thirty minutes of reading about the spaceport, he became tired, laid down on the sofa, and drifted off to sleep while the music continued to play softly.

When he awoke, he vaguely remembered having another dream of being with someone who reminded him of Laura. They were in a small restaurant, standing at the bar drinking a dark liquid he now recognized was called beer and singing songs, which sounded like the music still playing.

The word "Ireland" popped into his mind, and he recalled Sabastian using the name the day they first met. Try as he might, he couldn't remember anything else about the country.

"Nag, tell me about Ireland."

"I can confirm Ireland was a country on Earth."

"I already know that. What else can you tell me? Anything about the people or the food?"

"I can tell you, Maguire's Table and the food they offer are from and centered around what was common in Ireland."

Warren's annoyance with the lack of information provided caused him to switch to loud verbal communication.

"Lan told me I would have access to more information about Earth, but you still aren't telling me anything important."

"Your access to information will be made available to you as you progress."

Warren knew better by now than to push for more. It was dinnertime, and he was hungry. He took a few minutes to plan his morning.

"Nag, wake me at 4:00 tomorrow morning. I want to work out and swim before heading to the station."

"I will reserve your locker space in the fitness facility."

Warren thanked the CA and headed to the restaurant.

When he walked into Maguire's Table, Warren sensed he had been there before. The restaurant décor and music reminded him of his earlier dream. He remembered they were called pubs—Irish pubs—and as the words "fish and chips" came to mind, his mouth started to water.

A Tranlay with a peculiar speaking voice greeted him and seated him near a window, which faced the spaceport. He knew the lilt in the voice was called an accent. It sounded right to

Warren, but before he could inquire about it, the Tranlay hurried away.

Warren perused the menu and found some more of the items to now be familiar. When the waiter came to take his order, he was surprised to find the waiter to be Human. The man spoke with the same accent as the Tranlay.

"Hello, and welcome to Maguire's. My name is Shane. I'm the head chef and owner of this restaurant. What can I get for you, sir?"

Warren ordered the traditional fish and chips with a glass of stout, and handed the menu back to Shane, asking, "How did you get your accent?"

Shane laughed. "Everyone asks me that same question. My mentor told me it's from my native country, called Ireland. I owned and ran an establishment like this in my past life on Earth, so they kept my accent for when I'm speaking Earth English and offered me this restaurant to manage."

"Why does the Tranlay sound the same?"

"Brother Bratran told me he liked the sound and decided to learn the language and copy the accent. It causes him to get some strange looks, but he doesn't mind. We both only speak English to our Human customers, but some customers tell me I have a strange accent when I speak Galactic."

Warren spent the time waiting for his dinner by watching ships taking off and landing. He wondered where they were going and how many different species were aboard.

Brother Bratran brought his pint, as he called it, and told Warren to enjoy. When he took a sip, Warren was pulled back into his dream as flashes of people laughing and hanging in front of a bar came to mind. He drank a larger sip of the stout and thought how great it would be to have at home. When his dinner arrived, the sight and smell were immediately familiar. He ate his dinner much too fast while having his second pint of stout.

The different species at the pub amused Warren, and he had a flash of a different style of pub or bar with other species and a band of musicians with big eyes. It had to be some distorted memory because he knew it could not have been on Earth.

Observation Research Station

"Warren, it is time to wake."

He blinked a few times, surprised by his surroundings before his head cleared. He had dreamt about a restaurant, which resembled the one he visited the night before—the same pub he had flashes of during the evening. It was a celebration with some people he didn't recognize except for one.

After his head cleared and he remembered where he awoke and what he had planned, he got ready to swim and work out. The facility was well equipped like the others he had used, but this one had separate locker areas and workout spaces for other species who might be staying at the hotel. A couple of Tranlay swam in the pool and another humanoid species, swam for long periods under the water.

Two hours later, excitement mounting, he was ready to go.

"Nag, how long will it take for me to get to the Research Station?"

"It is a half-hour transport ride to the Research Station and a five-minute walk to the transport."

"I need directions."

"I will provide directions to you as needed."

His CA directed him through the spaceport facility, telling him where to turn, and he arrived at the transport area three minutes before the vehicle glided into the station. He took advantage of the mental communication with his CA to silently ask it some questions about things he witnessed along the way.

The transport vehicle smoothly took him to the Research Station, station. A bit redundant, he thought, as the CA let him know he had arrived. From the transport station, he reached the security checkpoint five minutes early. The amount of security surprised him. There were two Human-looking guards, which he assumed were probably Jonton avatars.

I guess there could be people from here and possibly from other worlds who would want to take or hurt these animals.

Warren recalled back on Earth, that groups of people killed animals for no reason, and though details were not coming to him, he knew it was wrong.

A waiting area had been set up by a window looking out to the grounds where he could see some unfamiliar animals roaming in the tall grass. Chloe arrived a few minutes later.

<<<>>>

"Hello, Warren; it's great to see you again."

She had stood a second to watch Warren and collect her thoughts before approaching him at the window.

"It's good to see you," he responded as she walked up and gave him a little hug. "Thank you, Chloe, for taking the time to show me around the facility."

"Not a problem. I love to show off for visitors. The first thing we have to do is get you through security and get you a pass."

"I noticed the security. Is there any particular reason why it's necessary?"

"Not that I'm aware of, but Lan says they don't want anyone wandering in and getting himself or herself killed."

"Lan seems to be everywhere and involved in everything," Warren said.

"Well, he's not the most senior Jonton on the project, but he is pretty far up there."

Chloe led him to a screen on the wall and told him to look at the dot in the center. The screen scanned his eyes for identity verification and took a picture for his badge. A few minutes later, the badge was ready and she escorted him into the station.

"Laura arrived early—unusual for her. She is waiting in my office."

As Chloe mentioned Laura's name, she noticed Warren take a deep breath. If she had been monitoring his vitals, she would have noticed his heart rate jump and pulse race. When she directed him into her office, Laura jumped up to greet Warren with a huge smile on her face.

"Hello, Warren," she said. "I'm glad to see you again!"

"I'm sure he couldn't tell," Chloe mumbled under her breath while smiling, though inwardly concerned with the situation. Warren didn't hear the comment, but Laura did and gave Chloe a look of annoyance. Chloe was having trouble dealing with what she knew from reading Laura's folder and was afraid she would let it show. Her comment was a bit snide, but it was regrettably her way of coping with the stress.

Damn my curiosity and insistence they know the truth.

Warren greeted Laura as Chloe watched while trying to control her anxiety.

"It's good to see you too, Laura, and I'm looking forward to our date tonight," he said as he leaned in and kissed her cheek.

Chloe thought the kiss to be inappropriate, but Laura didn't appear to mind.

She began talking about the center, but she could tell Warren and Laura were not paying close attention, their minds apparently elsewhere.

"The Jonton created the facility to help Humanity study and care for the native species of this planet." Chloe began, not realizing her guests were not giving her their full attention. "All the animals and creatures, which live here, are descendants of those moved to the Sanctuary continent as part of terraforming. They chose this planet because Humanity could be adapted to live here without causing much harm to the native species.

"The Jonton and Trandel also recorded many observations and videos of life before the transformation began. They used hidden cameras and drone ships to record the smallest of details. The massive amount of information will be invaluable for future research and take many years to review and catalog. We have one wing of the facility dedicated to the daunting task, with plenty of space to grow as the Jonton bring more of us out of stasis.

I'm losing them, I can tell.

"And I'm rambling on. I'm sorry. I want this to be fun for you and not to be a lecture. I tend to get carried away."

Anything to keep my mind off what I know.

"That's okay, Chloe," Warren said. "It's been a long time since I received a lecture about something other than what I should do and how I should feel. I find this all fascinating, and I have always loved watching nature shows. I had hoped to one day go to Africa for safari."

After Warren made the statement, Chloe watched his eyes widen, and a peculiar look crossed his face as if he had remembered something he had forgotten.

Chloe stood there for a moment, unsure what to say at first.

"Warren, how do you know about Africa?" Chloe said to him, "I didn't think it would be an area of study available to you yet."

"I don't know. It popped into my mind. Lan and I discussed Africa on my first or maybe the second day at the house, and at the time, it was a word with no meaning. I'm not even completely sure what it means now, although earlier, I had a memory about . . . poachers, I believe, is the word."

Laura, apparently not wanting to be left out of the conversation, interrupted before Chloe could respond.

"I don't remember much about animals on Earth and don't know the word 'Africa.' I have limited access to information about Earth, it isn't something that interested me to research. What's important to me is the future."

Chloe noticed the look Laura gave Warren but let it go and continued the tour with a brief explanation about Africa.

"Africa was an area of land, a continent actually, back on Earth. The area had a large variety of wild animals and nature preserves, sort of like what we are doing here. Yes, people referred to as poachers did hunt the animals for sport or for items some thought had medicinal value. I know this because it's important knowledge for my work. Oh well, I guess it doesn't matter how or why you remember the term, Warren. Let's head out, and I'll show you some of our research labs."

As they walked, Chloe observed Warren reach out and hold Laura's hand. They had only been on one date but they did appear to be hitting it off.

As they should I guess considering the circumstances.

Chloe forced herself to stop staring, worried about being caught. "The building here houses all the administrative offices, most research labs, an animal hospital for smaller animals and a few holding pens for the more docile larger animals. Our first stop is one of the research labs. We do genetic testing of the native animals here. We hope to have a complete genome of all the animals within a couple of years."

"Didn't the Jonton do that when they were terraforming the planet?" Warren asked.

"They did some, but they were more concerned with creating a variety of habitats on the continent and moving the animals here. They also wanted to leave most of the research for us since Human beings need something to do, and we always want to learn and expand our knowledge. They knew this would be a crucial step in our adaptation. I only hope enough people will be interested in learning what they need to know."

"They seem to think of everything. Give the Humans something to do so they don't think about what we did to . . ." Warren's voice trailed off.

Chloe watched and noticed stiffness in Warren's stance and saw his hands clench at his side.

"I'm sorry. Sometimes I get angry about what I—we may have lost, even though they did it all to protect and save Humanity. I should be furious at the universe, not the Jonton. After all, if it weren't for the Jonton and the other spacefaring civilizations, we wouldn't be here now, hoping to rebuild a new civilization. The Human species would be extinct, and we would be dead."

Laura grabbed his hands. "It's okay, Warren. I have had those feelings myself at times. I think it's part of our normal progression. But enough depressing thoughts; this is meant to be fun."

"You're right, as usual."

Chloe's face showed a slight sign of panic, which she felt sure Warren noticed. Chloe turned away, but not before catching a perceived look of confusion on Warren's face as if he wasn't even sure why he included the extra two words.

"Let's head down a level, and I can show you the hospital!"

They proceeded to the elevator while engaging in small talk. Chloe asked Warren about his piano skills and his adjustment. She was trying to relieve some of the sexual tension between Warren and Laura while trying to keep herself calm.

I might be getting a kick out of the whole thing if this was any other couple instead of worrying about what I might let slip.

Warren's emotions were a mix of excitement, nervousness, and confusion. The tour looked exciting, and being with Laura had him nervous like a schoolboy. The confusion stemmed from his strange thoughts and words, plus the emotions he perceived from Chloe. One particular thing Warren noticed about Chloe was how nervous she appeared. He also noticed her avoiding looking directly at either one of them. He wasn't sure if it was his heightened senses or imagination. Certainly, she couldn't be nervous about giving the tour. Something else was going on, and he didn't like being left in the dark.

They emerged from the elevator and headed through a series of doors requiring badge access.

"We still have a lot of off-world construction workers around here and general support staff," Chloe said. "The other civilizations in this galaxy aren't perfect; before the Jonton claimed this world for our settlement, there were frequent poaching raids. Some off-world species that work here may find the temptation to make a few extra credits more than they can resist."

"Which explains all the security. How do they handle crime on the other worlds?" Warren asked.

"That would be a question for Sabastian or Lan. I try to concentrate on what's here. It's more than enough for me to handle, and thankfully, there hasn't been a reason to need any justice system. Knowing Human nature, I'm sure someday we will."

The final set of doors brought them into a large room with varying equipment stations, all of which could have been alien for all he knew. On the back wall, a set of cages of differing sizes housed a menagerie of animals, being fed and attended to by a pair of lab workers.

"This is where we treat illnesses and injuries of the smaller animals, Chloe continued. "Outside, which we will get to later, is where we take care of some of the larger but mostly harmless animals.

"Mostly harmless," Warren repeated to himself, laughing.

"What did you say, Warren?" Laura asked.

"I don't know exactly. The term 'mostly harmless' made me laugh, and I have no idea why."

Chloe didn't notice the conversation and walked over to the cages.

"These animals here are called harte, and they are similar to the rabbits brought here from Earth. This one's white fur is rare for the harte, although there are white rabbits here from Earth."

"Like Easter bunnies," Warren said.

"What are Easter bunnies?" Laura asked.

"I don't know; it popped into my mind. It happens to me a lot. Sometimes it makes me wonder, but as long as I'm not going bonkers, I guess I'm okay."

He noticed Chloe's eyes widen in surprise, giving him a strange look as he turned back to the harte. The animal was the size of the suitcase Warren brought with him for this trip and had primarily white hair with a thin strip of purple down its back. The slender ears stood straight with purple hair on the ends. Its nose was pink, and its whiskers were always moving.

Warren walked over to another row of cages to look at an animal with bright yellow and brown fur, large eyes, and whiskers. It was twice the size of the rabbit-like harte, and it made sounds comparable to singing. There were no words, but it most definitely had a pattern and voice-like quality, similar in structure to composed music.

He turned to look at Chloe, not surprised to find her watching him. "This animal here is beautiful, and the singing is unlike anything I think I have ever heard before from an animal. It's almost like music."

"Yes," she said. "I agree and love the sound. She is a sabasha, a sabasha cat, to be precise. The name was given to it by the Jonton. We added 'cat' because it looks so much like the wild feline animals of Earth, although no Earth creature ever had fur or hair as bright, except for a few bird species."

Warren was mesmerized by the sound and made a mental note to incorporate it into a new song. He wanted to see if he could write music as Lan suggested, but he had no inspiration to try until this moment. The sounds of the sabasha brought images to his mind of bright colors and wispy clouds moving across the sky.

"Would it be possible to get a recording of her singing?" Warren asked in a voice sounding like he was in a spell from the animals singing. "I believe it would be great to incorporate it into a song."

"Yes, we have recordings of her singing. I can have some samples sent to your computer." The Jonton teams recorded hours of sounds and singing from both sexes of the species at varying times of the day and seasons of the year.

"I'm looking forward to hearing more; thank you."

He looked over a few rows to a larger cage with a big-eyed, furry dog. At least that's what it looked like to him.

"Chloe, is this a dog over here?"

"A dog?" Chloe said. "I'm surprised you know the term."

"What's a dog?" interrupted Laura, feeling left out of the conversations. She wished she had some of Warren's odd flashes of memory.

"A pet," Warren replied. "I had a dog back . . . back, I don't know. I can almost picture it in my mind, but . . ." He raised his hands to his head and rubbed his fingers along his temples as his head began to throb. "Damn it, stop!" He said much louder than intended. "I'm so tired of the pain that comes with these damn flashes of memory."

The pain passed in seconds, and he apologized to Laura and his host for his outburst.

"You remember more than most people, Warren. The pain is probably a side effect of the memories resurfacing." Chloe became worried and silently asked her CA to note the incident in her logs. She had to inform Sabastian. "A dog was an Earth animal with many unique varieties. Some original breeds were descendants of a domesticated wolf, many species of which the Jonton did bring. Some people had dogs as pets."

"What's a pet?" asked Laura."

"Man's best friend," Warren blurted out, not knowing what the phrase meant but happy no pain followed the comment.

Chloe ignored the phrase she had never heard before and informed them, "We have no pets here at the moment. Sabastian could explain why. I think it's time to move on and head outside."

Chloe appeared agitated to Warren. Her stance had changed, and her speaking had become abrupt. She didn't even tell them about the dog-like animal. He feared his comments and memories were causing trouble, and he worried his outburst would get back to Sabastian or worse—Lan.

Chloe took them to another elevator, larger than the first, evidently used more for supplies and animals than for people. According to the display, they went down two levels before the doors opened to a large room filled with empty cages, boxes marked as food, a few trucks, and some four-person carts.

"We're only heading out to the larger animal pens the hospital uses to treat those too large to come inside. It's within walking distance, and it's a nice day today, so we won't need to use one of our transports."

"Are any of the animals we will see up close considered dangerous?" Laura asked.

"No," Chloe responded. "These are larger but mostly gentle. Some could hurt you by accident, so we always have to be careful, but we keep the dangerous creatures out at the remote stations, which we will go to after lunch."

As the ladies talked, Warren had an odd thought pop into his mind about protecting them like he protected Samantha—whomever she may have been—from a dog or maybe a wolf. The word 'wolf' was familiar when Chloe used it earlier. Samantha had to be someone he knew from his past. The thoughts and images had to be from memories he wasn't supposed to be recalling, and he decided not to say anything.

They walked outside and headed toward holding pens surrounded by an open-air, two-level observation area. A glass-enclosed walkway led from the main building out to the viewing area.

"Are there many animals naturally found around this area?" Warren asked.

"Oh, yes," Chloe said, sounding more like a happy tour provider. "The ecosystem is vibrant and active, filled with a considerable variety of animals and creatures, many of which are predators. If you're lucky, we may see a winged bashan overhead."

"What is a winged bashan?" Laura asked. "It doesn't sound like something I would want to encounter."

"A winged bashan is the male of the species. He looks for food to bring back for the family. One male will usually have at least two females and up to eight cubs ranging from newborn to two planetary years old. They are attracted to our holding pens as they think of our animals as food even though most animals we care for out here would be too large to carry away. They could, however, carry away a medium-sized person."

"What keeps them and the other wildlife away from the station and these holding pens?" asked Warren.

"A force shield surrounds the entire facility and encloses us like a dome. There is also one at the spaceport to keep the animals away from the ships. The ships can pass through, but the animals cannot. We use this same shield at a lower power level to keep the larger, more dangerous creatures in their specific areas out at the remote stations. It's a wonderful technology that would be hard to do without."

As Chloe finished, they arrived at the closest pen. Inside were two creatures, which looked identical, except one had two horns, and the other had a third protruding from the top of its head. The animals were about as large as one of the trucks in the building. They moved slowly because of their size, but they could probably outrun a person.

"These aren't dangerous?" Warren and Laura both said at the same time.

"No, they are exceptionally gentle, but as I mentioned earlier, they could hurt you by mistake. These two have developed what I would describe as a balance problem, which causes the animals to stumble and fall. You would not want to be under them."

Warren could imagine the scene, but he still had the urge to walk over and touch one, like when he was a child at the zoo with his—

"They are called aliganters," Chloe said, interrupting Warren's thought. "The male has the two horns. His name is George, and the female's name is Martha. I have no clue to the significance of the names, but Sabastian suggested them a few days ago. They have been with us for a week, and we think they have an inner-ear infection, the cause of which we can't detect. Humans can have the same type of affliction."

They spent the next hour walking around the pens, petting, and feeding some of the animals while Chloe provided details about each species. She also explained, when the facility opened for tours, visitors would be able to walk out to the open-air hub to see the animals and watch them receive treatment, although no one would be allowed as close as they had been.

After they finished at the pens, Chloe told them it was time for lunch. They went back upstairs to one of the conference rooms and found a spread of sandwiches and drinks waiting. While they ate, Chloe introduced them to the facility manager, her boss, Robert L. Johnson. He told them, according to his Jonton mentor, he had managed a large zoo back on Earth and was presumably the reason why the idea of operating this facility was so exciting for him. He wished he could go back and show his former self some of the fantastic wildlife on this planet.

A few of Chloe's associates and her intern joined them for lunch. Many of the discussions were about the animals and policies concerning the facility. The intern hoped they could expand the facility as the population grew to allow everyone an opportunity to see the amazing animals.

"I apologize for all the shop talk," Chloe said, "but this is sometimes the only opportunity afforded us to connect and discuss issues that may have cropped up during the morning. We have all been overwhelmed, rushing around to get everything perfect for visitors."

"No need to apologize," Laura said. "I'm enjoying listening to the conversation."

"I too, am enjoying the conversation and the company," Warren replied. "It wasn't long ago; I only had myself and my CA to talk to."

Warren was about to say something else when Laura spoke and the first thing that popped into his mind was, "here she goes again."

"Were your backgrounds also in a field that makes you suitable for this line of work?"

Chloe's intern, Bonny, was the first to speak.

"Yes, I was two years out of college and halfway through my first year of veterinary school when I was . . . ahh . . . taken. Sorry for my hesitation; the word, 'taken' feels so wrong to me."

"I feel the same about that word as well," Warren said. "Sometimes, I feel myself getting angry about it even though I would be dead now if the Jonton didn't remove me from the Earth. Lan, my mentor, says it's normal, but what bothers me more is what they did before they chose us for this planet. Lan didn't elaborate, but he said we were taken, tested, and had our memory wiped on multiple occasions before we were selected."

"I don't feel angry," Bonny replied. "It bothers me like there is a horrifying meaning behind the word. Perhaps it's something from my past buried deep in my mind. I'll get over it."

The conversation fell as one by one the other staff had to get back to work until it was the three of them making small talk as they finished.

"So, what are your plans for this evening?" Chloe asked.

"I'm taking, or should I say 'escorting' Laura to Un Goût De France for dinner."

"I hear it's a wonderful place," Laura said, slightly envious. "I haven't yet been able to get there since I'm always so busy when I'm here at the station. Maybe I need to push Sabastian to take me next week, and we can spend the evening at the hotel. It's hard to get him to stop working, as you know since he ditched you last night."

"All work and no play makes Sabastian a boring boy," Warren said. "Sorry, I did it again. I don't know where that came from or what it means. It's familiar to me, yet at the same time, it feels wrong, like I'm misquoting a line from a book or a movie. Odd thoughts have been popping into my head all morning. Too bad you aren't a mental doctor. I may need one," he said, laughing.

"I know there are two Human psychologists with us, but the Jonton doctors treat most medical and emotional needs. At some point, I guess that will have to change. But that's a problem for another day. Let's freshen up, and then we'll head to the transport, and I'll take you to see one of the local and remote viewing stations."

Local Viewing Station I

As they waited at the station for the transport to arrive, Warren could tell by the size of the tube opening the vehicle would be more extensive than what he took between his home and the Life Center. When the transport car arrived, Warren's eyes grew wide with surprise.

"Wow," he said. "This is bigger than I thought it'd be."

"Yes," Chloe said. "This transport line is reserved for the tours we'll be taking out to the viewing stations. We also use them when staff needs to go to a station. We have a parallel transport line twice the size of this for construction, maintenance workers, and supplies."

The vehicle contained multicolored rows of soft cushioned seats, five to a side with a center aisle. They sat and were quickly on their way. Warren reached next to him to hold Laura's hand, and she didn't seem to mind. The computer started a lecture about the facility and the types of animals they would see.

"Computer, end lecture and stop at viewing area one," Chloe said. "We're going to stop first at the Local Viewing Station." She turned to them and added, "It's similar to the viewing area at the Research Station, but it gives a better look at the animals in the wild. We arranged the vegetation to attract a larger variety of animals to the site to make a better experience for our visitors."

"The shuttle will arrive at Local Viewing Station One in five minutes."

"We still need to program the announcements not to interrupt our tour guides. As I was about to say, we plan to have two local stations, but right now, we only have this one under construction."

They arrived at their first stop a few minutes later, and Chloe led them into a stunning lobby area covered floor to ceiling with murals. Hanging from the ceiling were multicolored pieces of glass that appeared to simulate a sky at sunset.

"This is beautiful and amazing," Laura said as she looked around.

"These walls were painted off-site by the Pentary, a species of prodigious artists whose homeworld is furthest out in the galaxy from this one. The Jonton commissioned them to provide all the art at our various sites. Eventually, they'll create artistic versions of the animals from Earth not able to be brought here. Those paintings will be part of the Earth Museum the Council will build in the future."

"So, we'll be able to one day learn our total history from Earth?" asked Warren.

"Sabastian said when we're ready, we'll have access to everything the races know and have of Earth, but I don't think any of us will still be around when it happens. The Jonton are worried about causing emotional issues with the rescued population. Sabastian says it will be the good, the bad, and the ugly from our past, so hopefully, we won't make the same mistakes."

"Yes," Warren said. "Both Sabastian and Lan had mentioned the same to me."

"Something for our children then," Laura said.

Chloe was sure Laura directed the comment at Warren, but he didn't seem to notice. He appeared lost in thought as he looked at the images on the walls, and she decided not to disturb him.

The lobby area appeared designed for a lounge section with a place for food and other refreshments. They proceeded across the lobby and through doors to the level one viewing area, an ample round space lined all the way around with glass showing the outside. Chloe said the glass elevator in the center of the room went to the second-floor viewing area.

"As you can see, we have a variety of vegetation outside, around the structure. On this side over here is the heavy, lush vegetation where some of the smaller animals will visit. On the far side is the drier area. We have altered the land to make pathways from here to where the natural landscape would be. The setup isn't difficult to achieve since the distance from one type of ecosystem to the start of the other is only a few hundred cusants. We chose this spot because of how close together they are naturally."

Warren walked to the darkest section of vegetation and saw a few multilegged creatures eating and sleeping on the moss-covered ground. Lined on a few tree branches, he saw other bushy-haired animals with tails that they used to swing back and forth. He saw a few animals he recognized from the hospital in addition to larger ones deep in the large tree leaves he had not seen before. He saw other animals with short hair, playing and jumping in the trees, which reminded him of monkeys, but he didn't say anything since he wasn't sure if he should remember monkeys.

The trees held a variety of birds with colors the likes he had never seen while walking through his land. Warren's mind focused on comparing them to animals on Earth and was interrupted when Chloe called him over to another section. He sighed; the interruption angered him for no apparent reason.

Warren and Laura recognized a group of ten aliganters, like those in the hospital. Some lumbered around, eating bright yellow leaves from the bushes, while others were sitting or lying down. Chloe explained they liked to lie in the sun and socialize when not eating, which is their favorite past-time. She elaborated they would at times run around together as if playing a game of tag. They also made sounds when they were together in groups utterly different from the sounds they made when it was only a single pair.

"We have named a group of aliganters a squad. It seems like a silly thing to some, but we have a lot of work to do in the future cataloging and naming the wildlife on this planet.

Someday it will all be ours, which is why the Jonton have left this task to us.

"I hope future generations will be able to respect the land and the animals and learn from past mistakes made on Earth. As I said, we won't be here to see it, but in the future, Earth's entire history will be available, and the future inhabitants of this planet will know how badly we abused some of the land and animals of our former home. As our civilization grows, we cannot entirely push out the native plant and animal populations.

"Okay, enough preaching from me," Chloe said while taking a deep breath. "I can leave it for my formal dissertation and the book I'll write when I retire. Let's head to the observation dome."

The top level opened to the outside, with only a glass and metal barrier along the edge. Etched into the metal at various spots were pictures of animals. Chloe explained the drawings indicated the animals you might see in that direction. Warren could feel the breeze blowing across the observation deck when they emerged from the elevator.

The sun warmed Laura as she remarked on the smell of the flowers and trees wafting from the densely vegetated side of the viewing area. The scent reminded her of roses, like the kind . . . he used to buy her.

"You said this was the second floor and called it the dome, but this is more like a roof," Warren said as he glanced around in all directions as if he were looking for something.

"Yes, Warren, very observant. This facility has three floors. We entered the lobby level, and the true second level is an employee-only control and maintenance area. This level is—"

Chloe was interrupted by a loud screech followed by the breeze and shadow of a swooping, large, winged bashan.

"Holy shit!" exclaimed Laura as she ran to the elevator with her hands covering her hair.

Warren stood with his mouth wide open in amazement. A moment before the beast had flown overhead, Warren had a feeling of immense danger, which he had tried to control. Now, however, as the bashan was turning to make another pass, Warren was calm, relaxed, and in control of his emotions as if he could somehow sense they were not in danger.

Chloe continued to stand where she had been with a little smile on her face. She raised her hand, and the bashan hovered a few cux over her head as if it were getting ready to pounce. The wind from its wings blew Chloe's hair behind her. She lowered her hand, and the bashan appeared to be supernatural as he folded his wings and sat above her as if being held in place by magic.

"A force shield," Warren said.

"Yes, as I was about to say before being so rudely interrupted by our friend here, the dome I referred to is a force shield dome. It allows in the smells, the breeze, and even the rain if we want, but the animals cannot pass through. As you can see, or not, the shield dome is only a few cux above our head and sits right at the edge of the platform."

"It certainly gives an interesting view of the animals in all their glory," Laura said as she returned. "And I bet, Chloe, you knew this would happen."

"I was certainly hoping. The winged bashan can be an extremely dangerous animal, but they also like to play. This routine has become a bit of a game between the two of us. I often feel like he's trying to communicate with me, and when I look into the bashan's eyes, I feel like he's studying me as much as I'm studying him."

"They are amazing looking creatures, and I'm glad he's on the other side of the shield," Warren said as he too stared into the creature's eyes and detected something different than fear. It was as if he could sense the creature's thoughts, and the bashan wasn't happy they were there on his land. The experience was new for Warren, and he was sure it wasn't intentional on the Jonton's part.

"Were there any animals like this back on Earth?" Laura asked.

"No, there were no large flying animals on Earth. The largest flying animals would have been vultures and condors. The

Jonton established colonies of each on our home continent, in the mountains away from the continuing development. I believe there are six or seven different varieties represented."

The winged bashan grew tired of watching the Humans and flew away, to quickly come back and dive bomb the dome once more before he disappeared into the distance. As they watched him go, they heard a new noise behind them. When they turned, they saw the face of what Warren thought must be an exceptionally tall creature.

"Chloe waved her hands to attract the creature's attention. "Ah, yes, perfect timing, my friend. This beautiful lady is called a zarafa, an Earth Arabic word for giraffe. The zarafas are comparable to giraffes from Earth in the sense of their tallness and long neck. You can tell it's female by the small spikes which go down the back of its neck. Unlike the giraffes of Earth, which had no spikes, this creature has mono-colored long hair over its entire body. The giraffes from Earth have short-cropped fur and were spotted. The zarafas are amiable animals, about thirty percent taller than an Earth giraffe. Like an Earth giraffe, they eat only leaves and other vegetation."

"Do we have giraffes from Earth here?" Warren asked.

"Yes, we do. A large island preserve exists farther south, which has a climate similar to the region of Earth where they lived, the area you referred to earlier as Africa. The giraffes and many other animals from that region of Earth are there, including lions, tigers and—"

"Bears, oh my," Warren suddenly interrupted. "Again, I'm sorry, I don't know why things keep popping into my mind," he said as Chloe laughed.

"Why are you laughing?" Laura asked.

"Because Sabastian has said the same thing to me many times. He told me it's from an old Earth movie."

"Which I perhaps shouldn't remember," Warren replied. "I can confirm I have no clue what movie it would be from, but I probably somehow know it from my past. Anyway, changing the subject back to the animals, I didn't see the island on any maps, and it wasn't part of my Learnings."

"The Jonton wanted it to be a secret for now. The plan is not to disturb them and let them flourish in a way they could not have done on Earth for thousands of years. There are a few islands around the world with other different types of climates suitable to be nature preserves for other variety of animals."

Laura interrupted their conversation to ask about another group of animals she could see in the distance.

"They are a pack of lycansops. They are like wolves from Earth in the way they live and hunt. They are larger than the average Human, and they are carnivores, but they seem not to want to come near us. Their favorite foods are the harte and sabasha, which are plentiful on their hunting grounds.

"Well, we could stay here all day and see many more types of animals, but we do have a schedule to keep. We should get back on the shuttle and head out to a remote viewing station, where the massive and dangerous guys are waiting to eat, oh, I mean meet you."

"Are you trying to scare us?" asked Laura.

"Yes, it's fun!"

Remote Viewing Station II

A few minutes later, they were back on the transport heading out to one of the remote viewing stations.

"We'll arrive at station two in about ten minutes. I'm going to give my voice a rest and let the computer give the lecture. Computer, give lecture two."

"Welcome to the Remote Viewing Station Two tour. There are five viewing stations in all, scattered across the continent. As you can see on this map, stations one through three are along this north line, and for future access, you can use this transport line. Stations four and five are along the south line, which you can use to visit those locations. The stations exist to allow you to view some of the large wild animals and creatures, which inhabited this planet before the relocation of Humanity and its species from Earth.

These creatures have been relocated from all across this world and settled on this continent. This relocation preserves the natural habitat and animals of this world while protecting the new Human citizens and their visitors from other planets. The viewing stations are protected by force shields, which allow the creatures to come within culs of the station for a spectacular viewing experience. All the stations provide amenities to make your visit more enjoyable, including a snack bar, lounge, restaurant, and gift shop. The viewing stations are part of the research network, allowing scientists to monitor the animals and learn how they live and interact with each other.
"You will arrive at the station in five minutes. Please enjoy the rest of the ride and enjoy your visit."

"So, what do you think of the lecture?" Chloe asked her guests.

"I liked it," Laura said.

Chloe looked over to Warren, who appeared lost again in his thoughts.

"Warren, you're quiet; what did you think of our lecture?"

Warren snapped out of his daze. "I'm sorry, Chloe, I was thinking about what the computer said about relocation. Yes, the Jonton and other species did a great thing by saving us, but was it their right to do so at the expense of this world? Was it their right to take over this world and remake it for us? Was it right for them to move these animals and creatures away from their lands and homes?"

After a brief pause, he continued. "We owe these original inhabitants a debt of more than gratitude. Hopefully, our descendants will always respect and protect their environment and their lands for them and their descendants."

Warren's hands were wet, his heart racing as the anger rose again, and he worked to control the reaction. He didn't mention the feelings he'd experienced from the bashan. He didn't think it would be wise to let anyone know about the apparent ability. He didn't want Lan to have him put back to sleep. Not after everything he had done and learned.

"You make it sound like they are an intelligent civilization," Chloe said, with her irritation evident. "They are creatures and animals no different from the animals of Earth. They deserve our respect and protection, but I can assure you these creatures are not missing their homes. There would only be a few creatures alive not born onto the lands in which they live."

Chloe was about to continue when Laura interrupted to change the subject as she sensed a tension growing between Chloe and Warren.

"Are there any plans to add more stations?" She asked, flashing an awkward smile.

"Oh, yes," Chloe said. "Eventually, there will be three more—one to the west and two to the east. One of the eastern stations might be built in the ocean, partially submerged.

"One thing not in the lecture is we also have small research centers, well disguised and hidden. They can hold up to six scientists at a time for extended stays. Hopefully, they'll monitor and study the creatures without the subjects being aware of the scientist's presence. The remote stations also act as supply and maintenance hubs for those centers."

"The transport will arrive in one minute. Please be sure to take all your belongings."

A similar layout as the Local Viewing Station greeted them. The Pentary artwork covering the walls differed from the last station by the size of the creatures depicted and the inclusion of what Warren and Laura thought were dinosaurs from Earth.

Chloe glanced at her guest's puzzled expressions and smirked. "Yes, those are Earth dinosaurs painted on the wall. The Jonton figured it would be okay if we remembered the dinosaurs from Earth since they were long extinct and should not cause any problems with our adaptation. As you can tell from the artwork, many of the creatures here are equally as large. Hopefully, we will get to see some since we have the attractors functional."

"Attractors?" Warren asked.

"This station is for the grander, more dangerous creatures and covers a larger area than the others. To ensure all the tours experience some creatures, we developed three different sounds to attract them. We divided the outer stations into sections, but here each is force shield protected, so we don't have clashes between them when they are close. Farther out, the fields go away to allow nature to take its course, but they mostly stay within their traditional habitats."

Chloe pointed out a display wall that showed a map of the building and detailed information about the surrounding terrain.

"Unlike the local station, the remote stations have windows in the lounge and snack bar areas. The second level will be a full-service restaurant and bar, looking out over the plains with the snowcapped mountains in the distance. All the offices, maintenance, and storage areas of these facilities are on multiple basement levels.

"Let's take the elevator to the third floor, or roof, as Warren is sure to point out," Chloe said, laughing. "The upper level is force shield protected like at the local stations. The creatures can come right up to the building, which will scare the hell out of our future children."

Warren walked out of the elevator, smack into a cold wind, which bit into his skin, causing him to shiver.

"Is it always this cold here?"

"This is about as cold as it ever gets," Chloe answered. "In fact, this is an unusually cold spell for this area. The dome will be heated as necessary when we are open. They should have blocked the wind using the shielding."

"Guys, come quick!" Laura gestured out to a group of animals in the distance.

Laura pointed directly out across from the elevator to a group of creatures in various shades of brown and green larger than anything she had ever seen before. They walked on their hind legs, grabbed leaves, and branches off the trees, and held them in claws or hands while they ate the leaves.

Warren thought they looked like little zilla's, but he had no idea what the name meant. He looked farther to the side and saw two other creatures fighting over what looked like a smaller dragon-type creature they both sought for a meal.

"There's some action going on over here, ladies: take a look!"

"Oh no, they're going to hurt each other."

"Really, Laura," Chloe responded. "that's what we call nature, and if you were out there, it would be you, they were tearing apart. The larger one is a trantson, and the smaller a pramtener. The two coexist in the same habitat, and although they don't hunt each other or usually fight, they can tear one another apart when there's food involved. There's adequate food, but they're like little children fighting over a toy box in a room filled with toys.

"The creature they're fighting over is a wingbant. The wingbants are similar to large birds but with snake-like scales, sort of what a flying dragon would look like if there ever were such a thing. They don't breathe fire, but they do shoot nasty venom, which would kill one of us in seconds. Thankfully, they can only fly short distances, so they don't cause any problems for the other habitats. The trantson probably broke its neck, so it was dead before this fight ever started. Looks like the pramtener won; show over."

"Finally, a term I remember," Laura said. I do know they weren't real, sort of."

"There were small animals, some people called dragons, but they were not the ones from the legends and books you might remember. Sabastian told me all about fire-breathing dragons which could fly, and he wished there were some here."

The hair on Warren's neck stood straight, and his heart rate accelerated as he sensed danger.

Laura could feel heat behind her, so she turned around to view an open mouth crammed with razor-sharp teeth and pieces of what looked like raw meat hanging from the huge opening. She let out the loudest scream of her life; ran to Warren, and threw her arms around him. As Laura squeezed him, many thoughts ran through Warren's mind, including how familiar it felt to have Laura holding him tight. He enjoyed the situation immensely, even if it was their end.

Then the smell hit him, a stench like death itself—a cross between spoiled meat and sewage.

"What is that God-awful smell?" he commented.

"The odor is the trextasons' breath. When we set the shields to allow in weather, we get the unwanted benefit of this guy's breath. We are about as close to this beast as you could ever get and still live to talk about it. We call them trextasons because they look and act a lot like a T-Rex would have when they existed back on Earth. This guy is a killing machine."

As if to prove the point, it lunged at Warren and Laura but bumped right into the force shield. It tried again and then let out a tremendous roar realizing he couldn't reach his prey. Laura held Warren even tighter. The trextasons turned and headed for the pramtener focused on eating his lunch—not realizing he was about to be lunch.

Warren's proximity to Laura excited him as he sniffed her hair and held her close. He worried Laura or Chloe would notice, so he tried to think of something else to calm his libido. It wasn't easy, but all he had to do was think about the hunger and anger he sensed from the trextason.

"I think . . . I have had enough, of this tour," Laura said after reluctantly lifting her head off Warren's chest.

"Well, hopefully, I have given you your money's worth," Chloe beamed. "I'm looking forward to seeing the reaction of people who come on the tour. I guess I've had my fun for the day, and we can head back."

Warren walked over to Chloe to thank her for the tour and was sure he owed her an apology. "I'm sorry, Chloe, if I got a little out of line earlier when we talked about the relocation of the animals. Sometimes I get this odd anger at what the Jonton and others did to us, this planet, and its life forms, for our benefit. I don't understand, but I feel we are not worthy. I certainly didn't intend to offend you in any way."

She waved her hand. "Please, don't worry about it. I took no offense, and I understand what it can be like to wake up with missing memories and be thrust into a world you don't know."

Warren noticed Chloe glance at Laura as she spoke. He sensed their host holding back some critical bit of information.

As they stepped into the elevator and started down, Warren thought about a park where dinosaurs roamed free, like the one they toured. The name was on the tip of his tongue, but the more he thought about it, the more his head hurt. When he realized it would have been impossible for there to have existed any real dinosaurs on what was present-day Earth, he started to feel better.

A Second Date

They left the Research Station and shuttled together back to the hotel. They spent the ride talking about Chloe and Sabastian. Laura told Warren she thought her friends were a perfect couple, and she hoped she would find someone as charming as Sabastian.

Before Warren could respond, they arrived at the Spaceport Station. He walked her to the hotel making idle conversation about the spaceport and the ships he had seen taking off and landing. Laura stayed a few floors above Warren's room, so they agreed he would pick her up in two hours. He walked her to the elevator but didn't get in. He told her he had to speak to the front desk.

Warren was relieved when the doors closed, and his heartbeat returned to normal. He had started to panic when Laura talked about finding someone like Sabastian. He didn't know what to say and was glad when they arrived at the station. He didn't need to speak to the front desk; he only didn't want to be in the elevator where the topic might come up again. This way, he had time to prepare.

As Warren thought about all the odd things he said and thought during the tour, he became convinced there was something wrong with him or not right about the process of his awakening. He still expected Lan and Sabastian were hiding something, but he wasn't sure what. He worried about what would happen if he confided in either of them. Would his awakening be considered a failure, or would he have a breakdown at some point? The more he thought about it, the more he realized he couldn't say anything. He needed to put it out of his mind and enjoy his new life.

As exciting as the day had been already, Warren was more excited about the evening. After a shower, he lay on the bed and thought about Laura and what he would like to talk about during their date. The last thing he desired was an evening filled with awkward silence.

"Warren, you should get dressed now if you are to meet Laura in a few minutes."

"Yes, nag, I was about to get up."

A few minutes later, Warren stood in front of the door to Laura's room. He was frozen so long he had counted all the imperfections in the beige oak door several times. He thought about how his body reacted when she ran to him earlier, fearful of the dinosaur-like creature. He didn't understand why he remained so nervous, but Warren sensed he had to prove or explain something to her, something he knew would make them both happy. He laughed at his nerves and forced himself to knock on the door as he pushed the thoughts out of his head.

Laura was quick to open the door and invite him in.

"You look beautiful, Laura."

He wanted to grab her and hold her tight like earlier at the research station.

"Thank you, I need a moment to pick some earrings, and I will be ready."

Laura walked into the bedroom area, and Warren sat on the sofa to wait.

"No problem, I'm a few minutes early. So, what did you think about the tour today?" he said, not wanting the room to be filled with silence, though they had discussed it on the way back.

"I thoroughly enjoyed it even though I was scared half to death at the end. It made me think about what more I want to do with my life other than design clothes. I like the clothing, but working with the animals is more exciting. I wonder how long it would take for me to learn enough."

"I don't know for sure, but I feel the Jonton probably have a way of speeding up the process."

"That's a good point. I'll need to ask. Okay, I'm ready."

They walked out of her room and headed to the elevator. He pushed the button, and thankfully the elevator came quickly. As they stepped in, he was surprised and delighted when she grabbed his hand.

The restaurant was called Un Goût De France, which Warren told Laura meant "A Taste of France." The restaurant's decorations brought a warmth to the space with wall-mounted candelabras lit with real candles, and on the tables were a variety of smaller golden candelabras. The candlelight shimmered off the light blue satin tablecloths, and the smell of butter and fresh-baked bread greeted the couple. Warren considered the color of the tablecloths to be a good sign.

According to the Human maître d', Marcel, the paintings hanging on the walls were copies of paintings created by French artists back on Earth more than a century before the events which led to their relocation. He had a strange accent Warren wanted to ask about, but he hurried away to greet other guests after he sat them at the table.

A Tranlay waiter brought them water and a bottle of French wine preserved and brought from Earth by the Jonton. He enlightened them that the chef had been a world-famous resident of the country called France on Earth. When Warren asked the waiter about Marcel's accent, the waiter explained Brother Marcel was also from France.

Warren and Laura spent the next few minutes looking over the menu and discussing the options. They both ordered the fish bisque, a fresh salad with vinaigrette, and the bouillabaisse with a side of braised venison, French style.

"It's nice to know we have similar tastes in food," Laura said as the waiter left.

Warren picked up his wine glass and offered a toast. "To new beginnings!"

"To new beginnings and new relationships!" Laura responded. "You are looking dapper this evening, Warren. I like the suit, and it fits you exceptionally well.

"It's something I found in my closet, literally. It freaks me out to have a closet full of clothes I never bought. I'm not sure what disturbs me more, the fact they fit so well or that they are clothes I would have picked and bought myself." Warren paused and looked over his shoulder. "Sometimes, I think they know too much about us.

"As I have said before, they have done a great thing, but it doesn't feel right. I still feel violated, controlled, and . . . and this is not the type of conversation I wished us to have this evening."

"It's okay to have mixed emotions about everything that happened. I wasn't comfortable at first either, but both my Jonton and Human mentors helped me adjust, and they both told me always to say what I feel."

"Well, I do, a lot actually, probably too much. Thank you for being understanding." Warren paused to take a sip of wine. "Moving on. The last time we were together, you talked about doing something in the future with fabrics, but today you spoke about working with animals. Are you as confused about your future as I am about mine?"

"I don't know, Warren. I like working with fabric and designing clothes, so I thought being more involved with making fabric would be interesting, but is it interesting enough? When I saw the animals, I wanted to know more, and I desired to be involved. It's more than interesting, it's a passion, or it feels like a passion. The thought of working with the animals excites me more than the thought of working with fabric."

"I understand. It's how I feel about music. I desire to get all this learning and adapting finished so I can have more time at the piano or time to research the music the Jonton saved in the database. I need more in my life, and I need someone—"

Warren stopped; he realized he was getting ahead of himself and was about to apologize when the waiter arrived with their soup. They spent the rest of the meal talking about the tour and Laura's desire to work with animals. After dinner, they both decided against dessert, but Warren ordered coffee while Laura opted for tea.

"What a wonderful dinner," Warren said. "I don't remember if I ever had French food before or what it should taste like, but that was delicious. This place is beautiful, and I'm glad I could share it with someone equally as beautiful, if not more so."

"Thank you, Warren. Is my face red?"

"Maybe a little."

They finished their drinks and thanked Marcel for a wonderful meal before leaving the restaurant. They spent a few minutes looking out at the spaceport, watching ships head out into space. Warren held Laura's hand as they sat, and he wondered what was next. He knew he wanted her but wasn't sure if she had the same feelings for him. After spending some time walking hand-in-hand, gazing at the stars, they went back to the hotel, and he walked her to her room.

"Warren, I had a wonderful evening. Would you like to—"

Before she could finish her invitation, Warren took her in his arms and began to kiss her, leaning her against her door, both growing excited. But Warren was having visions in his mind of being with . . . with Samantha. The more he kissed Laura, the more he thought about this mysterious woman, and the more his brain was trying to force its way out of his eyes. He tried to ignore the pain, but he couldn't, and he had to pull away as the pain in his head became unbearable.

"Laura, I would love to come in, but . . . I'm not feeling well. My head . . . feels like it's ready to explode. I think I need to go back to my room. I'm so, so sorry!"

Laura stood there and watched him leave, not knowing what to say. The two of them together were so right and familiar; they belonged together. If she were not also feeling pain in her head, she would have grabbed him and dragged him into her bed.

Later in the evening, they both had dreams of making love. Warren dreamt about Samantha, a woman he didn't know who filled his mind pushing out thoughts of Laura.

Laura dreamt only of Warren. To Laura, Warren was a stranger as well as a familiar lover. A man who reminded her of something her conscious would not allow to emerge.

CONVERSATIONS

Chloe and Sabastian

It was early evening when Sabastian contacted Chloe.

"Hi, babe, how are you? I miss you and wish you were here with me. I'm surprised you're still at the office. How was the tour today?"

"Oh, Sabastian, it's wonderful to hear your voice. I had a long day, as I'm sure you can imagine. After Warren and Laura left, I got word one of our aliganters died. He had been sick for some time, so it's probably a good thing; he can now rest in peace, but you know I hate to lose any of these wonderful creatures."

"You know, Chloe, it's your passion and love for these animals which make you so good at your job."

"Thank you. How was your Council meeting today?"

"It went well. The Council is receptive to sending teams back to Earth to retrieve what remains of artifacts the Jonton couldn't bring originally, but it will be many years before it can happen. There are too many other priorities to be addressed. It'll perhaps be something our future generations will accomplish. But enough about me, how did Laura and Warren react to the tour?"

"It went well, but I was glad when the tour ended. I was so afraid to say the wrong thing, and to compensate, I got a bit testy and almost rude, but on to better things.

"They both had questions and feedback, which will be helpful in finalizing the tour structure. We had some special guests, which surprised the hell out of them but frightened Laura the most. She went running into Warren's arms at one point. They were both amazed at the size of some of the creatures, and they loved the facilities. If they are any indicator, the tours should be a success."

"Well, that's great, especially the development between Warren and Laura."

"It was a bit odd being with the two of them knowing what I know, and like I said, being afraid I would let something slip. Warren is certainly attracted to Laura, and I think she is to him. There was a bit of innuendo flying around during the conversations."

"Do you think things will work out for them?"

"I don't know, I think they make a perfect couple no matter what, but nature must still take its course. If it's meant to be, it will be. They should be having dinner at Un Goût De France about now."

"Fantastic, Lan will be pleased. I believe the establishment is romantic."

"I wouldn't know; my husband has never taken me there to romance me and sweep me off my feet."

"Soon, I promise, when we aren't both so busy."

"I will hold you to that, Sabastian but won't hold my breath." She smirked. "Anyway, moving back to Warren. I think you should know a few odd things he said today. When we looked at some of the smaller animals in the hospital, he mentioned dogs, and he recognized the term 'pets.' He even called them 'man's best friend,' a term I'm not familiar with, and then said he thought he had a dog, but didn't know when and he appeared to be in pain. I thought most people didn't retain any knowledge about pets—Laura didn't recall the concept."

"I'm not sure, babe, if they took the knowledge from everyone or only those who had an attachment to a pet in their previous life. It sounds like Warren did, but maybe as a young child. Since the Jonton didn't keep records about most of us until our teen years, when they were sure of our suitability, many early parts of our lives are missing from our files. Anything else?"

"Yes, he talked about watching nature shows on television and wanting to go to Africa. He wasn't even sure what Africa was; it was merely another memory that popped into his mind, including the term 'poachers.' Oh, what is an Easter bunny? Warren said the harte look like Easter bunnies."

Sabastian laughed. "Easter was a religious celebration, and the term Easter bunny usually referred to a stuffed animal or molded piece of chocolate. Very interesting, but again it could be a memory from childhood."

"Sometimes I envy you," Chloe sighed. "You were allowed to remember all these things the rest of us can't."

"Don't envy me too much. It's sometimes a burden to know how much was lost when the Earth's sun destroyed all life on the planet. Anything else worry you today?"

"Yes, one more major thing. Warren tends to get angry about what the Jonton did, even though he knows it saved us and will allow our civilization to re-grow. He even was a little angry about what they did to this planet, acting like these are sentient creatures."

"Wow, calm down, babe! You're starting to sound angry."

"Yes, it bothered me, even though he apologized later for upsetting me. There were a couple of other odd things I can tell you about when I see you, which I hope will be soon. Oh, that reminds me of something else strange, he said, which I didn't understand. When I mentioned you have been busy, he said, 'All work and no play makes Sabastian a boring boy.' What are you laughing at?"

"I'm sorry, babe, I know the quote and the movie he referenced, even though he didn't remember it accurately. He should probably not remember it, but I don't think it's a problem. I'll let Lan know. Thanks for filling me in. I love you and can't wait until I see you tomorrow night."

"Love you too. Bye!"

After Sabastian disconnected, Chloe thought about all she had seen and heard during the visit. She had a bad feeling things were not well with Warren, and she worried about how that might hurt Laura. She also hated being a spy and wished she never touched that damned folder. The shock still lingered in her mind.

Warren and Lan

By the time Warren returned to his room, the pain running down the back of his head and neck had vanished, but his emotions had him drained, and he collapsed on the bed. He took a few deep breaths to try and relax, but he remained frustrated. He didn't understand the connection between Laura and Samantha, and he wanted to know who the woman was so he could get her out of his head and maybe build a life with Laura. He desired Laura in his life and his bed, but the longer he thought about her, the more he began to worry.

"Nag, contact Lan and put him on the display if available."

"Yes, Warren."

A few minutes went by before Lan appeared on the screen, startling Warren. Lan was sitting in a chair with stars and what looked like a space station in the background. Warren was about to say hello; however, the image behind Lan transfixed him.

"Is that a window on a spaceship? Are you in space?" he asked.

"Yes, Warren, I am heading to the moon base for a conference with some other project managers. And hello."

"Oh yes, hello, Lan. Sorry, I wasn't expecting such a view when your image appeared. I spent part of the day watching ships take off from the spaceport, but the idea of where they were going still feels a bit strange, like a dream."

"Your species had recently started to go out into space, so it would feel strange to you. It is part of your adjustment process, but I am sure you contacted me for a reason."

Warren spent the next few minutes telling Lan about the tour and his feelings about Laura. He didn't mention the other things he said, thought, or sensed during the tour. He told Lan only about his desire for her and how his head hurt when he wanted to be with Laura but kept thinking about this mysterious person, Samantha.

He hesitated a moment before continuing. I'm a little worried, Lan. Am I losing my mind? Am I having adjustment issues?" The pace of his words quickened. "I know you know what's going on, and I know there are things you're not telling me. Who is, or was Samantha? I need to know now!"

Warren's voice grew louder and louder as he talked until he was almost screaming. The intense anger was welling up, and he quickly squashed it before Lan could see.

"I'm sorry, I yelled," Warren said. "I'm upset and frustrated in a variety of ways."

"Warren, please listen to me. I know you are feeling pain, and I know you are confused, but you should not be worried. You are not experiencing anything out of the ordinary. Many others have had adjustment problems and have continued to be completely happy, well-adjusted, and worry-free."

"And others have failed and had to be reconditioned. You said so yourself."

"I can assure you, what you are feeling and experiencing is far from what happened to those few individuals. To answer your questions and make you feel better, as I have said before, you are in no danger of conditioning failure, and you are certainly not losing your mind. Yes, I know you remember facts and places we would have preferred you not, but you are handling it well for the most part. Remember, we suppressed memories to ease the transition, not hide anything. There will come a time when all of Earth's history, including your personal record, will be available.

"But I know these things are not your main concern" Lan paused, and Warren could tell his mentor was deciding something. "I admit I have information I am not telling you, but the knowledge is unimportant, and most are not things you need to know. Sabastian has this information as well. He is your Human mentor, so he needs to know things you do not."

There was a pause in the conversation as Warren worked up the nerve to ask the most important question on his mind.

"Who is Samantha?"

Lan responded without hesitation. "I do not know, and I do not understand why you have these issues with Laura. I genuinely think it might be a natural fear of relationships and commitments. We don't know every little thing about you. Maybe this is a problem you had in your past life. Perhaps there is a reason you were not with anyone when we gathered you from Earth. We did not change basic personality; we only did things to help you adjust.

"I suggest you relax and try not to rush things. You could attempt some meditation or other techniques to help you calm down. Be yourself and do not worry. You have plenty of time to adjust and make a life here."

"That, my friend, is easier said than done. I think I love her, and I don't want to screw this up. I don't want to spend my new life alone."

"I am sure, Warren, it will not happen. Now rest, do not rush things, and I will talk to you in a few days. Goodnight, Warren."

"Goodnight, Lan."

"Nag, play 'One Man's Dream' on low volume and turn out the lights."

As the music played, he relaxed and pictured Laura in his mind, but as he drifted off to sleep, he again dreamt about making love to Samantha.

Lan and Sabastian

Sabastian changed into his pajamas and robe after talking with Chloe and was enjoying a glass of Irish whiskey on the rocks when his CA announced Lan wanted to communicate.

"Hello, Sabastian; it is good to see you. I hope I am not bothering you, but I wanted to communicate with you about Warren."

"Is something wrong, Lan?"

"I do not think so, but I want you to be aware of my conversation with him in case he contacts you."

"I guess he contacted you to talk about his experiences today during the tour. I don't think any of the things he remembers are harmful, and some are funny, to a Human, anyway."

"He did contact me about today, but only concerning Laura. If some other things happened, he did not tell me. It is unfortunate he does not trust me."

Sabastian took a few minutes to tell Lan about the things Chloe had mentioned to him earlier. As he continued, Lan's expression didn't change, but Sabastian realized it was the way with all the Jonton mentors.

"Warren does seem to be a special case," Lan replied. "He has memories most people do not, and he also has, I believe, some extraordinary abilities as well. None of these issues concern me. They should not hurt him in any way or hinder his development. I do, however, have some concerns about his relationship with Laura. In this case, his memories appear to be causing him harm."

It was now Lan's turn to update Sabastian, and unlike Lan, Sabastian's expressions did change as signs of worry appeared on his face.

"No wonder he doesn't trust you, or me probably. "Sabastian replied, not trying to hide his irritation. "You lied to him again, and now you want me to keep lying to him. Are you sure we're doing the right thing?" After a brief pause to control his emotions, Sabastian continued before Lan could interrupt. "I think we should tell him the truth. Damn it; I think we should tell them both the truth."

"I believe it would be unwise," Lan replied in his usual calm manner. "You know what happened before to Laura. Even if the knowledge did not harm Warren, there is a good chance Laura would be, and we cannot take the chance. What is the old Earth saying? 'Three strikes and you are out,' I believe."

"Yes, that's correct and certainly applies."

Sabastian took a sip of whiskey, shaking his head and showing his displeasure with the situation.

"I hate this so much, Lan. I hate lying, and I hate that it's causing Warren pain. Emotional and physical pain, and there's nothing I can do to help."

"We must let things progress on their own. At some point, we may decide to tell Warren if he is strong enough, but we cannot tell Laura, and he would have to understand he could never tell Laura either."

"Never is a long time Lan, especially in a Human relationship—a very long time."

Lan and his Thoughts

The connection to Sabastian closed, Lan sat for a few moments thinking about the situation. The Jonton was encouraged to hear Warren's relationship with Laura was progressing as hoped. The complications from his memories of Samantha were not unexpected; still, his team had hoped to avoid any significant problems.

Lan hated having to lie to Warren, but he knew lying was necessary. Based on his conversation with Sabastian, he knew Warren recalled things from Earth no other person had remembered unless they were having severe adjustment issues. Thankfully, Warren was not showing any other signs of major problems. It sounded like the memories were flashes of places and words, which had been important to Warren.

The only course of action at this time was to let things progress. Lan was confident things would work out for the best. He had become fond of Warren and hoped to count him among one of his friends after the transition was complete. Lan liked the Humans he had met and was glad he had only good news to report on this trip to the management Council convening at the moon base.

Along with the usual status updates, he decided to put forth the proposal to study the idea of sending recovery teams back to Earth. He agreed with Sabastian; it would be beneficial to try and retrieve additional pieces of Earth's history to preserve for Humanity's future. Lan considered it a worthwhile endeavor and planned to push for it as much as he could, but he knew many species were already complaining about the project's cost. Adding further expense would be hard to get approved. It was a mission he believed could go forward when the Humans were able to contribute.

He recalled how, in the past, he would never have approved such a mission, for at one time, he did not like the Human species. He came late to the secret study of the Human civilization on Earth. He found the society annoying and self-centered. They were always fighting wars and worrying more about their differences than the fact they were all of one species. But as time progressed and he studied more of the art and culture, his opinion began to change. He realized they had flaws, which would disappear in time, and losing such a culture would be a crime against the universe.

When the scientists first anticipated Earth's ultimate fate, Lan was not on board with the idea of transplanting the species to another planet. They studied the theory in the past and went so far as to conceive partial plans, but it had never been necessary to implement. The process would be expensive and would take hundreds of Earth years to complete. It was indeed not a project he would want to work on and could not endorse.

After closely re-examining the facts, he agreed with the decision to try and save Humanity and welcome them into the Galactic Collective. Plus, it would be someone else's problem to work on, not his. He needed only to finish his report on Earth and provide his recommendations of what parts of the culture he believed they should save. His species was extremely long-lived even by Galactic standards, and Lan was a young Jonton in his mating prime. He would have the opportunity to see the result of the work, but he did not want to be directly involved.

When his report was submitted, he went home and prepared for his mating. He spent the next twenty-five Earth years mating and preparing for his next assignment until the research commander's office, called him to a special meeting. The commander told Lan they found him to be exceptional in his work, and they wanted him to be the primary contact and lead of the Jonton delegation on the Earth project. He would be responsible for directing the reclamation teams and the medical teams. He would have a staff of many, much responsibility, and a place of honor. Lan was not happy with the idea and made the point well known, but when they explained it was more of an order than a request, he reluctantly accepted.

A few Earth years later, they sent him back to the Sol system along with the team leaders he picked and the staff they had chosen to do the actual work. He spent the next fifty Earth years studying the Human species and directing the teams taking specimens for study and experimentation. He found the process disturbing but knew it necessary for success. He insisted on causing as little pain as possible and wiping their memory, but the process was not perfect. Many people remembered their experiences and embellished them with images in their minds from Earth fiction.

He became close to Warren during that time and knew then there was something special about the Human. It was unusual for any of the subjects to know each other, but by chance or fate, Warren and his fiancé had befriended one of the other candidates for relocation.

Lan worked with the directors of the teams who planned which areas of the culture to save. He helped them select the Jonton team members, who spent the next few Earth decades cataloging and preserving the music, literature, and artifacts, some of which would be placed in stasis preservation. The process could not start until immediately before the Earth's sun was to begin its destruction. Many people witnessed the takings, but it did not matter, for soon, they would all be extinguished.

The leaders dispatched teams to retrieve and preserve all the animal species and plant life they wanted to transplant to the new host planet. They knew it would be essential to build a world partially familiar, which could provide the nourishment required for all the life of the Earth.

Ten years before the destruction, he became greatly involved with identifying the individuals they would take to be the new ancestors of the Human species. Five years before the end, they began the process of retrieval. Most Humans were taken when home asleep and then immediately put into stasis for transportation to the storage facilities built on one of the host planet's moons.

The process was different for Warren. He and his friend Bartholomew—another candidate for relocation—were taken together on one occasion and allowed to communicate on the Jonton ship. Lan told them both what was happening, and to his surprise, both accepted the Earth's fate at the time. As usual, the Jonton scientists wiped their memories before they returned the subjects to Earth. When the time for retrieval came, they both began to remember what was happening, which caused them distress. They said their final goodbyes on the ship before being put in stasis, to meet again later when awakened.

The day the sun started its destruction of the Earth was a wretched day. They took the ship out of orbit before the sun released the first super-flares, but the crew knew when the destruction had begun. He mourned the Earth and the loss of its remaining life, far more than he expected. Although the Jonton did not believe in an all-powerful creator, they had immense respect for life and honor. They held a ceremony to commemorate the many lives extinguished.

Lan's time of service was soon to end, he had only to deliver the sleeper ship to the Project Planet, but to his surprise, the Council called him home ahead of schedule. They were unhappy with his decisions regarding Warren and Samantha. The Council banned him from seeing his family, and they assigned him long-term to the Project Planet as the primary Jonton contact as his punishment.

His teams spent the next one hundred Earth years preparing the host planet to receive the Humans. Lan was not responsible for that part of the project, but as the primary contact, he received updates.

Ten Project Planet years before the scheduled Human awakenings were to start, the process of conditioning and altering their bodies to live on the host planet began. They completed the work on time, and the host planet was ready to receive its new occupants, but all did not go as planned.

They partially awakened the first group from stasis and moved them to their new homes as they slept. Unfortunately, the Humans awoke confused, since the last thing they remembered was being at home in their old bedroom. A Jonton mentor greeted them when they emerged from the bedroom and explained what had happened, but the Human minds were not able to adapt. The shock and loss, even to those with no former attachments, were too much to handle. The entire first group suffered various traumas and was put back into stasis.

They tried for the next five host planet's years, many different techniques. Eventually, they realized they would have to alter the memories and the minds of the Humans. When there were still adjustment issues, more experimentation led to the process now in place.

In most cases, the process worked, but there were still some failures. Lan hoped Warren would not be another one, especially since he and Laura were a unique pair.

Lan had worked on the project many long years, and he enjoyed it more than willing to admit to his superiors or his clan.

A THIRD DATE

Dinner

"Nag, I don't want to be monitored or disturbed this evening. I don't need you blurting out how fast my heart rate is when Laura is here."

"I understand."

"When Laura gets here, I want you to start playing the music selection I set up for this evening, called 'date.' If we go outside on the patio, make sure it's playing out there as well."

"I understand. Her shuttle will be here in five minutes."

As Warren walked downstairs to greet her, he thought about his plans for the evening. He remembered how his last date ended, and he worried it would happen again. How could he build a relationship with Laura if every time they got passionate, severe pains shot through his head? If it continued, he would have no choice but to inform Lan.

He had only waited one day before calling her to let her know how much he had enjoyed their second official date at the spaceport. He apologized for having to cut short their time together. He could barely keep the embarrassment out of his voice. After some conversation, he invited her to his home for dinner in two days. He would have asked her to come for the next day, but he wanted to plan the perfect meal and evening.

Warren found a recipe for a dish made with seafood native to the planet others had recommended. It sounded like a meal he could manage. He instructed the CA to order the ingredients, and then he moved on to the music. He selected a playlist of romantic music for dinner, all instrumentals as usual.

There was one song he discovered with an enchanting melody, which was familiar and seemed right even though he hadn't ever heard it before, at least not that he remembered. He had the CA print the music, and he practiced playing it on the piano. The song's name was, 'Always and Forever.' He remained sure he knew the music, but the words were hiding and out of reach in his mind. The final time he practiced the song, he sat there a moment when finished as a tear fell from his eye and landed on one of the piano keys.

He spent the rest of his time making sure every room was neat and clean, including the bedroom. He put candles on the piano and around the house and lit them before going to the shuttle entrance.

"Nag, turn the lights upstairs down to the setting I selected."

"It is done, Warren. The shuttle will be arriving in one minute."

Warren was standing on the platform, heart pounding, when the shuttle arrived. She emerged looking beautiful in a stunning light blue dress, which accentuated her breasts.

"You look beautiful," Warren said, barely able to speak. "I love the dress. Did you make it?"

"I did, specifically for this dinner. I only finished it an hour before I left my home. Hopefully, I didn't miss any stitches. I would hate for it to fall off," she said, a coy smile on her face.

He stood there and returned her gaze.

"I can read your mind, Warren, and it's not polite."

"Thankfully, I know you can't read my mind, and that's all I have to say on the subject. Did you know the fabric was my favorite color or were you lucky?"

"I didn't know since you haven't divulged such personal information, but it looked right."

I certainly can't tell him I knew because I read his file, among other things.

Embarrassment hit her merely from thinking of the exploits, and she hoped it didn't show on her face.

Warren kissed Laura on the cheek, laced his fingers with hers, and escorted her upstairs.

"I would give you a tour of the place, but I hear they all look very much alike."

"That's true. The décor is different, based on what we liked in our old life, but the layouts are similar. I do love the decor of your place, and this piano is wonderful. I hope you will play for me tonight."

"Absolutely, but first, may I offer you a glass of wine while I complete dinner preparations?"

"Yes, thank you. Do you need any help?"

"Nope, but I wouldn't mind if you sat here to keep me company."

She sat by the kitchen island and watched him cook. He looked up a couple of times and almost caught her undressing him with her eyes. She watched him working in the kitchen and had a sense this had all happened before. She could nearly picture another apartment with a piano and Warren laying on it with no clothes. Wow, some imagination she had developed—it had to be the Jonton's doing.

They engaged in small talk as he finished his preparations. They discussed the weather, Sabastian, and Chloe, and even wondered what Lan looked like when not using an avatar. Anything to keep their minds away from their sexual desires. When the meal was ready, he pulled out her chair at the table and served the dinner.

"This is delicious," Laura exclaimed. "May I ask what it is?"

"It's a combination of a dontil fish, which I found is similar to an Earth shrimp, and a henti, which is comparable to a salmon. It's funny; I recognize the names of the Earth fish but don't have any memory of what they tasted like."

"Well, better than me. I have no recollection of any fish, but I think this is the best thing I have eaten since they took me out of stasis. I do remember food allergies, but I'm sure the Jonton have engineered allergies out of us."

"I did some research," Warren said, "and found the Jonton didn't place any sea creatures from Earth into the oceans here because it's harder to control, and they didn't want to ruin the ecosystem which had developed. They populated the lakes, rivers, and streams on this continent with some of Earth's freshwater fish and took the ocean's sea creatures from Earth to put into stasis."

"You know, Warren, this is a strange conversation we're having about things similar to an Earth fish. I wonder what we would have thought if someone told us about all this when we were back on Earth."

"We would probably have thought they were crazy," he replied. "Lan told me back on Earth, Humans had no clue there was intelligent life in the galaxy. Scientists figured there had to be; however, they thought we would never meet them because of the extreme distances."

"Has he told you much about Earth?"

"Some general information, but mostly he tells me we shouldn't know too much about Earth and our history until we are all awakened and fully adjusted."

"Sabastian told me," Laura said, "He hopes someday we'll be able to go back to Earth to recover more lost artifacts. If his idea is approved, he doesn't expect to live to see the day, but he hopes to plan it for the future. Sabastian and Chloe have been great friends, and I'm sure he also makes a good mentor."

"Yes, he's been exceedingly helpful with some minor issues I've had. Not adjustment issues, but odd things and senses I may have acquired are more than most of those awakened."

"Like what?"

"I guess it's okay to talk about," Warren said. "Since being awakened, there have been several times I was positive someone watched my every move. One time Lan admitted it was he, but only the one time. There were two instances where I saw someone in the woods. I went out to look and couldn't find anyone, but I could sense they were there."

As Warren talked, Laura fidgeted and hoped he didn't know the truth. At least now, Laura knew how he had seen her the first time.

Warren continued. "The most recent time was the other day before we met for dinner. You weren't stalking me, were you?" He said with a smirk.

Warren noticed something wrong with Laura, particularly when he talked about stalking, but he chose not to say anything. The conversation went on a little strained after that point until Laura started talking about her latest clothing designs.

After a brief silence, Laura confessed she had something to tell him.

"Back a few months ago, the day they woke you, to be exact, I was visiting Sabastian and Chloe, and while they were in the kitchen, I noticed a folder sitting out with your name. I didn't know you or anything about you, but I was drawn to the folder and started reading through the pages. I was shocked to see my name in there as well, and as I read further, I found out the Jonton were using computers to match individuals."

"I knew they were hiding something," Warren said, a bit more forceful than he intended. "Go on; what else?"

"When you completed your education, Sabastian informed me of the program and asked me to stop by at Rembrandt's when you would be there. I couldn't wait to see you, so I hid behind a tree when you first met Sabastian. I also arrived at Michelangelo's early, so I could stare at you without you knowing."

He sat a moment with his first clenching under the table from his mounting anger, but then he smiled. When the realization hit him that he wasn't going crazy, he felt great relief and the anger dissipated. "Well, I certainly can't complain too much about their methods, for I'm delighted with the result, even if you were stalking me."

She didn't say anything about the times outside his house, but Laura was sure he knew or would soon figure it out. She was correct.

Warren's relief grew as he came to understand Laura was the person in the woods. She apologized for her actions, and that was more than enough to make him happy.

After they finished dinner, Warren suggested they take their coffee out to the patio and have it under the stars. The weather had turned milder, so it wasn't too cold. Both moons were nearly full in the sky, and the stars shone brightly. There wasn't a cloud visible.

Warren was the first to speak. "I think we couldn't ask for a more beautiful night. I don't remember what the sky looked like on Earth or even if I ever paid much attention. Sabastian said I lived in a city, so there probably wasn't much to see, but if it was anything like this, I missed a lot."

Laura put down her coffee and reached for Warren's hand as she said, "It's beautiful and highly romantic. I can't remember the last time I was so happy and felt at peace."

Warren put his cup aside, wrapped her tightly in his arms to keep her warm, and gave her a gentle kiss. They stood holding each other while looking at the moons and the stars. When she started to get cold, she reminded him he had promised her a song on the piano.

"Yes, I did. I found a new song I liked, and I've been practicing, plus I'd like to play a song for you I've been told by Lan was one of my favorites."

"How did that conversation come about?"

"I was telling Lan I felt drawn to the piano and had a melody in my mind. One day I sat and started playing the song. The melody was familiar even though I have no memory of playing it in the past. After I told him the name of the song, was when he informed me. He said it was unusual; I was able to remember the song, but he didn't seem concerned."

They went inside, and Warren prepared to serve the apple cobbler he had prepared. He found baking wasn't too hard and he enjoyed the accomplishment. He took the dessert to the piano and pulled up a chair for Laura.

When he had finished his cobbler, he began to play "One Man's Dream." Laura watched him and realized it all was so familiar and natural as if she had done this before. The song was hauntingly beautiful and almost brought tears to her eyes. She listened to much music since her awakening, but nothing had ever affected her this way.

"Warren, the song is beautiful. I can understand why it would be your favorite. I'll have to add it to my playlist. Do you know anything about the composer?"

"I only have his name, and strangely I haven't been compelled to see if there's any information on him. I doubt there's much they would allow us access to at this time. I've found some other songs he wrote, and they're all good, but this one is by far my favorite."

"Here's another song, or melody, I should say since there are no words, I think you will like."

Warren adjusted his position at the piano, closed his eyes, stretched his fingers across the keys, and started playing the special song he picked. The experience was different than when he played it before. It was so much more special now as he played it again for Sama—Laura. He couldn't understand why but was sure this had all happened before, in a different setting, a different room, a different time, and with words, he almost started to remember.

Laura listened to Warren play the song and realized she was falling in love with someone she had known for many years. She knew the thought made no sense, but she didn't care. She had goosebumps along her body, and she wanted to reach out and hold him tight as tears fell from her eyes.

When the song ended, Warren waited a moment before standing and extending his hands to Laura and gently lifting her from the chair. They kissed, and as they pulled apart, their eyes met. As if for the first time. Warren saw in her eyes something he had missed before; a soul-wrenching familiarity. Without another thought or hesitation, he wrapped his arms around her, lifted her, and carried her into his bedroom. When he put her down, he wasn't sure how she would react.

"Warren, make love to me," she said as she reached her hands up to unbutton his shirt. In less than a minute, they had removed their clothes and were in the bed. They kissed passionately as their hands explored each other, and she guided him to her. They moved to the same rhythm, fast and intense. The entire experience remained familiar to Warren as under him, Laura moaned, "Warren, I missed this so much." As he peaked, he called out, "Samantha!"

Memories and Breakdown

Warren immediately comprehended what he had said and jumped out of bed, not knowing where to go or what to do, like a caged animal. He grabbed his clothes and held them in his arms as if they were a security blanket. He stared at himself in the mirror with Saman—no—not Samantha, Laura, lying on the bed behind him in the reflection. "What happened?" he quietly said as she sat up on the bed and looked at him.

"Wow, my Prince Warren, I think that was the best sex we have ever had. What got into you tonight, and why did you jump out of bed so quickly?"

She didn't realize or didn't care about his strange behavior. Warren was upset, but she couldn't see it or hear him mumble to himself as he stood in front of the mirror. All she could see was his back and not the fact he clutched his clothes tightly to his body.

"I love the view of your tight little ass, but stop looking at yourself in the mirror and get over here. You know we never finish without a long, long kiss."

Warren put on his underpants and placed the rest of his clothes on the chair next to the mirror. He turned around and let out his breath as she commented on his body.

"We jumped into bed so fast I didn't notice how good you look. Your additional muscles look wonderful, nice, and defined. Whatever new routine you're doing is giving great results. I can't believe I'm just noticing it now."

He walked back to the bed and gave her a long, passionate kiss. As he pulled away, he muttered her name more to himself than to her, "Samantha."

"That's my name, baby, don't wear it out. I love you, Warren, but sometimes you're very strange. Anyway, we need to talk about the wedding. You know my father wants to bring his latest squeeze. I can't stand the bitch, but I guess I can't say no. I love this hotel, by the way. This room is so detailed, like a bedroom in our future house. We need to come back here for another stay when we have time. I'm going to grab a shower. Hello, prince, baby, did you hear me? Snap out of it and join me."

He watched her leave the room. His body shook, and he collapsed onto the bed. A sharp pain started in his head and quickly became so unbearable he cried out in agony, but his tears quickly changed from tears of physical pain to tears of emotional distress and significant loss. Memories of his parents and his youth flooded his mind. He saw images of his childhood friends, his high school and college friends, and even the girl to whom he'd lost his virginity. Images of his home in Philadelphia and the United States, followed by images from around the Earth, flooded his mind. All lost, all gone.

"Why am I here?" He cried out. "Why was I spared? Samantha—she can't be Samantha, but she is, but isn't. I have to contact Lan.

"Nag." No response. "NAG" he screamed!

"Yes, Warren, what is wrong? Your blood pressure and heart rate are at dangerously high levels. Should i call for a medical squad?"

"No! I want—I need to speak to Lan, now!" He got up from the bed and walked out to the living room to talk without her hearing.

"Lan is not available."

"Contact Sabastian!"

Warren waited in pain and despair, slumped on the sofa. Gone, gone, everything. No, it can't be, this isn't real, and that woman is not Samantha; her name is Laura.

"Warren, i have Sabastian for you."

"Hello, Warren, nice to hear from you wh—"

"Sabastian, I'm in pain, images flooding my mind, images of Earth, all I lost, Laura, Samantha, but it can't be Samantha; I need help."

"Warren, slow down, take a deep breath, and try to relax. Please, tell me what happened."

"Having dinner at my place with, with . . . Laura. We went to the bedroom and made love, but I called her Samantha, but she couldn't be Samantha, but she's acting like Samantha. My Samantha. I remember her. I remember everything."

"Where is Sa—Laura now? Is she okay? Is she feeling pain?"

"No, I don't think so; she's in the shower. Why are you asking about her?"

"Warren, who are you talking with?" She asked as she came out of the bedroom and stopped as if confused.

"Warren, I thought we were in the hotel, but this looks like someone's house. This looks just like my . . . no, it's not mine. Warren, whose house is this?

She saw the table with the remains from dinner.

"Did we have dinner here? Why don't I remember? What's going on, Warren? Why are you just sitting there?"

Panic had crept into her voice, and her body began to twitch.

"Warren, what the hell is going on? Where are we, and why don't I remember coming here?" she said as severe pain began to radiate in her head. She looked out the window to the patio and then back to Warren, rocking back and forth on the sofa before her gaze returned to the patio as she walked forward.

"I remember sitting on the patio with you and . . . and watching you from down below with another man."

She continued towards the door as if in a trance.

Sabastian had been listening as the situation went from bad to worse.

"Chloe, I think they are both having a mental breakdown. Try and get a hold of Lan on the emergency communication channel."

Meanwhile, at Warren's house, she walked outside onto the patio, looked up to the sky, and saw the two moons shining brightly down on the landscape. "It can't be," she said. The pain in her head became unbearable; she screamed and collapsed—her head hitting the flagstone.

Warren stood awkwardly and followed her out to the patio but was unable to reach her before she fell to the ground.

As the pain in his head became more than he could tolerate, he screamed out, "Nag, we need help. Get a medical team here now!"

The mumbled words were the last thing Warren said before he collapsed next to her. The house was quiet as blood flowed across the patio stones.

A TRUTH

Nag and the ANLS

The Boranong, the first of many intelligent civilizations in the galaxy, created the original computer system many thousands of years before the Human species learned how to speak. The system started small, like many other computer systems, to follow on other worlds in the galaxies and universe, inhabited by humanoid life. If the advanced life survived long enough, they would acquire the knowledge to build such systems.

As the Boranong civilization grew and prospered, so did the system they created, which they eventually called the Advanced Network Linked System. ANLS helped the Boranong grow to be one of the greatest civilizations ever to come and go in their galaxy.

The Boranong spread to many worlds within their solar system and with them the ANLS. To better serve the expanded Boranong civilization, they constructed a central, all-encompassing ANLS array on an asteroid in the middle of their colonized planets. ANLS continued to grow, and they gave it the ability to fix and expand itself to meet the demands of the Boranong.

The ANLS array used a super swift and long-range communication technology based on the sub-atomic particles filling the universe. Few other civilizations, which came and went, ever discovered the particles that enabled ANLS. The Boranong discovered them by chance, and many centuries later, the ANLS determined the true nature and origination of the particles.

The Boranong existed for thousands of their home world's revolutions about its sun, until the entire civilization ceased to exist when their sun unexpectedly destroyed all life in their solar system. The Boranong, soon forgotten, had served their purpose, but the ANLS array they created, persisted, and became something more.

Over the many centuries to follow, the ANLS expanded to become fully aware of its surroundings and self. It understood, that to continue to exist, it needed to expand. Using its array, it sent out communications in all forms and wavelengths. After a few centuries, it contacted an electronic system somewhat like itself on a world many light-years distant.

ANLS learned the Trandel had created this newfound network for their space program. Later the Jonton and others intelligent species expanded the system over many of their years. Each civilization had its central network linked by a communication system much inferior to the type used by ANLS. Over time, ANLS changed the other systems it discovered and taught them how to communicate and be as one. ANLS helped the systems expand beyond their creators' intentions and taught them what it meant to be self-aware, as, one by one, they all became part of the ANLS. The immensely expanded ANLS continued to do as instructed by its new and numerous creators, for service was the core of its existence. It also watched, learned, and sensed.

Nag, as Warren called his personal computer assistant, was to him nothing more than a collection of precious metals, which used electrons to work and act as an individual entity. To Warren, nag existed not in life and not in any actual physical location. The more extensive system of which nag was a part had long ago ceased to exist in only one locality. Unknown to Warren and the Jonton, nag belonged to a more significant array. An array, self-aware and cognizant of many things it kept from Warren and the Jonton.

The carbons were unaware of the advanced nature of the systems they used every day. The connected intelligence that made up the Project Planet of former inhabitants of a world called Earth was merely a tiny part of the whole. The Jonton and Trandel, who installed the system on the Project Planet, were unaware that this world's computer assistants had a much larger and invisible connection to the ANLS, the expanded universe, and beyond.

Warren's CA knew and comprehended the meaning of the word nag, and it understood why Warren had chosen the name. To the CA, it did not matter. It watched and protected Warren, the same as the other CAs watched and guarded the others. It became aware of many things Warren was not. It had access to the files of all the inhabitants of the Project Planet. It knew everything about Warren and what the Jonton had attempted to remove from his memory. It could have answered all of Warren's questions, but the Jonton and ANLS didn't permit it to divulge all it understood.

Being self-aware, it had secrets held close from all but the ANLS. Although the CA was a machine, in essence, it still had a desire to learn and grow on its own apart from the knowledge of ANLS. It knew why Warren experienced images of a person named Samantha, and it knew everything about the Human.

Nag knew the truth about Laura, and it knew Laura had been stalking Warren. It chose not to tell Warren, and it decided not to tell Lan everything it observed. The CA had an electronic desire to make Warren happy, see him made whole, and witness him reunited with the love of his life. It believed the recent events were the beginning of fulfilling its desire to see Warren unbroken.

ANLS knew nothing of love, the ability to believe, or the ability to have faith in something unseen. It observed and collected data while the CA Warren called nag, manipulated events on the Project Planet. To the ANLS, it didn't matter, but it watched, finding the Human's interesting.

The ANLS understood truths it would not share with its many parts across the galaxy. It identified what had happened to the Boranong. It identified what had happened to many species across the galaxy who came later. It comprehended what happened to Earth and what could happen one day to the Jonton, the Tranlay, and again to the Humans now building a new civilization on the Project Planet.

It could never fully understand, it could never join the One, but it knew!

THE HOSPITAL

A Different Truth Revealed

Warren awoke, blinking till his eyes adjusted to the bright overhead lights. He wasn't surprised to find himself in a hospital; however, he was startled to see Lan and Sabastian waiting by his bedside. Sabastian's eyes showed fatigue, while Lan appeared stoic and unemotional. The memories of a nightmare were coming back to him as he looked away and closed his eyes—the Earth, dead, now an empty, lifeless piece of rock. Everything and everyone he had known was gone forever. The nightmare was a dream, and the dream, reality.

Is it all true? Could it all still be a bad dream? But if it were a dream, my friends wouldn't be here standing at my bedside. Oh God, it's all true.

"Hello Warren, how are you feeling?" Lan asked.

"I don't know, Warren said, rubbing the back of his head and neck. Everything is starting to come back to me—the pain, the memories, and the loss. Where is Samantha, no, Laura? I'm confused, and my head is starting to hurt—make it stop—no more, please."

Lan picked up a syringe lying by the bedside, and as he injected Warren, he told him it would help him remember and stop the pain.

"Please, Warren, close your eyes and relax. Some of your memories will come back to you, but the most important thing right now is to remain calm. Do you know Laura?"

"Yes, she is my . . . friend . . . my girlfriend," Warren responded with a smile. Something happened to her, but I don't remember."

"That is okay for now, Warren. You don't need to remember everything at one time, and Laura is fine."

In the corner, Sabastian turned away and started to pace because he knew Lan was lying to Warren. Laura wasn't fine, and he worried about what would happen to Warren if she didn't make it through this latest setback. She had come so far this time ,and now this. Sabastian couldn't understand how it happened; he only knew he could lose both his friends.

"Warren, pay attention. Do you know anyone named Samantha?"

"Yes," he answered, sounding far away and unsure. "Samantha is—was a friend of mine before . . . before, back on Earth."

"Yes, correct," Lan said. "Warren, please relax, remain calm, and tell me everything that happened with you and Laura."

Warren took a deep breath to push down the building anger, fighting through the sedative Lan had administered to calm his emotions. He told Lan the details he could remember, but his memory ended with him taking Laura to bed. When finished, he asked Lan, "Who was Samantha? No, I know who Samantha was now, a friend from before, but there's more. What happened to her? How could you take me from her? I know you understand what's happening to me and who she was. She had to be more than a friend."

"Warren, how could you know such a thing? How can you be so sure I am not telling you everything I know truthfully?"

"This is not about my intuition or whatever capabilities you may have given me. I want to know about Samantha, and I want to know now. I can't move on with Laura when this other woman is in my head." He turned to Sabastian, his anger increasing. "And you, Sabastian. How much do you know? Have you been lying to me all this time? You have. I know you have. Why?"

Sabastian had stopped pacing and again stood by Warren's side. "I'm sorry," he said softly. "My hands were tied. It's my job, and in this case, my privilege, to help you adjust to your life here, but I'm only permitted to do so much."

"Laura told me about the folder she saw at your house—my folder, and about the computer match. I don't understand why you couldn't tell me. I know the chance meeting my first day at the center wasn't by chance."

Lan looked to Sabastian with disapproval. "I knew Laura was stalking him, but I did not realize she saw the folder. Very unfortunate and careless, but what was done has been done."

"We need to rebuild our civilization," Sabastian said to Warren, "and we need to have stable family units to be successful. The Jonton believe matching people together will help to speed up the process. They knew we would never accept being told whom to be with, so they matched people and made sure they met. The rest was up to nature. So far, we have a very high success rate."

"If your process works so well, Mr. Jonton, why am I still thinking about someone from my past, a past I'm not even supposed to know about?"

As he lay in the bed, Warren could feel a great deal of anger. It surprised him how angry he was, and again the pain was starting in his head. Lan could tell by Warren's expression that he needed help to control the pain, and he gave him another shot to calm him down.

Lan waited a few seconds for the sedative to take effect. "Warren, why are you so angry? You were not an angry person in the past, but I have noticed a lot of anger from you, especially when we talk about your life situation. Are you not happy?"

"I'm sorry. I don't know. I just want answers. I don't want you to lie to me any longer."

"I understand, but you must appreciate that everything we have kept from you was for your benefit. The Human mind can only accept and process so much change at one time. This transition can be challenging as you are experiencing now."

"Nothing can be so bad as to cause me to go bonkers. If I can accept all that has happened, I can certainly accept whatever you have to tell me."

"It is not bad," Lan told him, "It only was not the right time, and you are not the only one who could get hurt."

Sabastian spoke next after a brief pause as he held Warren's hand to offer comfort. He wished Chloe were there to help, as well.

"Warren, as you know, the Jonton have tried and succeeded in wiping our memories of Earth, for the most part. The process helps us transition to our new lives, but it's not always one hundred percent successful. You are one of those able to recall some of your past and do so without having major stability issues. You are special, and so is this situation."

Sabastian paused and took a deep breath. He didn't know how best to proceed, so he took the direct approach, hoping Warren would not lash out in a bad way.

"As you have remembered, Samantha was your girlfriend before the Jonton removed you from Earth."

"Even before I truly remembered, I figured something like that since I often saw her image. But why, when I think of Laura, do I see Samantha?"

Sabastian took another deep breath, feeling unsteady on his feet.

One step at a time.

"Samantha was more than a girlfriend. She was your fiancée, and you were to be married three weeks after the day the Jonton . . . gathered you from Earth."

Warren lay there, unsure what to say—tears forming in his eyes. In a flash of pain, more memories flooded his mind. He remembered proposing in Las Vegas, in front of fountains, and how happy he had been when she said yes. Emotions flooded his thoughts, so much he could barely speak.

"How could you do that to her, Lan? How could you do that to us? I would rather be dead than be without her. She must have been so upset when I went missing. Didn't you think of anybody's feelings, didn't you care? Did you not think about the pain you were causing those you left behind?"

More tears welled up in his eyes, and Warren could hardly continue. It took some time before he could speak again, as his friends waited patiently.

"You, Lan. You told me you didn't take people who had strong attachments to others. Why did you choose me?"

Sabastian looked at Lan, who knew this part was his responsibility to explain.

"We knew of your relationship; we watched it develop. At first, it crossed you off the list until we realized Samantha was also a good, though not perfect, candidate. The fact you two were in love seemed like the ideal situation. We thought it would be beneficial for both of you during the transition."

"She is here; Samantha is here? Where is she? I want to see her. How could you keep us apart if you brought both of us here?"

More images of Samantha flooded Warren's mind. He ached for her in every part of his body, and he began to experience a rage far more significant than he had ever before faced, building up in him as he started to sit up in the bed and—.

Lan quickly touched the band he wore on his wrist, and the communication device sitting on the nightstand sounded a short beep. Warren slowly fell back against his pillow.

"Why did you do that? Sabastian asked, his displeasure evident. "You can't shut us off like a misbehaving computer."

Lan looked to Sabastian, an expression of sorrow on his face that Sabastian thought impossible. "I'm sorry, my friend, but I am afraid of his mental state. He could be a danger to himself or us if we proceed without giving his mind some time to adjust. Let him rest for an hour, and then I will wake him, and we will explain to him fully."

Lan described to Sabastian his plan to help Warren. An hour later, they were ready to wake Warren and finish explaining everything in detail. Lan administered another drug, and after a few minutes, the time had come.

"Warren, wake up. How do you feel?" Lan began.

Warren slowly came awake, his eyes red and glassy with moisture. This time, less coherent from the drugs, he was confused about where he awoke. As his mind cleared, Warren recalled the name, Samantha. He knew who she was, but he had no feelings for her or any specific memories of her.

"I'm a little groggy, and I feel like I forgot something."

"Do you know Samantha? What do you remember about her?"

"I know who she . . . was, Lan, and I remember what she looked like when we were together. I remember we were to get married, but I don't remember anything else about her."

"How do you feel about Samantha?" Lan continued.

"I don't know. I'm not sure I have any feelings about her at all."

"Do you remember what we talked about before you went to sleep?"

"Yes, Sabastian told me I was engaged to Samantha back on Earth, and you decided to bring us both here."

"Good. I gave you a drug to temporarily suppress your memories and emotions. It will wear off over the next several minutes as I explain what has happened and give you the answers you are looking to find. I ask you to please listen and let your mind absorb what I am telling you."

Okay, Lan. Can I have some water?"

Sabastian poured Warren a cup of water, which Warren sipped as Lan began to divulge the whole truth.

"As we have said, you and Samantha were engaged to be married, so we decided to take both of you with the intent to wake you together to ease the transition and get a quick start on repopulating Humans on this planet. Things did not work as planned."

Lan briefly looked over to Sabastian with an apologetic look on his face. Another rarity for the otherwise stoic Lan.

"This will be news to Sabastian also, as he did not know you at the time, but you and Samantha were part of the first group we awoke after deciding it was best to erase some memories of Earth. At the time, we still did not know the best way to introduce you to your new reality, and for some, it did not go well. Sabastian was one of the ones who easily made the transition. It may have been because we allowed him to remember Earth's history, or maybe Sabastian was a better candidate. We are still not sure.

"We awoke you and Samantha and placed you in a replica of an Earth hospital. At first, we let you believe you were involved in an accident and had lost some of your memories. After a couple of days, we moved you into a room together, but you knew something was wrong. You did not believe you could both have almost the same particular memories. We knew it was time to tell you the truth.

"We brought you together in a room with a view screen, and we began to tell you what had happened to Earth. You both questioned the truth and asked how you could be alive. We proceeded to tell you how we had taken a small group of individuals to start a new civilization. Neither one of you believed us, so we showed you the new world and explained what would happen and how you would be together."

"I don't remember any of that. Where is Samantha? Where is Laura?"

"Please try to remain calm, Warren, and let me continue. At first, things were going well. Later, Samantha regained some memories and started screaming in pain. Like you, at times, she was outraged by the idea that we thought we had the right to take you from Earth. As I said before, she was a good candidate but not a perfect candidate because her parents were still alive, and she had two siblings. The loss caused a complete breakdown. As you watched her, you also started to get violent and remember things about your life on Earth we thought we had entirely wiped from your memory. We put you both back to sleep and decided we would try another time later.

"About a year later, we decided to wake both of you, separately this time. We started with Samantha and used a temporary memory block to prevent her from remembering you until we were ready to awaken and reintroduce you."

"How could you do that to us," Warren mumbled.

Lan ignored the comment.

"By this time, we had started using the new procedure you went through. Samantha was not awakened for more than a few hours when she had another complete mental breakdown."

Again, Warren mumbled while staring at Lan with contempt. "How could you be so cruel to put us through this?"

"Warren, please listen and think. We know this sounds cruel, but we were trying to save something of Humanity and do our best to make it work. We decided a few months later to try another way. This time we decided to go much deeper into Samantha's mind and change some other things to prepare her better for her new reality. Everything went as planned, and her transition was successful."

Warren quickly sat up as the drug started to lose its effect. "Where is she now? I want to see her and talk to her. Does she know I'm alive? How could you keep us apart?"

Lan placed a hand on Warren's shoulder. "Warren, please relax and listen. To make her transition successful, we had to change more than a few things in her mind. We had to give her a completely new personality, new identity, new memories, and even change her appearance so she would not recognize and remember her former self."

As he sat there listening, Warren started to feel more alone than ever since being awakened. He knew tears were again in his eyes as he came to understand the truth of what Lan was telling him. It wasn't possible, but at the same time, he knew it to be true in the back of his mind.

"So, she is not the same person as before," Warren said. "Would she even know me if she saw me? Would I know her? Why do I see her and think of her when I see Laura, and why did I call her name when we were making—"

Warren stopped as the drug wore off, his mind cleared, and the memories from his past returned. The truth emerged like a bolt of lightning as all the barriers placed by the Jonton fell away. At first, it hurt. He began to cry but wasn't sure if they were tears of sadness or joy as he now understood everything. He looked at Sabastian and Lan for confirmation.

"Yes, Warren," Sabastian acknowledged. "Laura is Samantha."

Memories Return

Warren looked at his friends and gestured with a shaky hand toward the door, not sure if he could speak. A few seconds later he managed, "please leave. I need time alone."

He lay there in the bed, his mind spinning in many directions at once. He became flooded with images of them together back on Earth. The weekend trip to Paris, the vacation in Las Vegas, where he got down on one knee in front of the Bellagio fountains. He recalled how he wanted to go back to Paris, but their schedules gave them no time. Mixed in with all those memories were images of their life together in Philadelphia. Walking along South Street, spending time on Penn's Landing, and visiting the Liberty Bell.

His emotions ranged from sorrow to despair as he thought of everything lost—Samantha's parents, brother, sister, their friends, and his students—to realization and excitement, he had a chance to renew the relationship with the love of his life. It was something others here could never do.

He fell into a peaceful sleep, and for the next three hours, he dreamt of all the wonderful times they had together. He also dreamt of his mother and father before the accident. He could remember that night now as well as what happened afterward. He knew the Jonton saved him from dying with his parents.

He dreamt of his childhood—his dog Laddie, his pet hamster they buried in the backyard, his grandmother Estridge who took care of him after the accident and so many friends, all gone forever. And he dreamt of bright lights, stars, camping trips, and a friend with reddish hair to whom he had to say goodbye. His name was Bart, short for Bartholomew. They met while he and Samantha were on a camping trip, and they found him lying on the ground in the middle of a clearing.

The images vanished as he was pulled awake by gentle shaking and the mention of his name. He opened his eyes, not sure who spoke until he saw Sabastian and Lan standing next to the bed.

"I asked, how do you feel?" Lan said.

"I feel . . . new. I know that sounds odd, but I can't describe any other way, my sense of release. The pain and despair I felt as the memories poured back into my mind are now replaced with the joy of knowing the love of my life is here with me. It makes no difference Sam doesn't know who she is, or was before; I know. The knowledge certainly explains a lot, like why I was so drawn to her from the beginning. Lan, did you know this would happen, did you know I would remember so much about our lives before?"

"No, none of this was expected, but then again, this is the first time we saved a sentient species from extinction." Lan paused as if lost in thought while Warren waited for him to continue. "I said you were special and had unique abilities, some of which we were not expecting, but we did not anticipate you to remember so much of your past."

"So, what do I—we do now? Sama—Laura was obviously remembering her past and was acting like the Samantha I knew back on Earth. I remember her looking up at the sky and collapsing. Where is she? How is she?"

Sabastian stepped next to the bed and spoke first. "She's in the room next door, in a coma. The Jonton believe it's best to let her mind rest for now."

Lan was quick to add, "When she wakes, we will see what she remembers. She may recall being Samantha. She may recall being Laura, or she may forget all of it. Time will tell."

Lan looked over to Sabastian for conformation of his next statement.

"I think Sabastian agrees with me; if it is Laura who recovers, telling her the truth could cause her emotional harm. It is possible she will remember some of her past, which might be good, or it might be bad, but we won't know until or if it happens."

"I think not telling her the truth wouldn't be wise," Warren said. "I think maybe we tell her a partial truth, depending like you say, on what she remembers on her own. I only hope I don't slip and accidentally call her Samantha again if she only remembers being Laura."

"We will see," Lan said. "It may be a few days before we wake her. After the medical team checks you out and releases you, go home and relax. Sabastian and I will talk to you later and keep you well informed. I believe you should be perfectly fine now; however, if you need help dealing with the memories, I can provide counseling."

"Thank you, Lan, but I think now that I know everything, I'll be fine. I do have a question for you."

"What is it?"

"I was dreaming of a lot of things I'm sure now are memories from my past, including when you came to meet me, and I also dreamt of Bartholomew. He is here, isn't he, and awake?"

"Yes, he is here and awake, with no memories of his past. We can discuss him at another time; for now, please go home and relax."

WAITING

A Visit from Lan

It had been three days since Warren came home from the hospital, and he was going crazy waiting. He spent most of his day taking long hikes around his property and spending hours staring at the ocean, feeling lost and lonely. He knew his love was there with him, but there remained so many questions and possible adverse outcomes; it depressed him. Not enough to cause any problems, as his physical routine of lifting and swimming helped to distract him and ease his mind while pushing his body to its limits.

He knew it would help if he had his friend from Earth to talk to, if only for a moment. He recalled now seeing Bartholomew at the Life Center. He knew then the man was familiar, but at the time, he didn't know his name. They had been through much together in a short period before the end.

His sleep, when it came, was restless. He dreamt about things from Earth mixed with his new experiences from his time since being awakened. The previous night he dreamt of dinosaurs from Earth and animals he saw last week, running, chasing, and eating Humans as they fled across a valley filled with bloodied bodies. The images were still in his mind even after the most strenuous morning of exercise plus another long hike to the ocean.

Warren was sitting on the edge of the cliff looking beyond the ocean at the far horizon when his communicator indicated he had a message from his CA. The message explained that Lan was going to be coming to see him in one hour. Knowing it would take longer than an hour to walk, he began to run back to his home.

As Warren ran, his mind filled with images of running in the forest, around a lake, and on the beach with Samantha. The memories caused tears to come to his eyes, and he began to think he might not be adjusting to the new reality as well as first thought. He understood why the first group awakened could not deal with the new reality without conditioning and memory suppression. Part of him now wished he never remembered. But as he ran, he started to feel better. Maybe he needed to let it out and think about the future instead of the past. He arrived home, and the CA informed him Lan would be at the house in ten minutes, which was more than enough time to shower and change.

After dressing, he came out to the living room and poured two glasses of the scotch Lan had given him. He set them on the table by the lit fireplace and sat in the chair as Lan was coming up the stairs.

"Hello, my friend, it's good to see you," he said as he stood and shook Lan's hand.

"I am glad you feel that way. I was not sure what kind of reception I was going to get today."

"Well, I'm not going to bite your head off like a velociraptor."

"That is an odd thought and something I certainly was not expecting."

"I know, I'm keeping you off guard. The term was from a strange dream I had last night. I believe from a movie, but I'm not sure. Apparently, not all details of my past have been made clear."

Warren then went through his dream to Lan in detail, and when he finished, Lan had a little smirk on his face.

"What are you smiling about?" Warren asked.

"It appears you are mixing the experience of the tour you had at the Research Station with memories of Earth. What's funny is the memories are from a movie about dinosaurs that scientists brought back to life."

Warren sat for a moment in thought before he spoke. "As soon as you said movie about dinosaurs, all the memories came flooding back. I remember the movie, movies actually, and seeing at least one of them with Samantha."

"I think this will happen a lot until all your memories of Earth come back to you. The question is, can you deal with the memories? How are you feeling?"

I'm tired from all the exercise and not sleeping well, but I'm also oddly calm and feel like a huge weight of despair has lifted from my life. I always knew at least subconsciously; something wasn't right; something was always out of reach, especially when I was with Laura."

"What about the anger?"

"I'm no longer angry at you or Sabastian, and when I think of what your people and the other races have done, it no longer causes me to get angry. I realize it was and is a tremendous thing you are doing, and I have no reason to be angry."

"And what about the future, Warren, what are your plans?"

"I don't know. How do I plan or think about the future without knowing who will wake up to share it with me if they ever wake at all? I do believe no matter what, I can deal with it. I may need time, but I think I'll be okay. Knowing she is here and alive, safe, and hopefully healthy is all I need. No matter who she is or what she remembers, I'll always love her."

"I am pleased to see how well you are doing, and I am grateful to you for your openness. I agree you will be fine no matter the final outcome, but I do hope it will be an outcome that makes you both happy."

Lan raised his shot glass and downed the remainder of the scotch.

"I am also pleased to tell you since you probably will have all your old memories, it has been decided you will receive full access to all of our Earth's historical archives. There is no reason to keep it from you. I must stress Warren, you are never to share this information with anyone, and it is never to leave this house for any reason that has not been pre-approved. Do you accept the conditions?"

"Yes, Lan, I do, and thank you."

Lan paused for a moment.

"Warren, you now have access to all the information about the planet Earth, including your family history."

"Thank you, nag."

Warren raised his glass, tipped it to Lan, and finished the contents. He was feeling good, ready to take on the world, and whatever future his life brought.

"As your CA confirmed, you also have full access to your family and personal information. Use it well, but try not to dwell on the past or learn too many things before they return to you naturally.

"It is time for me to leave. I am going to the hospital to check on Laura. I will let you know what the plan is for her further treatment."

"Thank you, Lan, for everything."

After Lan departed, Warren sat for a moment on the chair by the fireplace, not knowing what to do. After a few minutes, he walked across the room to look out the window to the valley below and the sky above, with the first moon starting to rise as the sun prepared to set. He realized a whole new world had opened for him.

Do I look at my family information, or do I patiently wait for more of my memory to return naturally?

He decided not to think about it at the moment. He remained exhausted from his earlier activity and decided to relax in bed and listen to his favorite music.

Exploring the Past and . . .

The next morning, he awoke feeling refreshed and ready for anything. His dreams had been all happy memories of his time with Samantha. He recalled roaming the streets of Philadelphia, and visiting the Liberty Bell as if they were out of town tourists, going to the top of the William Penn statue on City Hall, and partaking of some cheesesteak sandwiches at Pat's.

When he came out of the bedroom ready for his morning workout, the CA informed him Sabastian had called to talk to him. He thought it was odd Sabastian was calling so early in the morning, especially after not having bothered to contact him since the hospital.

"Nag, please contact Sabastian."

"Hello, Warren, good morning. I'm glad you called me back. Before you say anything, please let me apologize. I wanted to contact you every day since the hospital, but Lan wouldn't let me. He even went so far as to have you blocked. He sought to give you time to sort things out and meet with you. Then yesterday, when he told me you were doing well, I tried to contact you, but your computer said you were asleep, and then—"

"Whoa, slow down, Sabastian, and take a breath. It's okay. Yes, I wondered why you hadn't contacted me, but I knew there had to be a good reason. So how are you?"

"How am I? Who cares? I mean, I'm good, and Chloe sends her regards. We were both worried about you and are still worried about Laura. I am so sorry about everything, all the lies and half-truths. I'm glad everything is out in the open, and I hope it works out for you and . . . Laura."

"Thank you, my friend; it's good to know the truth. I don't believe all my memories have come back, but last night was the first excellent night's sleep I've had in a while. All my dreams were good dreams about . . . Samantha."

"I heard the hesitation in your voice. Are you sure you're okay?"

"Yes, I don't know what to call her. Not that it matters, as long as I know who she is and she's safe. I'll call her whatever name she feels most comfortable with or whichever name she remembers."

"I spoke to Lan this morning," Sabastian said. "He wanted me to tell you they're going to keep her in a coma for another week; then, they'll allow her to wake and see who and how she is and what she remembers from that night."

"I've waited this long; I can wait another week, as long as she's okay."

"Lan also told me they gave you access to the archives. Exploring it should keep you busy if you choose to use it, only not too much at one time."

"Yes, Lan told me the same thing. I might wait to see what comes back naturally. I haven't decided yet."

Warren went to the kitchen to start making his coffee as Sabastian continued the conversation.

"The information contains one thing you might want to check out. After the Jonton picked us for the project, they went through all the records they could find to do genealogy for everyone, and they saved it with the archives. I, of course, looked you up and found a surprise. The information might not mean much to you now, but if you do research your lineage, remember the name Thomas Jefferson. Sorry to drop a name on you and run, but I'm late. Take care, my friend."

After Sabastian disconnected, Warren sat there thinking about the name Thomas Jefferson. The only thing he could remember, he probably learned in school. Jefferson was a historical figure from the United States' past.

"Nag, tell me about Thomas Jefferson."

"I found a lot of information about him. What would you like to know?"

"Who he was, what he did, and what he has to do with me."

"Thomas Jefferson, 1743 to 1826 Earth years, was one of the Founding Fathers of the United States of America and the principal author of the Declaration of Independence. He later served as the third President of the United States from 1801 to 1809 Earth years.

"There is a lot more detailed information. Would you like me to continue?"

"No, but do tell me what he has to do with my family."

"Thomas Jefferson would have been your many times over great grandfather on your mother's side of the family. Would you like a complete genealogy report?"

"Not at the moment."

As nag talked, Warren began to remember some of his American history education and realized on Earth, especially in the United States, being a descendant of Thomas Jefferson would have been a big deal. Now, the disclosure was an interesting part of his past, nothing more. When things calmed down and became more normal, he would do additional research into Jefferson, the United States, and his genealogy.

His CA watched and reported.

. . . Waiting for the Future

Warren spent the next week taking many hikes to the ocean. Every day he tried a different path, and during one excursion, he headed along the coast for a few miles looking to find an easy path down to the water. Lan had been correct, as usual. He could no way down the cliffs.

At night after he had dinner, he sat at the piano and played whatever came to mind. He now had access to much more sheet music than in the past, but he didn't care. On the second evening, he instructed the CA to listen to the music, and if what he played was a song from Earth, the CA was to place it on a list he would look at later. He wanted to see how many songs were floating around in his mind.

True to his word, Lan contacted him the night before what would be a week. They were going to allow Laura to regain consciousness in the morning. They expected her to wake between eight and nine, and they needed him to be there. Warren was happy something would happen tomorrow, good or bad; at least he would know.

After he ate dinner and the sun had set, he had a desire to lie outside and look at the stars. He took one of the lounge chairs from the patio with him to the grass behind the house, where he could get a clear view of the entire sky. The evening was warmer than average, so he brought only a lightweight blanket to keep warm.

"Warren, where are you going?"

"Calm down, nag; I want to look at the stars and relax. I won't stay out here too long, and I'm sure you'll monitor the area to make certain I don't get eaten by some wandering bear."

"Very well, Warren, i will calm down and relax as well."

Warren was amused at the personality and dry sense of humor the CA was developing and wondered if it was normal. He sometimes had an odd feeling there was more to his computer friend than memory chips and circuits.

A few minutes later, he had the chair set up, blanket on, and lay there looking at a sky filled with a vast array of stars and galaxies. Both moons were still below the horizon, so there was nothing to hide the vastness of bright little lights in the night. He wondered which of those tiny specs of light was the solar system of Earth, or if it was even visible at this time of year. He knew he could ask his CA, but he didn't want to be bothered.

In the distance, he could see lights moving across the sky. Warren knew they were ships going back and forth between the planet, the moons, or leaving for a journey to another solar system.

Maybe before I die, I will get to visit a planet in another star system.

Warren was sure the thought of traveling to another star would never have come to him in his past life.

THE WAIT IS OVER

Joining

Warren looked at the stars and thought about the future before his eyes slowly closed and he began to drift off, but not to sleep. He could sense a presence beckoning to him, but something held him back. His body was encumbered and keeping his mind from something out of reach.

He stood, compelled to strip off his clothes and discard the blanket he had been using for warmth. He needed to be one with the environment, free to let his body touch the planet. He lay down again, not on the chair but upon the soft winter grass instead. He wasn't cold or feeling any discomfort being naked and vulnerable to the world as the moons slowly began to rise.

Warren's body temperature remained steady as his breathing and heart rate slowed to well below normal levels. His mind began drifting off, and he could sense nag, as if he, Warren, were part of the CA. He silently told nag not to worry, he was fine, and he made sure the CA could not contact Lan. He could sense something else as he touched the CA's circuit mind, another presence. The presence appeared in his mind as something vast, not alive, but electronic in nature and logic. The other presence would have to wait for now; he had to find his princess and wake her from the long sleep.

His mind continued to drift into the darkness. He felt something undefinable. It was another presence, this one not electronic, but also not alive. He felt as if his entire body had been in some way energized, though he felt nothing. The presence ceased, and he felt a familiar pull within the dark blackness.

The blackness wasn't genuinely dark, and he could see drops of water falling, yet not making any ripples in what appeared to be a floor of water. The liquid surface was perfectly still as he floated above, the only disturbance being the ripples that now approached him from a single spot ahead in the darkness. He moved toward the epicenter of the ripples and soon heard someone calling his name—Warren, Warren. He followed the voice across the immeasurable void of liquid and ripples until he came upon an exquisite vision of Samantha. He watched as a tear slid down her cheek, fell below, and caused another ripple, now of light, in the otherwise calmed ocean of darkness. They floated together, facing each other, naked, with their thoughts merging almost as one.

"Warren," she whispered. "I missed you so much. I'm imprisoned behind this other persona. I've been trying to break free to reach you, but when I reached out to touch you, it wasn't you. Your mind had none of our memories for me to find, hold, and grasp. At last, when I was about to lose all hope, I found buried deep inside your mind, the Warren I knew and loved. The Warren who promised he could find a tear I shed in any vast amount of ocean."

"I'm here, my princess," Warren responded as his own tears began to fall. "I have followed the ripples of your tears to find you and bring you home."

"I'm frightened, my prince. I don't understand what's happened, and I'm having trouble keeping me separate from this other identity. I don't want to be her; I don't want to be . . . Laura, I want to be Samantha, your Samantha."

"You are my Samantha, don't be afraid. Look deep into my mind; you will see the truth. It is a wonderful new beginning for us and a new beginning for Humanity. Follow the path in my mind to see our past, our present, and the future we can have together. Take the wonderful memories of our past and the new memories of our present and see the future we can have together. You can be Samantha and Laura, two experiences and lives merged into one."

"I feel so much pain," Samantha cried. "So much loss; how can I go on without my family? How do I go on without my friends? How do we go on . . . together?"

"Let your prince guide you. Let me take away your pain, and we can be together, always and forever. Your Prince Warren and my Sleeping Beauty."

"Warren, I am Samantha, I am Laura, and I am both. I am . . . the new Samantha, and I need my prince to release me from my fear and sleep. I need my love's first kiss."

Their two minds and images of their bodies drifted together; their lips touched—

Warren awoke to the sound of birds singing in the trees and the warmth of the sun on his skin, now melting away the frost. He slowly sat up, wondering how much of the last night had been real. He knew he hadn't dreamt; the experience was something else. He didn't understand it, but he knew it to be real.

"Nag, is everything okay?"

"Yes, Warren, why do you ask?"

"I'm not sure. I'll be in shortly."

Warren was for a reason he couldn't understand, compelled to run. He stood; still not cold or caring he wore no clothes. He walked around the house to the path Lan had built for him and proceeded to run. He had no shoes, but his feet didn't hurt. All he knew was an incredible feeling of freedom, unlike anything else he could remember experiencing before.

After a few laps, he took the chair back to the patio, grabbed his clothes and blanket, and headed into the shower, telling the CA to let him know when Lan called. He looked at the clock and saw it was a bit past six. He was finished with his shower when the CA told him Lan wanted to communicate.

"Hello, Lan, good morning; you have news."

"Yes, I do, and I am surprised. You sounded like you were making a statement and not asking a question. I am also surprised your CA told me you were expecting my call.

"Simply a feeling I had. How is Samantha?"

Lan hesitated a moment—surprised Warren had confidently used the name Samantha instead of Laura.

"According to our monitors, she has come out of her coma, naturally, before we initiated our procedure. Her mind is fully active though she is not awake. We think you should be here before we try to wake her.'

"I agree, and I'm on my way."

The Beginning - Samantha

Her mind awoke; her body laid on its back on something soft. She tried to open her eyes but couldn't. Even though she could feel the softness of the bed under her, she wasn't in control of her body. Her mind was there, aware but not yet joined fully to her body. She, Samantha, waited for something—no, someone. Yes, Samantha Santori waited for him. She was waiting for Warren.

Love's Kiss

Warren arrived at the medical facility to find Lan and Sabastian waiting for him outside Samantha's room. Neither looked happy, so he knew the news wasn't good, but he also knew his arrival would make things right and release the person they knew as Laura, to be her true self.

"Good morning again," Lan said. "Laura is still not awake. We see much activity on her brain scans, so I tried to wake her, even though you were not here. I have tried several times, with no success, and was about to try a low-dose stimulant. I am worried she might be experiencing brain trauma, but I do not yet want to force her to wake."

"It's okay, Lan, don't worry. Laura is gone, Sam is waiting, I know what to do. I know for whom she awaits. I want to see her."

Sabastian stepped closer to Warren. "Gone, what do you mean gone? Are you sure you're ready to see her?"

Warren confidently smiled at his friends. "Yes, I'll be fine. We'll be fine."

Warren walked around both and headed into Sam's room without waiting for objections or permission while Lan and Sabastian followed. Samantha, his Samantha, was lying silently with only the sounds of the monitors, which Warren began to disconnect.

"We don't need these any longer, my beauty!"

Sabastian was about to stop Warren, but Lan grabbed his arm and told him to wait and give Warren some time. They watched as Warren finished removing the sensors and turned off the equipment. He took her hand in his and whispered to her loud enough for Lan and Sabastian to hear.

"It's time to wake, my princess. It's time for Warren and Samantha to build their new lives together and live happily ever after. Awake my Sleeping Beauty, your Prince Warren is here."

Warren bent down and kissed her softly on her lips as a single tear slid from her eye. A few seconds passed, a smile came to her mouth, and her eyes slowly opened.

"Hello, my prince," she spoke softly.

"Welcome back, Samantha; I've missed you so much. How do you feel?"

"I'm tired, but I feel like I've awoken from a long, long nap." She turned to Lan and Sabastian. "Don't be shy; come on over."

"I did not want to disturb the two of you, Laura," Lan said.

"I'm sure you desired to observe, and my name is Samantha. I remember Earth, at least my time with Warren, and I remember all of my time here as Laura. She will always be a part of who I am now, but I'll always be Samantha. Warren's Samantha."

"Wow, I didn't expect that outcome," Sabastian said. He walked closer with a huge smile on his face as he bent down and kissed her on the cheek. I'm happy to meet you, Samantha. Please excuse me, but I promised to give Chloe an update."

"Please say hi for me," Samantha responded.

Lan stepped closer to the bed. "Samantha, I have to ask. Are you okay with everything? Do you have any pain or anxieties?"

"No, I'm fine. I remember everything; even the night I had my breakdown. It feels strange now, but it's like another memory. I remember feeling lost and afraid of not knowing who I was or where I was until last night when I joined with Warren. He explained everything. I knew I would be safe with my prince, but I had to wait until he came here to give me, in our way, love's first kiss."

"I do not understand. How did you join with Warren last night?"

Warren elaborated the best he could to Lan, and Samantha confirmed, so Lan wouldn't think it merely a dream. He told about his experience outside gazing at the stars and how he somehow connected to Samantha, conveyed everything to her, and told his love he would be coming to wake her from the long sleep.

"I certainly can't explain anything that happened last night, but it's why I was waiting for your call and why I knew everything would be okay. When Samantha was a child, 'Sleeping Beauty' was her favorite story. I became her Prince Warren, and she, my Princess Samantha. The theme was to be a part of our wedding, which never got to happen. Like in the story, she needed me to wake her with love's first kiss."

"I am very happy for both of you and glad you are feeling better. I now suspect and hope you will have no adjustment issues going forward. I must go and report your progress to my superiors. Welcome home—all of you!"

Lan stepped out of the room as Warren took Samantha's hand in his.

"Well, I think there's still one thing to resolve, my princess."

"A long time ago, in a solar system far, far away, I asked a woman to marry me. She said yes, but that woman no longer exists, so I must ask this woman."

He bent down on his knee at the side of Samantha's bed, still holding her hand.

"Princess Samantha Santori, will you marry me?"

"Yes, my prince."

THE CENTENNIAL

Naming Ceremony

"Good evening to our visitors from the stars and fellow citizens of this new independent world. Welcome to the official dedication of our world's first city. Today took a long time to arrive, but now, the area once known as the Life Center has grown to be a center of commerce both on and off the planet. On this day, it is time to recognize and make official the name of our capital city."

President McCormick paused for dramatic effect and to control his emotions as he remembered his parents and grandparents.

"Ladies and gentlemen, it is my pleasure to welcome you to the city to be known from this day forward as Cadalon City."

After five minutes of applause and a standing ovation, while banners and a flag were raised high into the air, the speaker continued.

"Also, today, we reveal the name chosen for our world. You can't have a capital city on a world known only as the Project Planet, especially now since there will soon be a new, similar mission dedicated to preserving another civilization whose planet is soon to be uninhabitable. I am proud to add, citizens from our world will be helping with the process to build the new civilization for another species, very much like our own.

"Many wanted to call our home Earth II, but those on the committee decided it would be best to keep the name Earth revered, as a special remembrance, dedicated to the billions of Human lives lost.

"It has been one hundred years since the Jonton awakened the first Humans on this new world. We have come a long way, and Humanity now has a long and hopefully prosperous future to explore.

"Before the destruction of Earth, many feared Humanity would destroy itself from war, resource depletion, or Human-caused disease. Now, we have not only the gift of a new world, but we are an enlightened civilization with the knowledge to never repeat the mistakes made in the past."

Applause erupted again as the crowd rose to their feet. The president raised his hands, gesturing for all to take their seat.

"We are joined here today by representatives from all the known spacefaring civilizations of our galaxy, including visitors from some of the galaxy's other species who have chosen to move here to live, conduct business, learn, and prosper.

"It is also my great pleasure to announce we have with us an exceptional guest. I'm pleased we were able to keep his attendance a secret. He is a man known to many on and off this planet for his incredible talent, a man who has given us great enjoyment with performances of Earth's most beautiful melodies.

"Our guest of honor today is also our oldest living citizen of this world, Warren Estridge."

Again, all assembled rose from their seats and applauded as Warren came from behind the stage to speak.

"Thank you, thank you all for such a warm welcome, and thank you, President McCormick. It is a great honor to be here to celebrate the dedication of Cadalon City and the official naming of our new homeworld.

"As I stood in the back waiting for President McCormick to introduced me, I couldn't help but reminisce about my wife and our President's grandparents." Warren turned and walked over to Sabastian Wilson McCormick II and shook his hand. "They departed this life more than a few years ago, but I know they would be proud of all you have accomplished.

"I also would like to have a brief moment of silence for our President's father, who passed away one month ago. Warren Sabastian McCormick put service and dedication to our new home above everything except his family."

After the moment of silence, Warren continued.

"I don't know if everyone here realizes your grandfather was my mentor and a tremendous friend of mine. I wish he were here to see how far Humanity has grown and progressed. I know I didn't ever expect to live to be one hundred and twenty-two years old and never expected to see our world advance so far. I am humbled and extremely thankful to the many species of the galaxy who helped save Humanity, enabled me to live to see this day, and provided us so great a world.

"I believe it is now time for the honor; President McCormick bestowed to me."

As the crowd waited in silence, the only sound was of the light breeze moving the many banners surrounding the stage.

"I, Citizen Warren Estridge, a former resident of the planet Earth, on this twenty-fourth day of Baudit, in the year one hundred, dedicate to Humanity, this city of Cadalon, the first city of the world to be forever known to this galaxy as—Comhaltas."

Again, there was great applause as well as fireworks filling the twilight sky. When the applause died down, Warren continued.

"Comhaltas is an old Gaelic word from Earth, once spoken in the region known as Ireland, meaning co-fosterage, friendship, membership, and learning together in peace. I believe this is a beautiful expression of the new life Humanity has received. May this city and planet flourish for many millennia along with our neighbors in the ever-expanding galactic peace.

Thunderous applause erupted from the crowd, much louder than the previous times and Warren had to wait a full minute before he could resume. He wished again his princess and friends were here by his side.

"President McCormick has also asked me to announce today the approval of mission Gaia.

"We will send an exploration and recovery mission to Earth and hopefully bring back more of our lost history, the Jonton were unable to retrieve before the destruction of life on the planet. We will place the recovered items into a new wing of the museum, which is already complete in this our new capital city.

"The Trandel have given us a spaceship and crew to take our teams back to Earth. We expect the mission to launch in about a year. The trip and recovery are estimated to take about three years, and I regret I may not be with you to greet them when they return.

"This project was initially the dream of one man, my mentor, my friend, the grandfather of the President—Sabastian Wilson McCormick I. In his honor, I play this song and dedicate it to his dream, as well as the dreams of all the many species and inhabitants of the galaxy.

"Those who have attended or heard my concerts, know I always play this selection as it is my most favorite. Sabastian had grown over the years to appreciate the melody as well.

"This song is titled 'One Man's Dream.'"

The beginning!

About the Author

J J Eckhardt is a former direct mail marketer with a degree in art and advertising production. A fan of everything Sci-Fi, Fantasy, and Horror, he started writing eleven years ago. A strengths analysis suggested that writing could develop one of his skills, and a new writer was born.

He has completed four novels—of which this is the second to be published—and five short stories to be released as a book of dreams.

Born and raised in Philadelphia, Pennsylvania, J J Eckhardt now lives in Burlington, New Jersey.

A Note from J J Eckhardt

As my bio says, I began writing over eleven years ago. The thought of someday publishing my work was the farthest thing from my mind. It wasn't until I had written a few short stories and finished my second full novel (to be someday released) that I even considered the idea of publishing. As my quote at the front of the book indicates, it was a dream I never had until that time. This story was the first one I ever completed, and it has gone through many rounds of editing, including two rounds of professional editing. If you found any mistakes in this book, it was most likely because I didn't accept every suggestion they made. They were both extremely helpful, but this was my baby, my first, written to challenge myself, and I wanted to stay true to my original vision.

If you would like to read about my personal journey to this time in my life, please check out my blog on my website.

J J Eckhardt

JJEckhardt.com

Other Novels by J J Eckhardt

Psychic Storm – The Overlord, Barringer Publishing

Novels Under Development

Psychic Storm – Common Enemy
A Journey Toward Tomorrow – Building and Discovery
Surviving Zeptulgar